NIGHTMARES OF NIGHTFALL

ASPEN SHERWOOD

ISBN: 978-1-7382714-1-2

ISBN: 978-1-7382714-0-5

Book Cover by MiblArt

Map by Cartographybird

aspensherwood.com

For my parents who, I know, would fight the monsters for me. Every time.

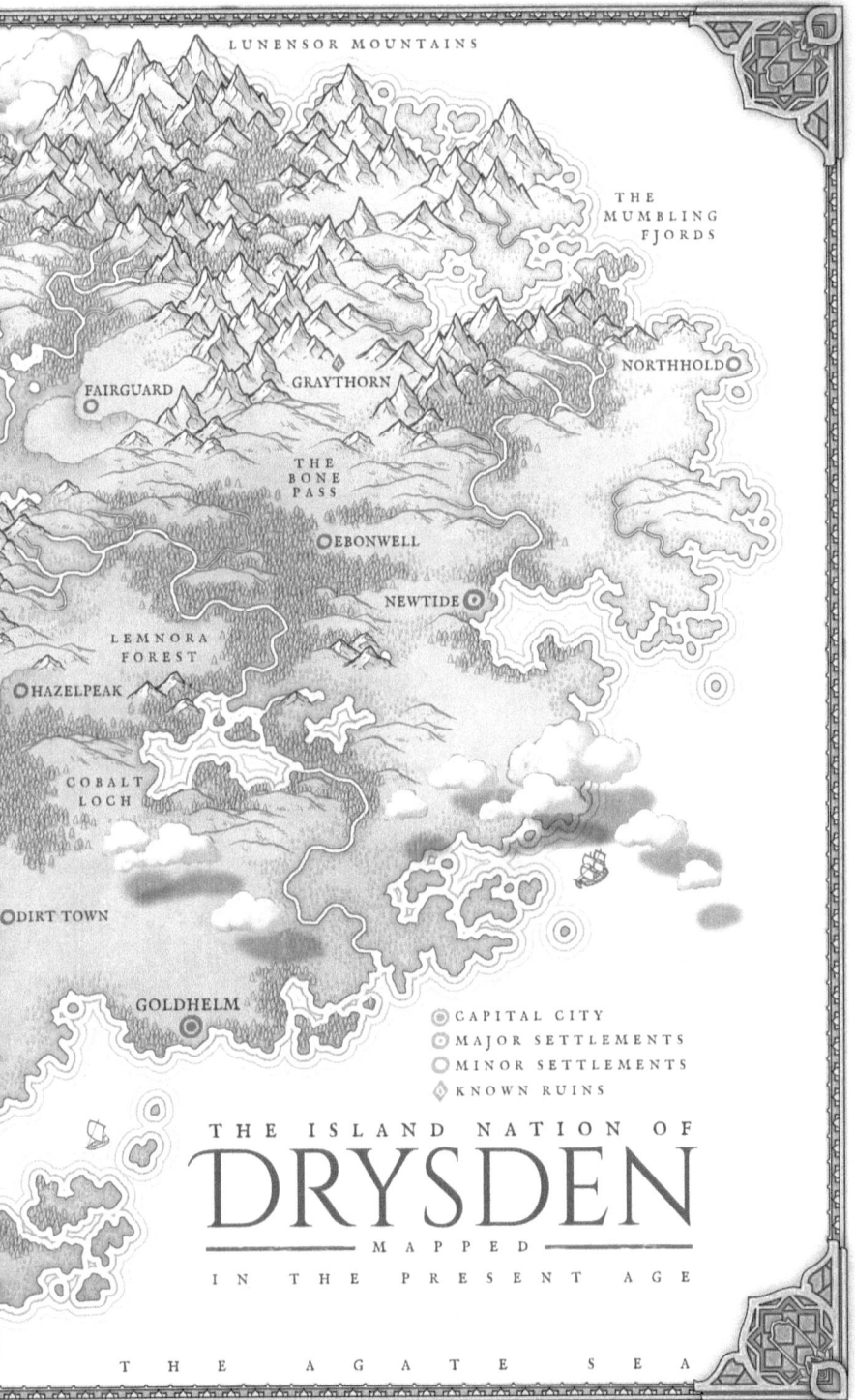

LUNENSOR MOUNTAINS

THE
MUMBLING
FJORDS

NORTHHOLD

FAIRGUARD

GRAYTHORN

THE
BONE
PASS

EBONWELL

NEWTIDE

LEMNORA
FOREST

HAZELPEAK

COBALT
LOCH

DIRT TOWN

GOLDHELM

CAPITAL CITY
MAJOR SETTLEMENTS
MINOR SETTLEMENTS
KNOWN RUINS

THE ISLAND NATION OF

DRYSDEN

MAPPED

IN THE PRESENT AGE

THE AGATE SEA

CHAPTER
ONE
BRYN

My clothes clung to my skin as the rain soaked me to the bone. The skies were a constantly shifting swirl of grey above my head. My boots landed in one of the many puddles covering the path, coating my clothes in mud splatter. The normally hard-packed dirt pathway was now nothing more than a slippery mess.

The land around me blurred as I pushed myself harder along the path. My chest burned as I reached the top of the hill, my breathing ragged. My village was finally visible in the distance, its details hidden in a shroud of rain.

I started down the hill, my feet sliding in the mud.

"Shit," I hissed under my breath as I tried to steady myself.

Da's footsteps splashed behind me as he continued to gain on me.

"Faster, Bryn! You've got to be faster!" Da called out. His voice was barely winded. I quickened my pace down the hill, stumbling for a moment before I managed to regain my already bad footing. "You'll never be able to outrun anyone if you don't get any faster!"

If I wasn't so winded, I would have yelled something back. Something that contained some heavy-handed sarcasm and one, or more, curses. But it was all I could do to keep running. My legs were a weight that I struggled to lift with every step.

My feet slid out from under me.

I landed hard on the path that was now nothing more than a mudslide. I tumbled down the hill, my body banging against the ground, not slowing until I reached the bottom.

I stayed sprawled on the ground, too tired to care if my muscles cramped. The rain let up, and only a mist still hung in the air. Da's mud-covered boots stopped beside me, but I didn't bother to look away from the churning clouds above me.

His chuckle rang through the air. "Alright there, Bryn?" Da's face blocked the sky as he looked down at me, his brown eyes twinkling. His red hair, now streaked with grey in his age, was plastered to his head from the rain. Grey stubble lined his cheeks and chin. He was soaked like I was but carried himself with more dignity than I could manage.

I raised an eyebrow. "Fantastic."

Da's chuckle turned into a full laugh.

"You need to get up and walk around. Otherwise, you will be walking back to the village with your muscles cramping up." He reached down a hand and helped me to my feet before he pulled the hood of his cloak over his head.

The top of my head only reached his chin, although what I lacked in height, I made up for with my hair. A riot of fiery red curls fell to the small of my back and seemed to have a mind of its own.

Da pulled two water skins from the bag he had slung across his back. He passed one to me as we started towards Ebonwell. Once I caught my breath, I turned to Da with narrowed eyes. "What was that for?" I said before I deepened my voice in a poor imitation of Da. "'Watch your pace, Bryn. You'll burn out if you go that fast. You're not running for your life, Bryn. Try to look a little bit less frantic.'"

I scowled as he laughed.

"Your speed needed some work," he said.

"Bullshit."

We started running together when I was only seven years old. Now I was twenty and the focus was always the same: endurance, stamina. Except for today.

"I thought it would be a good idea," Da said.

"You didn't even give me a chance to prepare myself for it."

Da took my empty water skin and put it back in his bag. Now that the high from the run had worn off, I regretted my decision to lie in the mud. I wrapped my cloak tighter around myself to try and ward off the chill that had settled over me.

"And how were you planning to prepare for it?"

"That's—" I paused, trying to find something reasonable to say. Nothing came to mind. "That's beside the point."

Da nodded to the watchman on the walls surrounding our village. The gate was open, as it usually was during the day. The gate only shut at sunset and remained barred until sunrise the next day. The message board stood beside the gates, the parchments on it protected from the rain by a little overhang. The parchments were in varying stages of weathering; some were yellowed, and some were completely unreadable. One, a missing person report, was new enough that it was still the same off-white colour of fresh parchment.

Ebonwell wasn't big. The walls were wood, not stone, and many of the houses looked as though they were part of the hills surrounding the village. We were too far from the water to have our own raiding ships, so people travelled to Newtide for the raiding season. Raiding was one of the few ways that poor country families were able to make enough money to survive the cold winter.

As we crossed through the gates, I asked, "Why today?"

"What about today?" Da waved to a young boy that crossed our path.

I tucked a wet curl behind my ear. "Why did you change the run today? We usually don't run in the rain like this either."

"It had to be done."

"But why—"

"—You'll find out when it's time, Bryn. Don't rush it just to sate your uncontrollable curiosity," Da said.

I grit my teeth. Whenever Da used that tone there was no use in trying to change his mind. He wouldn't budge.

We didn't speak as we made our way home.

Our house was one of the smallest in the village, without a shop or workshop attached to it, but the stone walls were clean, and the turf on the roof was a blanket of plush grass. The windows were all cracked open to let in the air while one of Ma's pies cooled on the sill.

We left our mud-covered boots outside the door.

Our house consisted primarily of a large room with the kitchen on one side and the living area on the other. There was only one other room in the house, my parents' bedroom, since I slept in the loft over the living area. The ladder up to my room was so broad that it bordered on being a set of stairs.

A large bowl of water sat on my washstand. Ma must have known Da's plans for the run.

The richer cities and citizens could get flowing water to work in their houses. Jarls and Warlords hired someone with a water bloodrite to make the water flow wherever they wanted. But in a smaller, out of the way village with about as much power as a muddy old boot, wells and pumps were the best there were.

I scrubbed the layer of mud off my body before pulling a loose, white, long-sleeved shirt over my head. I covered it with a dark green dress tied up on one side and a well-worn brown leather vest that clung to my chest.

I braided the front part of my hair back to try and keep it out of my face. Braids were the only thing that came close to controlling my hair, but even then, it was a close-fought battle.

By the time I was finished, Da had already left.

Ma was at the long table that divided the kitchen from our living area. Herbs were spread out on its surface along with a cutting board, mortar and pestle, and various tin jars.

With no healing bloodrites in Ebonwell, Ma was the closest thing to a healer. The medical salves and teas I made allowed her to treat everything but the very worst of cases.

When I was ten years old, Ma began to teach me all she knew about healing. Now, ten years later, I could treat people myself. Ma still preferred to handle the most serious cases, only allowing me to assist when necessary. Just recently she had allowed me to take over the creation of our ointments and salves.

One day, I would prove to her how much my healing had grown. I would prove to her that I was good enough to follow in her footsteps.

I pulled a stool up to the table. I chopped the herbs used for the burn soothers and added them into the mortar to crush them.

"Bad run?" Ma asked as she cut some potatoes.

I looked at her out of the corner of my eye as I continued to grind the herbs. "What gave you that idea?"

Ma finished the last potato and set aside the wooden

cutting board. She propped her hip against the table and watched me work.

If I got my eyes and hair from Da, everything else was from Ma. My small build, my dainty nose, and my full mouth were replicas of her.

"Your father was in a mood as he headed out for the day," Ma said.

"Da was fine until I asked why our run had changed." I scraped the ground herbs into a bowl. I wiped out the mortar with a cloth and began to crush the next batch. "When I called him on his bullshit answer and asked for more, he refused."

"Did you ask for an explanation, or did you demand answers?"

"I may have been a little blunt."

Ma turned back to the table with a twinkling laugh. She added the potatoes to a large pot and began to chop some carrots. "Your father wants nothing more than to ensure you have the best life possible."

"He doesn't need to protect me from the world anymore," I said as I combined the herbs with a cream I had finished the day before. When the once snow-white cream was a pale green, I divided it into small metal jars. After each was filled, I marked the top with a dollop of wax to identify what it was meant to do. This one was red for burn soothers.

"You don't know that. Your father is going to continue to protect you regardless of whether or not you feel as though you have outgrown his protection."

My cheeks warmed. "I just want to know what's going on."

"I'm sure your father will tell you when the time is right," Ma said.

I placed the majority of the tins in the boxes we used for

market day before I stored three jars in the cupboards where we kept our healing supplies.

Ma turned to me with a small smile on her face. "He isn't doing this to annoy you. Give him a couple more days to tell you himself before you push him for answers again."

I grumbled under my breath.

We spent several hours together in the kitchen. Jams, medical teas and ointments were packed into the baskets and set by the door, ready to be carried down to the village square. By the time we were done, not only were the boxes full, but our personal stores were completely refreshed.

Da returned home just as we were finishing. He didn't say a word as he hugged me, pressing a kiss to my forehead as we sat down to eat.

Once we cleared the table from dinner, Da pulled out our old, weathered game board. I sat down across from him, the fire crackling beside us. The game board was filled with spaces connected with intersecting lines indicating different movement patterns. The differently shaped playing pieces each moved in unique ways, which made capturing all of your opponent's pieces and making sure your own weren't taken even harder.

In a country *ruled* by its military and *defined* by its military, it was no surprise that even our games reflected battlefield tactics and strategies.

It had become a bit of a nightly ritual in our house for us to play at least one round after dinner. When I was younger, I could never win against Da, but now we were evenly matched.

We traded pieces pretty evenly until Da was left with a single piece, and I only had two.

I studied the board, surveying my options.

I moved one of my pieces two spaces.

"Are you hoping to corner me or surround me?" Da asked as his eyes darted around the board, no doubt weighing the various moves he could make.

"I'm pretty sure that if I told you what I am doing, it wouldn't work," I joked.

"It was worth a shot," Da said as he moved back a spot.

Perfect. I moved one of my pieces once to the right.

"I learned this game from you, Da. I won't cave so easily."

Da took his turn with a chuckle. "My little strategist."

Got him. I moved my piece in behind his, cornering him. "Got you," I said with a grin. Da shook his head laughing.

"Nicely done." He began to pack up the game as I stifled a yawn. "Go to bed. You look like you are about to fall asleep sitting up."

"Are you sure?"

"Of course. I've got this."

I dragged myself up to my room and only bothered to pull off my boots and vest before I flopped down on my bed. I pulled the furs up to my chin and let my parents' soft voices below me lull me to sleep.

I RAN THROUGH A FIELD OF FLOWERS WITH DA BY MY SIDE. BIRDS chirped as they swooped through the blue sky. Ma knelt in a garden in the distance, plucking plants from the ground. I tilted my head back to allow the sun to warm my face. I laughed as I leapt off of a rock in my path.

"Race you," Da said.

I surged ahead, my hair streaming behind me as my laughter danced away on the wind. We charged across the distance between us and Ma faster than ever before.

Ma turned towards us. The lines around the edges of her mouth deepened as she smiled, her eyes sparkling. As I got closer, the sparkle disappeared from her eye. My eyebrows furrowed as Ma's smile morphed into a frown.

Her mouth parted to let out a shrill scream, her hands pressed tight to her stomach.

Right where long, razor-sharp talons had punched through her skin.

Blood began to spill over her fingers.

She slumped sideways, blood trickling out of her mouth.

I scrambled to try and get to her, but each step seemed to take me further away.

"Ma!" I screamed.

CHAPTER
TWO
BRYN

I lurched out of bed with a strangled scream to see that the sky was dark outside my window. Rapid footsteps thudded beneath me.

The flickering light from a candle began to light my room as Da climbed the ladder. Ma was close behind him.

"What happened?" Ma asked softly. "Are you hurt?"

"No," I said. I wiped at the sweat that beaded on my forehead.

Da set the candle on my table. "Then what happened?"

"I don't know," my voice cracked. "I've never had a dream like that before."

My parents shared a look. "What do you mean, Bryn?" Ma reached across the bed to interlace our fingers.

"It was like any other dream, but all of a sudden, there was a scream and so much blood."

"A nightmare," Ma whispered. I almost missed the words as Da sucked in a loud breath.

"What—?" I cut myself off as Da shook his head roughly.

"No," he said gruffly. "Do not ask about it in the darkness. Never do that."

Da tightened his grip on the edge of the table, his knuckles whitening in the candlelight. "We'll talk about it in the daylight." He picked up the candle again and checked each shadowed corner in my room before he placed it back on the table.

Da left the candle burning in my room as he climbed down the ladder. Ma pressed a kiss to my forehead before she followed him. "Try to get some sleep. You should be safe now," she said.

I laid back down, but I made no attempt to fall asleep. My eyes focused on the small flame. It danced, casting long shadows on the walls.

Da cancelled our run the next morning.

Or, rather, Ma did it for him since he had already left the house by the time I woke.

I ran a couple of laps around the village walls, unsettled at the thought of not running in the morning. We always ran unless we were sick, hurt, or the weather was too dangerous. I needed the normalcy of it to try and forget what had happened the night before.

Luckily, there was no rain today. The rainy season brought storms and rain showers that lasted for days on end. They would be followed by a dry spell almost long enough to dry up the massive amounts of water before another storm hit.

But it was never quite long enough to fully dry everything. It certainly made the winter very icy.

Market day was always a busy day in the village. Well, as

busy as Ebonwell could be. Usually, Da would help do house calls to deliver medical supplies to those who couldn't get to our stall on their own. But since he left so early, I had no choice except to stop and ask Fannar to help me after my run.

I was just finishing packing the basket for the morning deliveries when Fannar showed up at the house. He didn't bother to knock before he let himself in and joined Ma and me in the kitchen. Fannar hadn't had to knock since he was a child.

He had left his long brown hair loose for the day, and his face was cleanly shaven. His brown leather vest was similar to mine, but his shirt and breeches were much lighter in colour. A black cloak edged with fur was settled around his shoulders to ward off the morning chill.

"Good tidings, Fannar," Ma said from her place at the bin where she was washing the dishes from breakfast. She didn't need to look up to know it was him.

"Good tidings, ma'am."

"You've done it now," I said quietly as I tried to avoid getting dragged into the fire alongside Fannar.

Ma shot him a look as she set her rag down and crossed her arms. "You know better than that, Fannar. I'm never ma'am to you."

"Of course, Ma," Fannar grinned, causing a dimple to appear on his cheek. "But sometimes it's just too good of a chance to pass up."

"Off you go, you scoundrels." Ma flicked the rag towards Fannar playfully, forcing him to dodge out of the way.

Fannar took the basket from me before he pressed a kiss to Ma's cheek and led the way out of the house. I pulled my cloak tighter around me as the cold morning air started to work its way through my shirt. My hip ached from my tumble down the hill the day before, and my run this morning hadn't helped. I tried to hide the soreness as much as I could. Fannar could be worse than Ma when it came to me getting hurt or sick.

He bumped his shoulder against mine. "Why the face, kid?"

"Kid? You're not even a year older than me."

"Yet I have the worldly experiences of an old man."

I rolled my eyes. "I wouldn't say that being abandoned in a snow drift as a baby counts as a worldly experience."

"Sure it does," Fannar said as he raised an eyebrow. "Not many people get to experience it."

I led us through the village since Fannar didn't know the path for the day's delivery. "Or they do, and we simply never talk about it."

"My parents do," Fannar said. "How many times have you heard them tell the story of them finding me?"

"Too many times."

"Exactly. You're just jealous that you've never gotten to experience the world like I have."

I smirked at Fannar as I led the way up the lane to a small cottage. "It really is a shame." I knocked on the door.

The door opened to reveal Marta and her screaming newborn. She quickly waved us into the house before closing the door behind us.

Marta's husband was out of the village on one of the raiding ships from Newtide, leaving her alone with a newborn that refused to be soothed. When Ma heard, she packaged up a few things to try and make it easier for her.

Marta stood in the doorway as she slowly rocked her baby back and forth. Fannar placed the basket on the large table in the main room. I held up the items that he passed to me so that I could explain how they should be used.

"This is a cream filled with soothing herbs. Rubbing it on your baby's inner wrists and around his ankles should help calm him down." Marta took the tin from me and rubbed the cream on her baby. His cries became whimpers before they stopped entirely. "And these are two jars of Ma's strawberry jams. Ma said they are your favourite."

Marta smiled. "They are. Thank you."

"Ma also said that you were having trouble sleeping without your husband home, so she told me to bring this tin of tea, too. It should help calm you."

"I really appreciate that, but I can't—"

I shook my head with a smile before Marta could continue. "Don't worry about it. Ma says that she remembers what it was like when I was little. She just wants to help you out a bit." Marta considered me for several moments before finally nodding.

"Your family is a gods send," Marta said. She laid the now-sleeping baby in his bed before rejoining us in the kitchen. "You two are being careful, right? No travelling on your own outside of the village."

"We're always careful, ma'am," Fannar said.

"Don't call me ma'am, Fannar. I'm only a few years older than you."

I snickered. Fannar's manners, combined with his mischievous nature, were proving to be rather dangerous for him today. "Ignore him, Marta, that's what I normally do."

"Hey!" Fannar cried, causing Marta to chuckle.

"Oh, of course, I'll do that from now on," Marta smirked before becoming serious again. "Be careful. They posted a new missing person parchment a week or so ago. They were travelling on their own and never returned."

I smiled at her. "Don't worry. We'll be careful. We only ever travel as a family, so I'm sure we will be fine."

THE MARKET WAS A LARGE SQUARE IN THE CENTRE OF EBONWELL. IT was surrounded by houses, all with stores or workshops built into them. The only tavern in the village was here, the merriment of its patrons spilling laughter and the sound of clanking tankards into the square. The symbol of the King Commander hung on the wall, dull and tarnished. A few stands were scattered around the square for people whose houses didn't back on to the market. In the centre was the Burning Circle, which stood out from the rest with its elegant engravings. Everyone gave it a wide berth.

No one was allowed to walk through the sacred circle.

Our stall in the village centre was busy as usual. Fannar sold Ma's jams and preserves so that I could focus on the medicinal ointments and teas. I had always been more drawn to Ma's healing than he was.

The sun had begun to set as we closed the stall. We packed away anything that hadn't sold into the baskets and crates. By the time we finished, the sky was almost completely dark.

Fannar went to buy us some drinks from the tavern so that we could enjoy a moment of peace before we carried everything back home. When he returned with the drinks, Fannar dropped down on a bench beside me and passed me a skin of water. I took a sip, the crisp taste of mint rolling over my tongue. I rested my head upon Fannar's shoulder and enjoyed the quiet nature of the square. The sky darkened to an inky black pierced by the light of several bright stars.

A large shadow passed overhead. "Did you see that?" I asked. My voice was quiet as I lifted my head to look around.

Fannar glanced around the square. He scanned the sky before he turned his attention back towards me. "Yeah, but what could it have been? All the large birds are asleep at night."

"All the large birds are asleep at night? Real impressive analysis of the situation," I snorted. "What about the fact that none of the birds in the area are that big?"

"Sard off," Fannar said with a laugh. Another shadow passed overhead, quickly followed by a third. "What in the name of the gods—"

A scream tore through the air as a light blazed over the rooftops of the houses that lined the square.

We rushed towards the light.

People raced around us, everyone running in different directions as they either fled or rushed to help.

We tore around a corner, flames reflecting off the windows of the buildings around us.

The smoke was thicker as we reached the house.

It had already been consumed by the flames.

Grass always burnt fast, and once it caught, the wood wouldn't be far behind it.

The young couple that lived in the house stood in the path. Their clothing was streaked with soot and torn in places. Fannar started towards them, but I grabbed his arm to keep him beside me.

His head snapped back to me. "They need our help. We can't just stand here and do nothing."

"There's something else going on," I said as my eyes swept across the scene. "Their clothes are torn. If it had just been a fire, they shouldn't be like that. Burnt, yes, but not torn." I focused on the couple. Their faces were pale, their eyes wide as they watched their house burn. They were even stopping the people who came forward to try and put it out. "Look at their faces; they're haunted. I don't understand why they would stop the people trying to help them."

Another scream tore through the air. The man pushed the woman behind him as she cried.

A large creature landed in front of the couple. I sucked in a breath as Fannar swore. The creature wasn't a bird at all.

It was a monster.

It had a large head topped with long curling horns and a mouth full of fangs that glinted in the firelight. Large wings tipped with sharp claws that had flared out when it landed now hung loosely at its sides. It had a broad chest with a ring of glass bobbles around its throat. The legs were massive, with long feet ending in more claws. The monster was still crouched from the landing, but if it stood to its full height, it would certainly tower over me.

I stumbled back a step.

A woman beside us scooped up her child, holding him close to her chest as she and her husband fled from the monster.

It surged forward on its powerful legs and cleanly beheaded the man with a single slash of the claws.

The woman screamed again as the people around us fled in all directions.

Someone fell to the ground, nearly getting trampled by the chaos around us.

The monster seemed to ignore the woman as it stuck a claw clean through the man's chest. One of the glass bobbles around its throat began to fill with a light-blue coloured light.

Fannar grabbed my arm and pulled me away. The glass bobble was almost completely full.

"We need to go," Fannar breathed, tugging on my arm until we were hidden in the shadows of an alcove.

I peeked around the corner.

The woman took off down the road, screaming, and the monster was quick to follow her once the bobble was filled.

I ducked back into the shadows.

"What was that?" I murmured

"I don't know," Fannar said. "But I don't think that it's over yet. There were three shadows. I'd be willing to bet there are three of those things somewhere around here."

I ran through our options for a moment, trying to come up with a plan. "We have to get to my house," I said.

"Okay." Fannar didn't even bother questioning me. Tonight, with everything happening, I couldn't have been more relieved not to have to explain myself. "You lead. I'll be right behind you."

I took off at a sprint, focused on the road in front of me. The light of fires sparkled in the corner of my eyes. Screams seemed to echo through the village.

A series of coughs forced their way out of my throat as I ran through a thick cloud of smoke. I charged into my house with Fannar close behind me. The door slammed closed behind us.

"Bryn!" My parents rushed towards us. Da looked me up and down, searching for injuries, before he pulled me into a tight hug. Beside me, Ma had Fannar wrapped in her arms. Da stepped back and placed a hand on each of our shoulders. "What took you so long?"

I swallowed thickly. "We saw one of those monsters, and it —" My voice broke as the images replayed in my head.

Fannar wrapped his arm around my shoulders and pulled me close to him. "It killed a man in front of us," Fannar explained softly.

My parents shared a look. "I should have known after last night," Da said.

Ma left the room without a word.

"You mean my—," I paused. "What did Ma call it?"

"A nightmare."

"Hold up. What in the gods' names is a nightmare?" Fannar's voice was loud.

I bit my lip. "I don't know. I was sleeping—*dreaming*—but there was all this blood, and Ma was screaming."

"We have to leave," Da said before Fannar had a chance to speak. "We need to get out of the village. Our best chance is to follow the wall until we reach the gate and make a break for the hills. If we move fast, we should be able to disappear into the darkness and be safe until morning." He pulled what looked like daggers from a bag he had slung over his back. He began to strap them to his waist and legs as Ma rejoined us.

She had changed into an outfit very similar to what I was wearing. Da handed Ma two daggers. She strapped one to her belt and the other to her leg. Her eyes met my own. "It'll be easier to run without having to worry about getting tangled up in my skirts."

"Your mother will go first, followed by you two. I'll be last," Da said. He stood at the window. The light from the fires cast shadows across his face.

"My parents—"

Da cut Fannar off with a frown. "We would never find them. It's chaos out there. We have to go now."

Ma tore out of the house with Fannar close behind her. I left just before Da did. There was an odd comfort in the sound of his footsteps behind me. If I ignored the screaming and crackling of fires, I could almost imagine that we were simply doing our morning run.

Almost.

We made it to the gates without seeing another monster. The gates hung off the hinges, badly charred. Ma charged through the gates, heading straight for the hill I had tumbled down the day before. The pathway was still muddy, but it had dried enough that I was able to find solid footing. We had just reached the top of the hill when two loud thuds sounded in front of us.

I slammed into Fannar's back as he froze in front of me. I moved out from behind him, and my heart thundered in my chest.

There, in front of us, stood two of the monsters with their claws stained in blood.

THREE

BRYN

"Skolli," Da said gruffly, his face pale in the moonlight. The only Skolli I knew about were the monsters from the stories I had grown up with. Demons that attacked at night and left death and suffering in their wake.

Fannar turned towards him. "Like in the stories?"

"Exactly like the stories and just as hard to kill."

Ma pushed Fannar and me behind them.

"The tales you were told to scare you were once the stories that taught people how to survive," he said as they drew their daggers from their sheaths. Da spread his feet evenly, bending his knees as Ma hesitantly followed his lead. "And it's time that our family remembers that there is more at stake here than our normal livelihood."

I scrunched my eyebrows. "What do you mean? What else is at stake?"

Da ignored me and focused his attention on Ma. She was pale, her daggers quivering in the air. "I know you're scared, but try to remember what my father taught you." His words were soft, the same tone that I had heard him use when Ma had burnt her hand a few years ago.

The Skolli charged towards us, and my parents stepped forward to meet the monsters. The Skolli wedged themselves between them. They each had to face a Skolli on their own.

I scrambled back from the fight, searching for somewhere to hide.

The ditch off the side of the path was mostly shrouded in shadow, and with the tall grasses in front of it, it was the best that we were going to do.

If we kept going into the hills or into the forest, there would be more options, but I refused to leave without my parents.

I dropped to my stomach in the ditch, my ribs smarting, and eased my body up to the edge so that I could see what was happening.

Fannar lay beside me, his body warm against mine.

I groaned, watching the fight, unable to do anything to help. Ma was struggling already. She barely managed to avoid the Skolli's attacks.

"Where did Da learn to do that?" Fannar asked, his voice barely above a whisper.

Da had a dagger in each hand. He used them to block the Skolli's claws. He spun and ducked to avoid the claws before he slashed it with his blades.

I shook my head. I had no answer to give him. Da was fast, but many of his moves were delayed—like he hadn't done them in a while. His dodges were too slow at times. Cuts on his arms bled from the blows the Skolli managed to land.

A sudden scream tore through the air. I turned back to Ma's fight. My jaw clenched as my heartbeat pounded in my ears.

Ma was slumped on the grass. Her left arm lay on the

ground several feet away from her. Only a trail of blood connected it to her body. She dropped her dagger and cradled what remained of her arm to her chest.

Blood quickly began to spread over her clothing.

Da screamed for Ma, trying to get to her.

But his Skolli stood firm.

He couldn't get around it.

I pushed myself from the ground and ran towards Ma, searching for anything I could use as a weapon. Fannar called out for me, but I ignored him. I needed to get to Ma. I had to protect her.

My arms shook as I scrambled to find something—*anything*—that I could use. Ma's daggers were too far away, and I had no idea how to use them. A sharp rock, half covered in mud, was my only choice. I tore it free of the edge of the path. Fumbling, I struggled to get a good grip. I started towards Ma, my stomach a knot of dread.

I screamed as the Skolli approached Ma.

My terror turned to fire in my veins that burnt its way through my body, pooling in my fingers and in my mouth. My body burned hotter and hotter as my skin broke and spread. Blood filled my mouth as my gums tore, but the inferno in my veins covered most of the pain as I felt my body shift.

The burning stopped as my body settled into its new shape.

"Gods' bones!" Fannar cried.

I glanced down at my hands. Where my fingertips should have been were long, sharp claws. I gently raised the back of my hand to my mouth. There were massive fangs where my teeth should have been.

I risked a glance towards Fannar. He stared at me with wide eyes.

I turned back to Ma as the Skolli raised its claws in the air. I charged towards them.

I jumped in front of her and raised my own claws to catch the Skolli's.

It was quick to jerk its claws free from mine before it slashed at me. The claws cut into my skin as I tried to jump away. I couldn't regain my footing as the Skolli lashed out at me with a vicious backhand. I crashed to the ground. Hard.

Fannar screamed, but the thundering of my heart drowned it out.

I struggled to my feet before I surged towards the Skolli, my own claws extended. I sliced at it, but it dodged my swing. It attacked me again and cut into my arm with its talons. I had no idea what to do.

I swiped at it again.

And again.

I was reckless, desperate to protect Ma, ignoring the fact that my arms and legs were covered in cuts. The monster seemed to anticipate my attacks, so I did something that I hoped it wouldn't expect.

I took several steps back before charging towards it.

I leapt at it, ripping out its throat with my fangs.

I spat out the chunks of flesh before I turned towards Da.

His movements were sluggish, and the ground around him seemed to be stained red. His eyes caught mine and widened. Fannar rushed towards Ma, but I didn't turn to help him. There was still another Skolli that had to be dealt with.

The Skolli beat Da away with a brutal swipe of its claw. Da hit the ground before he struggled to his knees. The monster's focus was on him as I covered the last few yards between us at a sprint and jumped onto its back.

The Skolli reached back and threw me off. I screamed as its

claws tore into my back. I hit the ground near Da and forced myself to my feet.

We would not die here.

My limbs were heavy, and every time I hit the ground, it was harder to get up. I needed to end this. I leapt at the Skolli and wrapped my legs around it. I allowed my momentum to carry me as I crossed my claws over its throat.

I carved clean through it.

I turned my attention towards Da, trusting Fannar to look after Ma.

Da slumped to his side before rolling slowly onto his back, his face pinched in pain. I dropped to my knees beside him and scrambled to remove the bag he wore. My claws caught and tore at the fabric. Once I got the bag free, I lifted his body to slide it under his head to prop him up. I scanned his injuries before my vision began to blur with tears.

I knew what injuries could be healed and what couldn't. Ma had taught me when it was best to simply ease the pain.

This was one of those times.

I knew there was nothing I could do to save Da, but I didn't want to admit it. I placed my hands over the wounds on his abdomen and pressed down.

I had to try.

My tears began to fall. The burning spread through my body again—we both watched as my claws turned back to normal fingers. As my fangs became my teeth once again.

"Da." My voice broke as Da's eyes began to fill with tears.

He laid his hand on top of mine as I kept pressure on his wounds. We were stained with blood. A combination of Da's red blood and the black blood of the Skolli that still covered my hands. The two colours mixed until they became one.

"My darling girl," Da said softly. Everything was a blur. I furiously scrubbed my eyes on my sleeve. I refused to have my last few moments with Da be nothing more than a tear-stained blur.

"I'm sorry. I don't know what to do." My voice was a broken whisper.

Da gave me a sad smile as he brushed my hair out of my face. It left a trail of wetness behind. "Promise me that you'll do your duty. Promise me."

I nodded, coughing to clear the thickness in my throat. "I will. I'll do my best." I had no idea what he was referring to, but I agreed anyway. I would agree to anything—promise anything—if it brought Da some peace.

"I can't imagine how hard this is for you, but you have more love in your life than you know. You will have your ma and Fannar. Look after them, and they will look after you," Da rasped. My tears coursed down my face as I nodded, unable to trust my voice. I blinked the blurriness from my eyes to focus on Da. He coughed, and blood bubbled up on his lips. "I'm so sorry that I won't be there. But I am so proud of you. So proud," Da whispered before his voice broke. "I love you, my girl."

Coughs racked Da's body as I clutched his hands tightly. "I love you, Da." A small smile broke across his face as he closed his eyes.

His body stilled.

He was no longer breathing.

I let out a wail, and my tears became sobs. My chest ached as I held tight to Da's hands.

If I held on, he wouldn't be able to leave me. But even as I thought of the impossible, I knew it would never become true.

I collapsed on top of him, my body shaking. The warmth of his blood soaked into my clothes, but I didn't care. Someone crouched down beside me, but all I could focus on was the pain.

Hands on my shoulders slowly pulled me off of Da's corpse. They untangled my fingers from his.

I dashed away the tears in my eyes as Fannar pulled me in close. He wrapped his arms tightly around me, but I couldn't focus on what he whispered.

I couldn't feel the pain from the wounds I knew I had.

I hadn't been able to protect them.

I had failed.

CHAPTER

FOUR

BRYN

Fannar struggled to help me to my feet. I stared blankly at him as he rushed towards Ma. He ripped the bottom of his shirt off and tied it tightly around the stump of her arm.

It was stained red within moments.

"Bryn," Fannar said. I blinked. "Bryn."

I didn't move.

Fannar stormed towards me. His hands landed on my shoulders before he shook me. *"Snap out of it!"* Fannar shook me again. "I know everything has gone to hell, but it will all go to absolute shit if you don't snap out of it and do something!"

"Okay." My voice broke. I cleared my throat. "Okay."

I limped towards Ma with a wince. Now that I was no longer as focused on my fight, I was painfully aware of every slash and blow I had taken. Fannar wrapped his arm around my waist when I stumbled. We made our way slowly towards Ma. I used the short distance to try and figure out what I was supposed to do.

I rested a shaky hand against my throat as I got a good look at Ma's arm. I turned towards the village, still burning in the distance. "We have to get her back to the house. All the healing supplies are there. It's our only chance."

Fannar gently scooped Ma up into his arms. She whimpered but was otherwise silent.

He took off down the hill towards the burning village, leaving me to stumble along behind him. A singed teddy bear lay in the entrance to an alley. Holding onto the teddy bear was a little hand.

It wasn't moving.

As we made our way deeper into Ebonwell, more people were sprawled across pathways. I let out a cry at the sight of Fannar's parents splayed across the steps of their house.

By the time I reached my house, Fannar was already there. His eyes were red and pooled with tears.

"Can you put her on the bed?" I asked as I limped towards my parents' room. "Close to the edge so that I can reach her."

Ma's eyes fluttered when Fannar set her down. He was quick to leave the room but returned just as fast with a stool that he placed beside the bed. I sank into it gratefully. I winced as my body smarted at the movement. My eyes scanned over Ma. The longer that I looked at her, the more light-headed I became. My shoulders curled forward as I finally looked away from her.

Ma would never have let me heal something as critical as this. At best, she would have let me hand her supplies.

But now I was on my own.

Fannar gave my shoulder a squeeze, reassuring me that he was there. "Where would Ma start?"

"What?"

"Think of what Ma would do first," he said softly. "You already know what to do. You just need to remember that."

My hand came up to his to return his squeeze as my fingers trembled. "Can you make a cup of knockout tea? Use two scoops instead of one. I need it to be strong. It's the one—"

"—with the green ink, I know. What else do you need?"

"Ma's healing basket."

It didn't take long for Fannar to return with the basket. It would take longer for the tea to boil. He drew a small table towards the bed and placed a candle on it. "I knew you would need the candle too. I've seen Ma heal enough times to learn that much."

I nodded, grateful that he thought of it. The candle had completely slipped my mind. What else was I going to forget? I sent him a smile. It was the smallest twitch of my lips, but it was the best I could manage.

His eyebrows drew together. "Can you handle this?"

"I have to," I said. I didn't mean to be short with him, but I was barely holding myself together.

Fannar considered my words for a moment. "I'm here for whatever you need. I'm not going anywhere."

"I'm here too." My eyes searched his face. "Did you see—"

"—my parents? Yeah. I did."

I had no idea what to say to him. I was saved from answering by the screech of the pot as the water boiled. Fannar was quick to leave the room. When he returned he passed me the tea before he made his way to the bed. He gently lifted Ma into a sitting position as I leaned painfully forward to pour it down her throat.

Since I had him use double the dosage, it only took a minute or two for Ma's head to fall slack against his shoulder as she slipped out of consciousness. Fannar eased her back down to the bed before backing away to allow me to reach her.

I reached for the basket Fannar had brought in. The first tin I grabbed was the most used by my family; the seal was easy to open. I untied the ragged scraps of his shirt from what remained of Ma's arm and smeared the cream over the stump. Within a few moments, the salve began to bubble. Once the bubbles stopped, I took a cloth from the basket and gently wiped it across the stump to remove as much of the cream as possible.

I pulled a spool of skin thread and a needle from the basket. Once the needle glowed red over the candle, I began to sew the jagged pieces of skin together, creating a rounded end for her stump.

I covered the stitches in a thin layer of salve designed to keep infection at bay. I tightly wrapped a roll of bandages around her arm, tying it in a knot over the freshly stitched stump. I lowered Ma's arm to the bed and buried my head in my hands. She had lost so much blood, and I couldn't remember what to do to fix it. Ma just had to keep fighting.

"Where are you hurt?" Fannar asked softly. I lifted my head to look at him. My body was one solid ache, so it took a moment for me to remember where I had been hurt.

"My arms and back are the worst. Maybe my stomach, too. I think the rest are just bruises."

Fannar loosened the ties on my leather vest and eased it off me. He moved behind me, allowing me to maintain some form of privacy as he healed me. Fannar drew my tunic over my head before he did the same with my shirt. He had to peel it from my cuts where the blood had caused it to stick.

"Gods, Bryn."

I swallowed thickly. "What do you see?"

"The cuts are mostly shallow, except for one gash, but there are so many." Fannar's fingers lightly traced down my back. "I can't use the knockout tea; you need to be awake for Ma in case she needs you."

"There's numbing cream in the basket. Pink ink."

I winced as Fannar rubbed the cold cream into my back. Once my skin was numb, I nodded to him. I could feel the weight of Fannar's fingers as he rubbed the cleansing cream into my cuts and the pressure of the needle as he stitched up the gash.

"I'm not as good at stitching as you and Ma. It will probably leave a scar," Fannar said softly.

"That's alright."

Fannar eased my shirt back onto my body before he pulled a knife from the basket. He cut off the sleeves of my shirt to get to the scratches on my arm. These weren't nearly as deep, so he only needed to numb them before he cleaned them out. When he lifted my shirt to reveal my stomach, the tightness in my chest eased a little. No injury was too serious.

I was going to be okay.

I didn't bother to change after he was done. Fannar helped me pull my tunic back on before he re-laced my vest. My clothes, while torn and missing sleeves, were in decent enough shape that I didn't want to waste what little energy I had changing. I found an old shirt of Da's for Fannar to replace his torn one.

When the sun began to peak over the horizon, I finally left my parents' bedroom. I made a cup of tea and stood in the open doorway of the house. I watched as the sun rose over the still-smoking village.

Fannar had spent hours soaking the outside of the house with water. Everything from the grass covering the roof to the walls. If it was too wet a rogue spark or flame wouldn't be able to catch. We didn't know where the last Skolli was, but there was nothing we could do about that.

We were in no shape to flee.

And in no shape to fight.

The village pathways were stained red. Countless broken doors hung off their hinges. But it was what I couldn't see and wouldn't hear that made my throat tight.

There were none of the early risers starting their day who always waved to me and Da as we left for our run. There would be no children's laughter in the middle of the day. No clinking of tankards as the sky darkened and the adults began to relax.

I closed the door before I slowly made my way back towards my parents' room. Ma still hadn't woken even though the strengthened knockout tea should have worn off by now. But she had survived the past few hours, and that was all that I could wish for right now.

As long as her heart still beat, there was still hope.

I had to cling to that.

I settled back onto my stool by the side of the bed. Some time during the night I had convinced Fannar to move it so I could hold on to Ma's hand. With Ma's hand in mine and my head pillowed on the side of the bed, I could almost imagine that everything hadn't happened.

By midday, Ma still hadn't woken.

Fannar brought in a simple meal he had managed to scrape

together a few hours before, but it sat on the small table, untouched. The very thought of food made my stomach roll.

I picked up the dish and carried it into the main room to dump it outside. There was no point in worrying if it attracted animals. The scent of smoke that covered Ebonwell like a blanket would keep them away for days.

"You need to eat," Fannar said. He sat in front of the fireplace with one of my family's old books in his lap. The pages were yellowed from age, and the spine cracked as he moved.

"I can't." I dumped the food before I dropped the wooden dish onto the kitchen table with a clatter. My eyes settled on the book. "What are you doing?"

Fannar leaned back in his chair to reveal a piece of parchment and a quill on the table beside him. "Reading. Da mentioned that the stories were originally about survival. I thought that if I reread the stories, then something would become clear."

"Like what?"

"I don't know. Maybe how to protect ourselves from them or how to detect them. Something. Anything. Things are seeming pretty desperate right now, Bryn."

I clenched my jaw. "They're gone."

"You don't know that."

"They're gone," I said. My hands gripped the table in front of me so tightly that my knuckles turned white.

Fannar sat back in his chair with a sigh as he placed the book on the table beside him. "There was something that Da said that makes me think that this isn't over."

"And what would that be?" I forced out the words through gritted teeth.

"Something along the lines of remembering that something more is at stake instead of simply the life your family is living."

"Was."

Fannar raised his eyebrows. "Sorry?"

"It should have been *was* living." My words were harsh.

"I know what happened to Da was awful—"

I clenched my hands into fists and slammed them on top of the table. "You don't know how it feels!"

"Of course I do!"

"I literally felt the life leave his body, Fannar!" I screamed. "I'm not entirely sure what happened to me—what let me fight them—but it wasn't enough!"

Fannar stood from his seat. "Bryn, you did everything you could."

"It doesn't matter - I didn't do enough. All I can feel is the blood on my hands," my voice quivered.

"I can't imagine how horrible that would have been, Bryn," Fannar said softly, approaching me carefully as though I were a scared animal that would attack him. "Our entire village went through hell tonight. I only found out that my parents were dead as I ran past them carrying Ma to safety. Ma lost not just her arm but also her husband. You fought two of those monsters and walked away with your life, which is more than I can say for anyone else right now." I whimpered, my hands shaking. "I have always promised Da that I would look out for you, and that's what I'm trying to do."

He had promised Da.

Just like I had.

I couldn't breathe.

I had to get out—I had to run. I couldn't care less that my body still ached or that the stitches were nowhere near healed.

My hand gripped the handle as Fannar reached for me. "Where are you going to go? Everywhere is destroyed."

"I don't know." My words were sharp.

"I'll look after Ma." My eyes slid shut as Fannar's footsteps moved away from me towards my parents' room. "You can't outrun everything, Bryn. Eventually, you have to let someone in." Fannar's words chased me out of the house.

CHAPTER

FIVE

BRYN

I didn't know how long I ran. Or how long I spent up a tree in the forest as I stared at the still-smouldering village. The sun had begun to set when my feet finally carried me to where I had fought the Skolli.

My hip ached, and my wounds throbbed. Yet as I reached Da's body, my pains were the furthest thing from my mind.

Da still lay where we left him. There was no one left to pillage his body. There was no one left to give him his burial rites.

No one but Fannar and I.

There was no way that I would be able to carry Da to the Burning Circle in the heart of the village, if it even still stood. Where he lay would have to do. He needed his burning to ensure he went on into the afterlife instead of remaining tethered to his body.

The forest near Ebonwell had plenty of wood for me to use for the pyre. I had never had to build one before; I hadn't even had to light one. I carried an armful of smaller sticks and twigs from the forest and piled them near Da's body before I returned for more.

A few of my wounds began to bleed again, but I refused to stop. Da deserved his burning, and I would be damned if some scratches prevented that from happening.

It took me longer to drag over the bigger, sturdier branches from the forest. I had seen people in the village use similar branches to build the base of the pyres in the Burning Circle.

I built a frame using the larger branches that I lashed together with a length of raw rope. I filled the inside with the smallest, driest pieces of wood. When the pyre was as high as my waist, I began to lay some of the thicker branches across the middle so that I had a place to lay Da's body.

The moon was high in the sky as I turned towards where Da lay. I froze as my eyes landed upon him. He was still covered in blood.

I could almost feel the warmth of it covering my hands.

My knees began to quiver. I didn't notice earlier, or perhaps I had intentionally ignored the fact. My stomach threatened to rebel.

"Bryn!" I didn't move at the sound of Fannar's voice. "Bryn." His hands landed on my shoulders before he gently spun me to face him.

"What?" My voice was soft. Defeated.

"What can I do to help? You never came back, but when I noticed it was nightfall, I knew I would find you here."

I stepped closer to him and rested my forehead against his shoulder. His arms wrapped around me. "I'm sorry, I shouldn't have said that. I was so wrapped up in how I felt that I never considered that you would feel the same."

"I wouldn't say I feel the same as you, just like you can't say you feel the same as me. But we are both in pain right now, and we can help each other through that," Fannar said. "The reading could have waited a day or two. I could have let our hearts heal a little first."

I shook my head. "No. You were trying to protect us. I know that. I'm just so scared. My last moments with Da were spent making a promise that I don't even fully understand, let alone know how to accomplish."

Fannar's arms tightened around me. We didn't speak. We didn't need to. We understood each other and knew that we were there for each other.

Always.

"Ignore the fact that everything has gone to hell." Fannar's voice rumbled under my ear. "What matters the most to you right now?"

"That Ma is healed."

"We've done everything we can for her, and now we must wait. What is something we can do right now?"

I swallowed thickly. "Da deserves his burning."

"Then that's what we will do."

I tilted my head back towards the sky. The stars pierced the harsh darkness where only the moon hung to light the black abyss. Da deserved to find his place among the stars.

"Can you lift him onto the pyre?" I asked.

Fannar pressed a kiss to the top of my head before he pulled away from me. "I'd be honoured."

He knelt by Da's body for a moment, his head bowed, before he lifted him. Fannar placed him on the pyre and neatly arranged his arms and legs so that he appeared to be sleeping. He pulled a water skin from his shoulder and poured some water onto a scrap piece of cloth from his pocket. Fannar wiped the blood from Da's face and skin. His eyes met mine. "He is not—*was* not—the type of man that would deserve to burn with blood still on his hands."

"Thank you." My vision blurred as I moved forward to join Fannar. My fingers slid Da's eyelids shut before I covered each with a silver coin.

Fannar pressed his flint and striker into my hands.

I knelt down and reached into the centre of the pyre. It took me three tries for the spark to catch. Fannar lightly grabbed my arm and pulled me up to join him.

We were silent as the flames began to spread. Fannar's hand squeezed mine. "He had no sons. It's your duty to guide his journey on."

I swallowed thickly. "No. He raised you just as he raised me. It's your place, not mine."

He pulled me close, letting go of my hand to wrap his arm around my shoulders. His strong tenor filled the air. A sad, lilting song meant to bring Da honour as well as guide his journey to the afterlife.

I didn't move as the flames engulfed Da. It wasn't until the fire was almost done that my attention drifted.

The bodies of the Skolli lay untouched on the ground.

I pulled away from Fannar and drew Da's dagger from my belt. My ears pounded as I made my way towards the monsters that had torn my family and village apart. I knew that they were dead, that they could no longer hurt anybody, but that wasn't enough to quench my thirst for revenge.

I sank the dagger into the first body with a satisfying thud. I pulled it out to stab it again.

A strong hand wrapped around my wrist. Of course, Fannar would stop me. He was always the one who guided me towards the right thing to do.

I tried to pull out of his hold."Let me go. I need to—"

"—No," a deep voice said.

I froze.

The voice didn't belong to Fannar. I turned my head towards the pyre where Fannar stood.

"Let me go!" I cried. I tried to yank my arm free again, but the hand on my wrist held firm. Fannar ran towards me.

"When I let you go, you cannot deface the bodies."

A second man grabbed Fannar by his shoulders to stop him.

"You have no right to stop me," I snarled. "They destroyed my home and my family. I was the one that killed them. That means I have the gods-given right to do whatever I want to them."

The hand around my wrist slackened. "Impossible."

"How did you do it?" The second man asked. He turned to face me while he kept a gloved hand on Fannar's shoulder.

"Who do you think you are?" I wrenched my wrist free, leaving my dagger lodged in the Skolli's body. "You have no right—"

"—I would suggest you rethink your tone," the deep voice said. "I am Gier, the newest member of the Striking Shadows." My eyes turned to study the man beside me. The moon was behind him, hiding any of his distinguishing features in the darkness.

I had heard of the Striking Shadows before—everyone had. Mainly because everyone knew you never wanted to end up on their bad side. They were a small-knit, handpicked group of people tasked with gathering information and fighting from the shadows.

It was never a good thing when they showed up unannounced.

Gier's head nodded towards where the second man stood

with Fannar. "And that is Hákon, second-born son of the King Commander."

My wide eyes met Fannar's. The subtle shake of his head told me everything I needed to know—he didn't know what to do either.

Fannar cleared his throat. "I'm embarrassed to say that I don't know the proper protocol for this."

Hákon chuckled before releasing Fannar's shoulder. "That's alright," he said. "My family hasn't visited this village in a long time."

"There is no reason to waste time with talking," Gier said as he moved closer to the body of the Skolli. "We have more important things we should be doing now." He brushed his long hair out of his eyes. "Where are the other survivors?"

"Gods, Gier. This is one of the times that you need to display some emotion instead of being a calculating asshole," Hákon said with a sigh. "Are there any other survivors?"

"As far as we know, we're all that's left," Fannar said as he grabbed my hand. He ran his thumb over my knuckles. It was a nervous habit he developed as a result of the countless scoldings from my parents for all the times we pushed the boundaries. "Except for Ma, but there isn't much more we can do for her."

Hákon stepped forward and began to roll up his sleeves over his gloved hands. "Take me to her. I'll see what I can do."

CHAPTER
SIX
BRYN

Hákon and Gier made their way towards a pair of horses.

"You might want to guide the horses through the village. The pathways are a bit—*messy*," Fannar explained.

Messy was certainly one way to describe it.

They led their horses by the reins towards the village. Fannar seemed content to lead the way back to the house, so I followed behind the group without a word.

Hákon walked beside Fannar and asked questions about the night before that I desperately tried to block out. I kept my eyes on Gier's back so I wouldn't have to look at the bodies that littered the pathways. Someone drew in a harsh breath as we entered the village, forcing me to blink away tears.

They brought the horses to the gated back garden of the house. Hákon took both sets of saddlebags as Gier began to care for the horses. He took the saddles off them as Hákon followed Fannar into the house and set their bags by their door.

In the light of the house, I finally got my first true look at him. His hair was a cross between blonde and brown, cut short on the sides but left longer at the top. He had a full beard, but it was kept neatly trimmed so it didn't become messy. His blue eyes danced around the house before they landed on me.

At Hákon's nod, I led him into my parents' room. He cursed softly as he made his way to the bed. "Who healed her?"

"I did."

"You saved her life," Hákon said as he laid his gloved hands on Ma's arm. Something that looked like blue lightning began to spread under her skin. He must have a healing bloodrite.

At least one thing had finally gone right.

I let my shoulders slump as I turned for the door. "It still wasn't enough."

I shut the door behind me and made my way out into the main room. Fannar was in the main room, his hands braced on the edge of the table as he glared at Gier. I took a moment to study the man as he surveyed my family's modest collection of books. He had long dark hair that fell to his shoulder blades and piercing brown eyes.

I joined Fannar in the kitchen.

"I offered to make some tea," Fannar said through clenched teeth. "But I was told I would be informed when needed."

My eyes widened. "Actually?"

"Yes." Fannar turned to the shelves and pulled down a couple of tankards. "I made a pot anyway. Your favourite."

"Thank you." I smiled softly as Fannar poured the tea into the tankard. I waited until he handed me mine before I headed towards where Gier stood. "We've been through enough without you treating us like we are lesser people than you are."

"Bryn, just leave it." Fannar's voice was resigned. "I'm hoping he won't be here long enough for it to matter."

Gier set the book that he was flipping through back on the shelf. "Are you two related?"

"If I call him a brother, it does not matter if it is through blood or choice." I arched an eyebrow. "Especially not to someone that we just met."

"That's where you are wrong. It matters to people far more important than yourselves."

"You listen here, you little—"

Fannar cut off my words with a gentle hand over my mouth. His voice was a whisper, "Careful. It's never good when higher-ups in the fortress come calling. Especially around here."

Hákon let himself out of my parents' room and closed the door softly behind him. He replaced his gloves with a clean pair before he turned towards us. "She's awake."

I placed my tankard on the table and headed into my parents' room with Fannar close behind me.

Ma lay still in the bed. Her stump looked like an old wound. Hákon had healed her.

I searched for any injuries I may have missed before noticing that she was staring at us.

"Ma," I said as I made my way to her side. Fannar lingered in the doorway.

"Where's your father?" Ma's voice was raspy. I swallowed, my eyes welling with tears. I shook my head. "Where is he?"

Fannar joined me by the bed. "There was nothing we could do—"

Ma's wail cut him off. I reached for her remaining hand, but she pulled away. Fannar gently tugged me back into his chest as we watched Ma curl in on herself in the bed.

I rubbed at my wrists as I watched her helplessly.

Hákon appeared in the doorway. "What happened?"

"She didn't take the news of Da's passing very well," Fannar said.

Gradually, Ma's sobs subsided, giving me the strength to pull myself from Fannar's arms. I turned back to her. She lay in the bed, her eyes staring blankly out the window, tear tracks still wet upon her face.

"Ma," I said. Her eye didn't even twitch. "Ma, please," I pleaded. But she didn't answer me.

She didn't even move.

"What's wrong with her?" Fannar's voice was rough.

Hákon laid a hand on Ma's arm, and the blue lightning flickered under her skin. "She's healthy. There's nothing wrong with her, medically speaking."

"That's not normal for her. There has to be something wrong."

"It may be her way of coming to terms with everything that happened," Hákon said. He tucked his gloved hands into his pockets. "With the loss of both her arm and her husband, her mind may well believe that this is the only way for her to cope with it."

I pressed my quivering lips together. "I was the one that had to heal her. I was the one that had to watch Da die. Gods, I killed last night, and I'm not shutting down."

What did that say about me?

"No one is minimizing what you have gone through. Everyone has their own way of facing the terrors of life. Your mother distancing herself is not a sign of weakness," Hákon said as he crossed his arms over his chest. "And forcing yourself to keep going to ensure everything gets done is not something to be ashamed of. It's admirable, not cold."

I swallowed thickly and nodded. I led the way out of the room—I couldn't handle being around Ma like this. She may be lying in a bed ten feet from me, but right now, she felt as lost to me as Da was.

Fannar wrapped an arm around my shoulders as he led me to the couch by the fire. Hákon and Gier took the seats across from us.

Gier pulled a leather tie from his pocket and braided his long hair into a horsetail. He cleared his throat. "Are you going to answer my question about whether or not you two are related by blood?"

"Bryn has already said that she didn't feel the need to answer your question," Fannar said. He stretched his legs out in front of himself and crossed his ankles. "I'm not going to force her."

"You have to."

I narrowed my eyes at Gier. "I don't have to do anything."

"I have to know," Hákon said.

Fannar tightened his arm around my shoulder. "No, I am not blood-related to Bryn and her parents. Would you mind telling us why it was so important that you know?"

"She shifted that night," Gier said, scratching at his chin.

"What do you mean by shifted?" I asked.

"Shifting is a bloodrite that many believe was lost a long time ago. It allows a person to alter their body. They can shrink in size, grow wings, or even change into something else entirely."

"I never told you how I killed them. How could you know that?" I questioned, Fannar tensing beside me.

Hákon leaned forward and braced his arms on his legs. "We were alerted at the fortress the moment that you shifted."

"How?"

"We have a map that is keyed into the Verndari bloodlines that flares wherever a Verndari uses their bloodrite."

Fannar drew me closer as he ran a hand through his hair. "What do the Verndari have to do with anything?" Fannar asked.

Gier sighed. "Don't tell me that you know nothing of the Verndari?"

"We know of them," I said harshly. I clenched my hands, frustrated with how the story was being dragged out. "Plenty of people in the villages surrounding our own think so little about them and the Commanding Family that they often have plenty to say about them. Very little of it is complimentary. I just don't see how that has anything to do with what happened."

Hákon stood from his seat and made his way towards the window. He surveyed what remained of Ebonwell as he spoke. "From the end of the Great War, there were always five Verndari. Later, a trainer was added, which increased the unit to six warriors. About a hundred and fifty years ago, one of the Verndari disappeared."

"How can one of the most public warriors in the realm just disappear?" Fannar's voice was threaded with doubt.

"Verndari trained from a very young age in all the skills that a warrior may require: fighting, basic healing, tracking, and strategy," Hákon explained as he turned back to face us. "The lost Verndari knew that as long as he didn't use his power, he wouldn't show up on the map. He also knew exactly how to hide because he knew all the methods that would have been used to track him." Hákon began to pace in front of the windows.

No one really spoke of the fifth Verndari anymore. The family had been lost for so long that many figured they would never be found.

"For a long time, we assumed he never had any kids

because the map never flared. But he must have simply taught his kids control, or maybe he didn't even tell them about their bloodrite. Perhaps they were just never in the situation where it would have awakened in them." Hákon stopped pacing and locked eyes with me.

My heart raced as I waited for him to speak.

Deep down, I knew exactly what he would say—I was smart enough to put the pieces together.

"Not many remember the bloodrite of the lost Verndari's line. But the family of the King Commander and the Verndari have been taught about the lost line since it disappeared," Hákon said.

"The lost line of the Verndari were able to shape-shift their bodies into other creatures," Gier said as he leaned back in his seat and crossed his arms over his chest. "We called them shifters."

CHAPTER
SEVEN
BRYN

I understood exactly what Gier and Hákon were implying. I was the last descendant of the lost Verndari line—but it was impossible to believe. My whole life, I had simply been Bryn. Nothing more, nothing less.

"That's impossible," Fannar said. "There's no way that can be true!"

Hákon moved towards the mantle where the family books sat. His fingers brushed along them. "How else can you explain that she shifted last night?"

"It was daggers, wasn't it?" I asked.

Fannar turned towards me with raised eyebrows. "Where did that come from? How does that even apply to the—"

"Each Verndari has a specialty weapon," I continued, cutting him off. "I know that much. The lost Verndari's was daggers, wasn't it?"

Hákon nodded.

I stood from my seat on the bench. I made my way towards the teapot and refilled it with water before I placed it over the fire. I needed to think. I needed space from the two people who sought to change my life more than it had already been.

I poured the hot water over the tea leaves that still sat in the bottom of my tankard.

I turned back around to face the others and placed my tea on the table in front of me. I leant forward, bracing my forearms on the table. I brushed a rogue curl behind my ear before wrapping my hands around my tea.

"I don't know what you expect from me," I said softly. My eyes drifted over Hákon and Gier before they rested on Fannar.

"You have to come to the fortress," Gier said. He was really starting to grate on my nerves. The man acted like he had never spoken to another person in his life.

"I don't *have* to do anything."

Gier began to rise from his seat, but Hákon rested a hand on his shoulder to keep him seated. "You have a duty," Gier said. "You can't simply turn your back on centuries of tradition. It's treason. No, it's more than that—it's abandonment of your post. It's cowardice."

I glared at him. "You may call me many things, but a coward is not one of them. I can't abandon a post I haven't even taken yet."

"From the moment you were born, the post was yours, even if you weren't aware of it at the time," Hákon said. "For you to not accept your post, or to accept it and then abandon it, is a terrible crime. One that is punishable by death."

I studied Hákon for a long moment. "You can't afford to kill me. Otherwise, someone much less important than one of the King Commander's sons would have been sent to find me. Especially here. This area seems largely forgotten by all the people in power."

"We can't kill you, that's true. But we can imprison you

until you decide to take your position. I'm afraid that my father and brother may insist upon it when they see the bodies of the Skolli," Hákon said.

Fannar joined me at the table and rested his hands on my shoulders. "I'm with you. Whatever you choose."

I considered my options for several moments. The room was silent. Tense.

As much as I didn't want to go, I had promised Da that I would do my duty. There was no way that I wasn't going to fulfill my last promise to Da. As much as I tried to ignore it, a seed of resentment began to take root in my heart. I had no idea what I was agreeing to when I made him the promise, and now I was about to be swept away by my duty.

"I'll go with you to the fortress, but Fannar and Ma are coming with me," I said.

"That isn't how it is done," Gier said.

"Well, now it is."

Gier leaned forward in his chair. "It can't happen. With the political climate the way it is at the fortress, we can't handle bending the rules for an untrained, unappointed Verndari."

"Ma and Fannar are all I have left." My voice broke. I cleared my throat viciously, angry that my control over my emotions faltered. "If you want me, then you have to take them too."

"Alright," Hákon said. Gier turned towards him with furrowed brows. "As the family of the Verndari, your mother has every right to be at the fortress. We'll have to find an appointment for Fannar in order to bring him with us."

"It seems like you are going to have Bryn on the front lines if there is another attack. I want to learn to fight in order to protect her back," Fannar said immediately.

My heart stuttered at the thought of Fannar learning to fight. How long until he was forced to fight on the front lines of some conflict? Even if that was what he wanted, could he survive it?

Hákon was silent for several moments. "That's the best solution we are going to find. I'll train you myself. Your mother is not up to the pace which we need to travel. Your mother and Fannar will follow us at a slower pace, with Gier to guide them. You and I will ride ahead and meet up with one of the Verndari on the way," he said. I nodded. I didn't have another choice. He studied us both for several moments. "Were either of you hurt?"

"Bryn was. I healed what I could, but I would feel better if you would take a look at the cuts yourself," Fannar said.

I glared at Fannar. "I can speak for myself."

"Were you going to tell him about your cuts?" No, I wasn't going to tell him. But I wasn't going to give Fannar the satisfaction of being right.

It didn't take long for Hákon to heal the wounds I had reopened. My back was going to scar like we thought it would, but I was okay with that. I had survived, and the scar was there to prove that.

I figured that I got off easy.

Gier disappeared out the door, claiming he needed to examine the Skolli and send in his reports. Whatever that entailed, I didn't know. I did know that I didn't want to spend more time with Gier than I had to. Hákon stayed for a quick meal that Fannar was able to scrounge together while I was being healed.

"Sometimes," Hákon explained as he made his way to the door after he had finished his food, "you can learn the most about the enemy by what they leave behind."

"Gods," I said after Hákon had left. I rested my head in my hands.

Fannar gave a weak chuckle. "I suppose that's one way to put it."

"I don't want this for us."

"I know you don't. Neither do I."

"But I don't think we have another choice," I said.

Fannar gently grabbed one of my curls. He pulled it down until it straightened before he released it, allowing it to spring back up. "We will do whatever we have to do. We have each other's backs—that will never change."

WE WOKE BEFORE DAWN THE NEXT DAY TO PREPARE EVERYTHING FOR the journey. By the time we managed to get Ma loaded into the cart, the darkness of night had lightened into a pink-tinted dawn.

I turned to Fannar and wrapped him in a tight hug. He chuckled. "We aren't saying goodbye, Bryn. We will just be a couple of days behind you."

"Be safe," I begged, causing his eyes to soften.

"Of course. As long as you do the same."

I nodded before heading toward where Ma lay in the back of the cart. The body of one of the Skolli lay beside her, covered by blankets so that it was hidden from view. The other Skolli had been burned after Gier had gotten all the notes he needed.

"Can you look at me, Ma? Please? I asked, but she didn't move. I bit back my cry of frustration and simply wrapped my arms around her. "I'll see you at the fortress, okay?"

Still no response.

I sighed and joined Hákon by the horse that was saddled

for me. Gier finished hooking the donkey up to the cart and climbed into the driver's seat. I swung into the saddle and followed Hákon out of the city at a walk. Once we were clear of the walls, we kneed our horses into a canter.

Judging by the position of the sun in the sky I guessed it was almost midday as we reached the closest town to my village. We hadn't had much of a chance to talk during our travels. The speed of our horses made conversation difficult. But that didn't stop Hákon from constantly scanning our surroundings even though he seemed completely at ease on his horse.

Newtide sat alongside the edge of the ocean, allowing them to easily participate in the raiding season each year. The main buildings were built from stone rather than wood, even though their walls weren't much better than the ones in Ebonwell.

Hákon drew a hood over his head, which, combined with his simplistic travel clothes, made him look like any other commoner coming into the town. He led us towards the gates, dismounting his horse and passing the reins to me with a gloved hand. Hákon approached one of the guards and bowed his head in greeting. "Good tidings, sir."

"Good tidings," the guard said. "Haven't seen you round these parts before."

"The early rains made the road we typically travel impassable earlier than it is supposed to be and extended our travels by a few days. We weren't planning on the delay and found ourselves needing to restock our supplies."

The guard shook his head. "Sorry to hear that. The rains caught all of us off guard," he said. He pointed down one of the roads leading into the town from the gates. "Follow this road until you get to the Loundry Marketplace—it's pretty hard to miss. That's where you'll find the best prices on rations and the like."

Hákon flipped the guard a couple of copper pieces. "I appreciate it."

"Safe travels," the guard nodded towards me as he tucked the coppers into his coin purse.

Hákon made his way back to me and re-mounted his horse. He led us into Newtide and down the winding road the guard had gestured to. The road was fairly narrow and lined with boarding houses and small shops. It didn't take us long to reach the marketplace. The road opened into a much larger common area lined with shops while stalls were spread throughout the middle of the square.

Hákon guided us towards a small stable tucked into the corner of the marketplace. He nodded at me to dismount as a stablehand came out to meet us.

"How much for our horses for an hour?" Hákon asked the young woman.

"One silver, sir," she said.

"If I give you two silver, can you make sure they get a good brush and some food, please?"

She nodded. "It would be my pleasure."

Hákon passed her the coins and led me out of the stable. He paused for a moment, searching the marketplace before he turned back to me. "This way," he said. "Gil was supposed to meet us at the tavern at midday today. He should be there shortly if he isn't already."

The tavern was near the stable. It had a dark brown bar that had been polished until it shone. Tables were spread throughout the space, and a staircase was at the back of the room. A small raised platform was near the large fireplace. There were only two windows by the front door, so the space was lit with lanterns that hung from the rafters and candles that were in the centre of the tables.

Hákon headed straight for the table that was tucked in the back corner. A man sat in it, his back to the corner so he could see the entire room. He had neatly kept brown hair that looked like he had brushed it back from his face with his fingers. His vivid green eyes seemed to pierce through me as he waited for us to join him. His shoulders were broad, and even with the harsh shadows on his face from the lighting, I could still tell he was handsome. Incredibly handsome.

He studied me for one more moment before he turned his attention to Hákon, who took the seat across from him. I took the seat between the two, and the man shifted ever so slightly away from me.

Hint taken.

"Where's Gier?" the man asked in a deep voice.

"He's behind us. He's travelling with her adopted brother and mother as well as an important package," Hákon explained.

I shuddered. That was one way to describe the Skolli corpse.

"And this is the one then?"

I bristled. "This one has a name, and it is Bryn." The man nodded at me.

"Gil," was all he said.

CHAPTER
EIGHT
BRYN

After three long days on the road, we finally reached Goldhelm, a large, sprawling city that stood between the fortress and the ocean. In the early hours of the morning, we made our way through the streets that had already begun to fill with people starting their day. The women curtsied while the men bowed, staying still until we passed them.

The gates to the fortress opened as soon as Hákon was near them.

The fortress was an impressive structure. It was a large stone building that stood as tall as three houses stacked on top of each other. Four sets of stone and wooden buildings zigzagged off the four corners and stood slightly shorter than the main building. As we reached the courtyard in front of the entrance, a handful of young boys came forward to take our horses.

A pair of elegantly dressed women stood on the steps leading into the fortress. Their dresses were the finest I had ever seen. They were made from rich fabrics embroidered with gold and silver threads and hemmed with fur. The older woman had her golden brown hair elegantly pinned to her head while the younger's matching locks were curled and left hanging loosely down her back.

Hákon stopped just before the steps to bow his head. "Mother. Sigrún."

The Queen and the youngest princess.

Gil had already sunk into a deep bow while I scrambled to curtsy but stumbled over my feet. He stayed still, making no move to help me regain my balance. I ducked my head, my cheeks burning.

"Please, there's no need for that. I've heard you were injured. You must be sore," the Queen said. I slowly straightened, Gil and Hákon doing the same. "I just wanted to see you. There will be time for formal introductions later. I'm sure the Verndari are anxious to meet you." I nodded in respect before the Queen and the princess headed back inside the fortress.

Hákon turned back towards me. "This is where we part for now. I have to go and update Ragna on everything that happened in your village. Gil will lead you to the Verndari wing."

"Thank you for everything," I said.

Hákon smiled and waved goodbye to us before he started across the grounds.

Gil turned towards one of the buildings that branched off the main structure. I stayed where I was.

He looked back over his shoulder at me, but I still refused to move. Gil tilted his head back to the sky as if asking for patience before returning to my side.

"What's wrong? Why aren't you following me?" he asked.

"I am not a dog," I bit out. "If you want me to follow you, then you should ask."

He was quiet for a moment. "Would you like to join me? I will show you to the Verndari wing."

I didn't bother to answer. I simply started walking in the direction he had gone. It didn't take Gil long to reach my side, his long legs allowing him to catch up easily.

A man, no older than I was, joined us partway across the grounds. He was tall and lanky. His dark brown hair was pulled back from his face in many small braids tied at his neck with a leather tie. He had the sleeves of his loose white shirt rolled up around his elbows, causing it to stand out against his dark skin.

He fell into step on my other side as he studied me closely.

"Who are you?" I asked.

"Óskar of the most honourable Verndari at your service. Do you deem me worthy enough to learn your name, young maiden?"

"It's Brynja, but everyone calls me Bryn."

"Honoured to meet you," Óskar said with an exaggerated bow.

We walked through a set of large double doors. "You can get to the Verndari buildings through the central area of the fortress, but sometimes it's quicker and easier for us to use these doors instead," Óskar explained. Gil separated from us with a nod, leaving Óskar to lead me through a long hallway filled with many doors.

"Is he always like that?" I asked quietly.

"Gil? He comes across as cold and withdrawn—but he also cares more than almost anyone I know. It just takes him some time to...warm up to people."

He began to point out some of the doors we passed. Some of them led to our private rooms, others to meeting rooms. By the time we reached the end of the hallway where the shared areas were, voices carried into the hallway from the common room.

Óskar walked boldly into the room. "I am back; no need to fret."

"Why would we be 'fretting'?" a deep, rich voice asked.

"Who uses the word 'fret'?" A female voice rang through the air.

"Your words stab deep into my heart," Óskar said; his joking nature somehow grounded me in reality. He reminded me a bit of Fannar, loosening the tension in my shoulders. I took a deep breath before I entered the room as Óskar continued to talk.

Everyone stared at me as they ignored everything Óskar was saying. He shook his head with a small smile on his face. "Great. One lost Verndari returns, and suddenly, you are yesterday's news. I get it."

"We've seen your mangy face plenty of times; you're nothing special anymore. Besides, the fact I am no longer the only girl is much more exciting than you, Óskar," a young woman said. Her long, golden hair hung loose over her simple clothes. Judging by her tan, she spent a lot of time outside. She smiled at me; her brown eyes sparkled. "I'm Rúna."

I nodded my head, too overwhelmed to think of what to say.

An older man, older than any of the others in the room, shook his head at Rúna, causing the firelight to flicker on his dark-skinned bald head. A scar stretched from the corner of his eye to the bottom of his ear. "Don't mind Rúna or Óskar. Sometimes they can be a little too much to handle, even if you have been around them most of your life," he said with the same deep voice I heard from the hallway. He held out a hand to me. "I'm Georg, the trainer of the Verndari."

I clasped his hand, the roughness of callouses scratching my palm. "Nice to meet you."

Georg nodded towards a man lounging in a seat by the fire with a book open in his lap. His shoulder-length hair was pulled back from his face and knotted at the back of his head. "You've already met Gil, so the last Verndari for you to meet is Pétur."

"Heard you tangled with a couple Skolli," Pétur said. His brown eyes landed on me briefly before returning to his book. "Pretty impressive to see you in one piece."

Georg led me towards a couch in front of the fire. "Normally, I would give you time to settle in a little bit, but we don't have a choice." He took a seat across from me. "There's a lot to go over and not much time to do it."

"What do you mean?" I shrugged off my cloak.

"You are to be officially appointed as a Verndari in two days."

THE NEXT MORNING, I SAT ACROSS FROM GEORG AT A LARGE TABLE IN one of the meeting rooms in the Verndari wing. Parchments were spread between us, a mess of family trees, titles and bloodrites.

Georg ran a hand over his head.

"Normally, we would train you slowly, over the years, so you would be ready to take your place as a Verndari around the time of your sixteenth birthday," Georg said. "Obviously, we don't have that luxury anymore. I will have to give you the most basic of information and then hope we have time for the rest after the appointment."

"Why is the King Commander in such a rush to have me

appointed? Is it because of the return of the Skolli, or is it because I will be easier to control once I'm appointed?"

Georg studied me for a long moment. "You are quite clever —you'll need to be to survive in this position," he said. "To answer your question, it is probably a combination of factors. The Skolli play a large role in it. It would be incredibly informative to have someone with us who has fought them before. There is only so much you can learn from written records and passed-down tales."

"And the other factors?"

"He presents himself as more powerful by finding the lost Verndari. And power is very important to the King Commander."

"You make it sound like we are things for him to collect."

Georg braced his forearms on the table in front of him. "That's because that's pretty close to what we are, to him at least. The King Commander and some of his children believe we are nothing more than something that is there to reinforce their power. An extension of his fighting arm, if you will."

I stared down at the table and didn't say a word.

"The Verndari have answered only to the King Commander and his family since the end of the Great War. Over time, very specific rules regarding the Verndari were developed. If these rules are disobeyed, it is considered the highest form of treason and is punishable by death," Georg said.

"What are these rules? I would hate to bow wrong and end up with my neck literally on the chopping block."

"Well, I can reassure you that bowing wrong doesn't result in beheading—most of the time, at least," Georg said. He spread five parchments filled with family trees on the table between us. "Most revolve around ensuring the Verndari fulfill their duty to the King Commander."

There was that word again. Duty.

Do your duty. Fulfill their duty.

And I would—I had promised I would. There was no other option.

"The most powerful child of a Verndari must take over their parent's position. This typically occurs between the ages of sixteen and eighteen. There are very few exceptions to this rule. If the child does not inherit the bloodrite required, they cannot accept the position. In this case a different child would take their parent's place. If the eldest child, who is typically the one to take the position, is weaker than one of their siblings, they will be replaced by whoever is more powerful."

"Do those kinds of things happen often?" I asked.

"It happens more often than you think," he said as he tapped one of the family trees. "Gil is the oldest of three children. Neither of his younger sisters inherited their mother's bloodrite, so Gil was the one appointed." He tapped on another tree. "Pétur is an only child like you. As a result, he had no choice about his appointment. Where it gets interesting is with Óskar and Rúna."

I studied their family trees. "How so?"

"Óskar has a twin sister who also inherited their father's bloodrite. As a result, they were watched from the time they were young. Óskar was determined to be more powerful, but just barely. It could have easily gone the other way."

"And Rúna?"

"Rúna's little brother showed great potential from a very young age. As they got older, it became apparent he was going to be more powerful than Rúna," Georg said. He tapped his fingers against the table restlessly.

My stomach quivered. "Then why is Rúna a Verndari?" I asked hesitantly.

"Heimir, Rúna's brother, died when a fire engulfed their family cottage. Her mother died as well. It was a stroke of luck Rúna stayed with Gil's family that night."

I swallowed thickly. "And her father?"

"Dead. Killed by an illness a few years after Heimir was born."

Rúna was even more alone in this world than I was.

"Rúna was their last choice then," I said.

"Yes, but she has worked incredibly hard to prove she deserves to be a Verndari." He cleared his throat and gathered the parchment. "Sadly, I don't have enough time to teach you everything you need to know about the court. I only have time to briefly cover the ranks."

My head felt like it was spinning.

"The King Commander and his family are the highest-ranking people in the realm. People can challenge for the position, but that hasn't happened for over a hundred years," Georg said.

"Why would someone challenge them? Don't they get born into the position?"

"They do, but that's not all that matters. Power and strength are the most important. If the King Commander isn't powerful, it would weaken everyone below him. As a result, if someone believes they are stronger, they can challenge the King Commander for his position. It's a risk, though. If the challenger loses, they are beheaded. Many believe it isn't worth the risk as long as the King Commander has a bloodrite to wield."

A knock sounded, and Óskar popped his head inside the room.

"What do you need, Óskar?" Georg asked.

"I was going to see if Bryn wanted to walk around the

fortress with Rúna and me whenever you two are finished here," Óskar said.

"Well, I think we covered everything we will be able to today. If she goes with you is up to her, though."

I stood from my chair. "I'll go. I should try and get to know the place in which I'm going to be living."

Óskar grinned and opened the door fully. A black dog, whose back came to about his knee, bounded into the room. A large canine grin was on its face as it jumped up on me to get my attention. A large patch of gray fur on his chest stood out against the rest of his black coat.

"Down, Yugar," Óskar said. The dog sat down, his tail still wagging against the floor. "Sorry about that. Yugar gets excited when he meets someone new."

"Is he yours?" I asked as we made our way out of the room.

"Yes, he's almost always with me," Óskar said. "My family's bloodrite revolves around wildlife. I have a few other animals my family breeds for specific purposes."

The conversation flowed easily as Óskar, Rúna, and I wandered through the fortress. Some people nodded as we passed by, while others ignored us entirely. One woman around our age stopped in front of us. Her skirts skimmed the floors as she propped a hand on her hip.

Her incredibly dark hair hung loose down her back, and her brown eyes glinted. "My, my. If it isn't, the long lost Verndari finally returned to her rightful place," she said.

"Leave it, Emilía," Óskar said.

"Leave what? I simply wanted to say hello."

"Well, now you can leave," Rúna said; her words were almost a hiss.

Emilía sneered at her for a moment before she focused her attention on me. "Too bad there's no way you will survive long enough to enjoy being here. The group of fools who call them-selves Verndari will once again be down to four. Such a pity."

Emilía swept passed us, bumping into Rúna's shoulder on her way.

Óskar opened his mouth to say something, but I grabbed his arm and shook my head. There was no point.

CHAPTER
NINE

I sat in front of the mirrored glass as the maid tried to gain control over my curls. She carefully gathered my hair on the back of my head with intricate braids.

Today was my official appointment as a Verndari.

The maid turned me to face her and carefully applied the barest amount of colour to my cheeks to hide how pale my nerves made me. She darkened my lashes before she painted my lips a deep, blood-red colour. She dipped her fingers into the paint pot and dotted it from the corner of my eyes to my hairline.

My uniform for the ceremony was the most beautiful piece of clothing I had ever worn. The main gown draped effortlessly over my body before gently sweeping the floor. The black fabric had golden threads woven into it, causing it to glitter in the light. A black fur cloak clasped to the sides of my shoulders and a patch of embroidery was attached to the cloak with the Verndari crest in golden thread.

I slipped on a pair of black slippers before I drew back the curtain that separated my bedroom from my small living area. My fingers shook as I made my way towards Fannar.

"You look wonderful," Fannar said softly from where he stood by the fireplace.

"I don't look like me."

"You still look like the girl I have always known, just dressed a bit fancier than normal."

I smiled sadly. "Are you sure?"

"Of course I am," Fannar made his way over to me. "I ran into someone on my way to your rooms."

"You mean the guards stationed at the doors to the wing?"

Fannar flicked me gently in the side. "No, smart ass. I don't remember his name, but he was a tall guy. Strong looking with a bald head."

"That must have been Georg, the trainer of the Verndari. What did he want?"

"He wanted me to give something to you." He pulled an ornately decorated dagger and sheath from his pocket. The sheath was strung on a gold chain. "Apparently, the Verndari wear ceremonial weapons at political events as a reminder of their role. Traditionally, they are given them by their parent who served as a Verndari before them." Fannar rubbed the back of his neck before he cleared his throat. "Georg asked me to give it to you because with Da dead, he thought I would be the closest thing you have to family."

I gave him a watery smile. "He wouldn't be wrong."

Fannar attached the gold chain around my waist like it was the most delicate of belts. He took a step back, assessing me before he nodded.

"Make them bow to you, Bryn."

I led Fannar to the entrance chamber of the Verndari wing. Ma sat upon one of the benches with Georg nearby. Fannar pulled me into a tight hug before he guided Ma out into the fortress.

The other Verndari began to make their way into the room. Rúna was dressed in the same outfit as me but with an elegant whip attached to her hip. Gil was stunning in his elegant black trousers that were tucked into black leather boots that had been polished until they shone. He wore a dark shirt under his formal jacket. The jacket was made of a stiff black material that hung open to his knees. The same fur of my cloak hemmed the edges of his jacket. The other men wore the same outfit, and all had the Verndari symbol embroidered on the side of their arms. Pétur and Gil had swords on their hip. Georg had a war axe attached to his back, while Óskar had a quiver of golden arrows and a bow swung over his back.

Georg arranged us into pairs to enter the ceremony. Óskar and I were in the back of the group as Georg and Pétur led us into the fortress.

By the time we reached the Gathering Room, my stomach was completely knotted. Óskar allowed me to take a breath to calm myself before we entered the room.

Long tables lined with benches filled most of the space. A raised wooden platform held the thrones of the King Commander and his family. There was an open space in front of the platform that was ringed with people dressed in their finest furs and leathers. Banners with the King Commander's crest hung from the ceiling. The family crests belonging to the Verndari were nailed to the walls.

I didn't recognize a single face that we passed. Once I came to a stop beside the other Verndari I could see Fannar and Ma in the front of the row closest to the thrones.

The King Commander's family entered the room through a

door behind their thrones. The Verndari all sank into bows and curtsies along with the rest of the room.

"Friends, we gather together today to celebrate the long-anticipated return of the lost Verndari family. Today, not only has the family returned to court, but they will also finally occupy their rightful spot as Verndari once again," the King Commander announced. Cheers erupted throughout the room. The Verndari stepped back to flank me. "It is my honour to introduce Jarl Brynja to court as the head of her family."

Hákon beckoned me towards the platform.

I held my head high as I walked towards the platform. I knelt on the steps that led to the thrones and bowed my head. The King Commander's boots rang through the room as he descended the stairs. I unfastened my dagger from my belt with fingers that shook. I held it out to the King Commander hilt first.

"King Commander, I was always under the impression that the members of the Verndari were required to demonstrate the skill needed to hold their position," a man said.

My eyes slid over to a man as he stepped out of his place in the crowd and into the cleared space in front of the platform.

He was shorter than Da had been, yet his arms and legs were much more muscular. His head was bald, but a ragged black beard showed what colour his hair would be. His eyes were dark and filled with hatred.

"That's true, Jarl Ottó. Jarl Brynja has revealed that she does have the abilities expected of a Verndari."

"Forgive me, My Commander, but as far as I am aware, she was just discovered a matter of days ago. There is no way that the many years of training required of a Verndari could have been completed within those days."

"If I am not mistaken, what you are saying borders on

insubordination," the Queen said. Her sweet tone disguised most of the venom in her voice but not all of it. "While the Jarls of Drysden reserve the right to make their own choices regarding their personal fighting forces and staff, they do not have the right to interfere with the Verndari."

"I'm well aware of the laws that govern my behaviour. Yet, as a member of the Council of Higher Jarls, it is my responsibility to protect Drysden. I believe appointing an untrained and untested girl as a Verndari puts us all at risk. I suggest that my daughter, Emilía, would be a better candidate for the position than this girl," Ottó said.

I bowed my head, my cheeks burning.

Silence descended on the room before the King Commander's voice roughly broke it. "Everyone except the Verndari, Emilía, and Jarl Ottó are to leave this room. Immediately."

I backed up to stand alongside the Verndari.

Óskar placed his hand on my shoulder as Rúna gently rubbed my arm. Pétur, Gil, and Georg moved to flank me.

"I knew that you had a dislike for the Verndari, Jarl Ottó, but it surprises me that you would go this far," Georg said with a bite in his voice. "Not only is it unprecedented, it is completely illogical considering that Emilía does not have the skills required to serve as a Verndari."

"I wouldn't want to fight with Emilía by my side," Hákon added. "Bryn may not have had years of training, but she shows potential and a desire to survive. The things that she could do with the proper instruction are endless."

The man that sat between the King Commander and Hákon shifted in his chair. The hair on the sides of his head was cut close to his head while the rest was long enough to be braided back from his face. A short cropped beard, the same colour as Hákon's hair, covered his chin and cheeks.

He must be Hákon's older brother, Commanding Son Baldur.

"I don't know about you, dearest brother, but all we know about her is hearsay. No one here has witnessed an ounce of skill or potential, as you call it, from the girl. While Emilía still leaves much to be desired, at least we have witnessed what few skills she does possess," Baldur said.

"A core aspect of a Verndari, tactically and traditionally, is their bloodrite. Emilía doesn't possess one. It would leave us vulnerable in battle," Georg argued.

"We should just announce that Emilía is the last member of the Verndari and move on. It doesn't matter that she doesn't have a bloodrite because the other girl can't even control hers," Baldur said, ignoring Georg completely.

I sucked in a harsh breath.

"We are trying to decide whether or not to consider Ottó's contest, not to automatically cave to his wishes," said a woman who sat between Hákon and his sister Sigrún. She looked very similar to Sigrún with her delicate facial features and brown braids that hung down her back. I didn't know much about Ragna, the oldest daughter of the King Commander, because she was never mentioned much in Ebonwell.

"Why wouldn't we follow his advice? Emilía may not have the same potential as the lost Verndari, but at least she has grown up at the fortress and can act like a civilized person rather than a bumbling idiot like the other girl probably will," Baldur said.

"Bryn did not even know she had a bloodrite when she awakened it to defend her family. She did it without any training. If that does not warrant her the chance at her rightful spot as a Verndari, I don't know what does," Hákon argued.

I opened my mouth, desperate to defend myself, but Georg silenced me with a small shake of his head.

"Hákon's right," Ragna said as she studied me. "On the political side of things it puts us in a vulnerable position if we cave to his wishes. It will paint us as weak when we cannot afford to do so. We cannot risk losing any support by presenting ourselves as pushovers."

Sigrún turned to her sister, her lips pressed in a thin line. "You claim that we would appear weak by caving to other people's demands, but you were quick to suggest a marriage alliance between me and a neighbouring country instead of war, Ragna."

"If we went to war, it would mean hundreds, if not thousands, of lives lost. That's too great a price to pay. So yes, I suggested we follow their ultimatum and have you marry their heir to the throne. I am focused on protecting our people; can you claim the same?"

The King Commander cleared his throat. "Sigrún, we have already agreed there is nothing we can do now. The marriage will not happen until you are twenty, which is still two years from now," he said. "Stop acting like you are boarding a ship in the morning and focus on the problem at hand."

"Perhaps we can compromise," the Queen suggested. "We can have them earn the position. Allow Brynja a few moons to train and then have them compete to determine the best candidate for being a Verndari. Until then, Brynja should serve as a Verndari, as is her birthright, but should she lose, Emilía would take her place."

Ragna turned towards the King Commander. "It would show that we still have control over the Jarls while making us seem understanding at the same time. It could work."

The King Commander took several moments to consider

their words. The longer he took to announce his decision, the more I began to fidget. Óskar rested a hand on my shoulder to try and steady me. I took a deep breath and tried to calm down.

"Very well. It is decided," the King Commander's voice seemed to bounce around the mostly empty gathering hall. "In three moons, you will both compete for a chance to earn the title of Verndari. Do you agree to the terms?"

"I agree to the terms," Emilía said with her chin held high.

I dipped into a curtsy. "Of course, My Commander."

After all, what else could I have done?

I had made a promise.

And by the gods above, I was going to keep it.

CHAPTER
TEN
BRYN

I sat in the common rooms, waiting for my lessons to start. Óskar was lounged across one of the benches with an arm tossed over his eyes to block out the midday sun. Pétur had a plate of food in his lap that Yugar was desperately trying to steal from.

Georg was in the middle of his weekly weapons maintenance and had roped Gil in to help him. Rúna had gone for a short trip right after training that morning and wouldn't return until tomorrow.

I still hadn't been cleared by Hákon to train, and my forced stillness was getting on my nerves. My legs were twitching for a good run.

A maid knocked on the doorframe. "Sorry to interrupt, I have a letter for Jarl Pétur and a note for Jarl Brynja."

"Thank you," I said, taking my small, folded note from the maid's hand.

In the note were directions to the library with instructions to meet Ísak there. Ísak had tutored both the Verndari and the

Commanding Family and had taken up the monumental task of getting me caught up.

I gave Yugar a scratch goodbye and waved to Óskar on my way out of the room. Pétur was already several steps ahead of me, his own letter clenched in his fist.

The hallways of the fortress were crowded as people went about their day. Jarls with their large war axes strapped to their backs greeted each other with hand clasps. Some people stood on the edge of the hallways, their heads bent towards each other to be heard over the ruckus around them.

I read over the directions one last time as I came to a stop in front of large wooden doors. With a sigh, I tucked a scrap of parchment in my pocket before I pushed the door open.

Many large windows filled the room with bright light and bookcases towered from the floor to the ceiling that looked to be two floors higher. Geir shared a small table with a girl that looked close to my age. Her hair, braided over her shoulder, was the same raven black as Emilía's.

Ísak arrived not long after I did and looked exactly as Rúna had described him. He walked slowly, his shoulders slightly hunched. His long grey hair, a lot thinner on the top of his head, was pulled back in a horsetail. His beard was just as grey as the rest of his hair and was long enough that it brushed along his chest. Wrinkles spread across his face and hands, while dark spots showed his love for the sun.

Ísak moved towards me with a sense of deliberateness in his slow and careful movements.

"Should I find us a table?" I asked.

Ísak shook his head as he made his way deeper into the library. I followed him to a back corner where the light barely reached. We came to a stop in front of an old bookcase that was stained a rust-red colour. When Ísak passed me a small knife, my stomach rebelled.

"It doesn't require very much blood; just a drop or two should be fine," he said with a voice that crackled like a fire in his old age.

I pricked my finger with the end of the knife and shut my eyes. The blood dripped off my finger. The unpleasant sound of wood scratching against stone made my teeth clench.

Ísak tied a bandage around my finger. I waited until his hands had dropped from mine to open my eyes.

He opened a door that had been hidden behind the bookcase.

"Where are we?" I asked.

"One of the few places in the fortress that many cannot access," Ísak said as he led us into the room.

"And the blood is what? A key?"

"Precisely. Only the blood of the commanding family's bloodline or that of the Verndari can reveal the door."

Ísak sat at the small table in the room, leaving me free to explore. Two walls were dominated by bookcases stuffed full of books with cracked spines and yellowed parchments. Opposite the door, a map spanned the entire wall. It was obviously of Drysden and the surrounding lands, but it was different than any map I had ever seen.

"Why did you have me meet you here? Surely, there are plenty of easier places to meet. Places that don't require my blood as payment." I studied the almost illegible spines of the books.

"I could not risk being overheard."

"Surely lessons would be harmless to whoever heard them."

"Being overheard could spell out both of our deaths. I

couldn't risk it," Ísak said. He watched as I sank into the chair across from him. "What do you know of the Great War?"

"Very little. Just that it was the war that split the people in our country in two."

"Yes, but that is just the barest of facts. Many have forgotten the true history of the war."

I studied his face carefully. He looked tired as he pressed his lips together, his wrinkles deepening. "What do you mean?" I asked.

"Back in the years leading up to the Great War, every night was filled with fear. Ógn ran rampant across the realm, leaving nightmares in their wake. Every other night, there was a Skolli attack somewhere in the kingdom. Naturally, people turned to the King Commander for protection. When it came to light that the King Commander and his wife were responsible for the attacks, many were outraged."

Were monsters responsible for my nightmare, then? Why didn't I see them? Many questions raced through my head, but I had to be patient.

Instead, I asked the one question that I thought I would get an answer to. "How is that possible?"

Ísak leaned forward in his seat and braced his forearms on the table. "How can you shapeshift? How can Hákon heal? It was in their blood."

"No," I whispered, intertwining my fingers in my lap to hide their shaking.

"Queen Valdís was able to create and control the Skolli. She sent out the Skolli to slaughter her people and bring their souls back to her. The Queen was able to use the harvested souls to extend her life and the lives of anyone else she deemed worthy."

One of the Skolli who attacked Ebonwell had stuck his claw

into the dead man's chest. Was the light that filled the glass bobbles around his throat the man's *soul?*

"So with these souls, she could extend life?" I asked. The idea was hard to wrap my head around. "So if she had a never-ending supply of souls, then she could live forever?"

"Yes," Ísak said. "King Commander Haraldur was the one that controlled the Ógn. He could use the fear they generated to increase the power of himself and others that he trusted."

"Did they have any children that inherited their bloodrite?"

"Bloodrites, as you'll learn, are not a precise thing. Some inherit from their parents, some from other ancestors in their family line, and some may not have enough power to wield whatever they inherited. In this case, their children inherited their grandparents' bloodrites instead." Ísak ran a hand through his beard. "Katrín, the Commanding Daughter, was able to control and wield pain like a weapon. Her brother Leifur was able to manipulate people's minds. He could force them to relive memories or even show them whatever he created."

"Their people turned to them for help when all along they were the threat," I said as I chewed at my lip anxiously.

"When the truth was revealed, a lot of people were horrified. They called for their heads. The Jarls and Warlords became divided when they realized some were aware of what was happening. They kept silent because they were offered extended lives or increased power."

I held up a hand. "Wait," I said, my head spinning. "So they let people suffer and die just so that they could profit from it?"

Ísak nodded as a ball of dread settled low in my stomach. "After that was revealed, the Jarls and Warlords became fractured. Some supported the people, while others supported their King Commander. We now call the war that followed The Great War."

"It was brother fighting brother."

"Yes, and it lasted six years before the King Commander was overthrown. In that war, six people, each from a different walk of life, stood out as commanders, warriors, and protectors. Five of them became the first generation of the Verndari while the sixth became King Commander."

"And what happened to the overthrown King Commander?"

Ísak's eyes drifted to the map on the wall. "After years of death and destruction, the new King Commander didn't want to start his rule with executions. He banished them to the north-eastern tip of Drysden and trapped them behind a barrier with all their Skolli and Ógn. Without access to people to extend their life, they would eventually die, their monsters with them."

"Then how are the monsters back?"

"That's the question, isn't it?" Ísak ran his fingers over his beard. He gathered it in his hand as he gently stroked down it. "When the barrier was made, it was decided that a powerful Jarl would tie the strength of their bloodrite to it. They would remain unknown to ensure the security of the barrier. The only thing the King Commander insisted upon was the introduction of a fail-safe. A second family was added to the barrier. Both families' blood—blood that was *willingly* given—would be needed to dissolve the barrier."

I closed my eyes, resisting the urge to rub at my temples. Everything that I had seen, everything I had been told, tied together in a way I knew I wouldn't like.

The monsters should have died behind the barrier alongside the exiled commanding family. The fact that they were back meant that they were still alive. Shivers ran down my spine. The very idea that the exiled queen could simply create more Skolli made me want to flee, taking Fannar and Ma with me.

But I couldn't. Not with the promise I made with Da and certainly not with my commitment to the trials to be appointed a Verndari.

It was too late to run.

The commanding family had not returned to claim their thrones, so I had to believe that meant the barrier still stood. But that also meant that someone, or many people, had been weakening the barrier enough for them to get new souls.

"There's a traitor in the fortress," I said. My hands clenched into fists in my lap. Ma and Fannar were meant to be *safe* here. *I* was meant to be safe here. Or, at least, as safe as a Verndari could be.

"Yes. It's the only thing that would explain the situation," Ísak said softly. "Let me ask you one more thing. If you had been so careful for four hundred years, why would you suddenly allow yourself to become visible? Why send out the Ógn when they aren't needed to survive?"

I had never seen a Skolli before the night that they attacked Ebonwell. I hadn't known that it was possible to have a nightmare until I had one the night before the attack. They had been so careful to cover their tracks that not even a whisper about them had surfaced.

Yet suddenly, they returned with no intention of remaining hidden. No more missing people assumed to be lost in the wild. Entire villages were being destroyed now.

I could only think of one reason that they would do so.

"They believe they are going to be free soon. There's no need to be hidden or forgotten if they intend to return. They are simply gathering power while they wait for the best time to strike," I said, swallowing thickly. "There has to be a second traitor. They wouldn't commit themselves without being confident they would succeed."

"That is what I believe."

"Why tell me this? I might not even be appointed a Verndari in the new year. Why me?"

"You weren't raised in the fortress. You won't be blinded by friendships or love. I had no time to wait for you to adjust to this life or give you time to train. Emilía has challenged your position as a Verndari, and she is backed by her father, who is a very powerful Jarl. A Jarl whose side did not win the last war."

"His family supported the exiled King Commander."

"They did."

I wrapped my arms around myself. "What do you expect from me?"

"Find the traitors, and we will ensure they are stopped before they can dissolve the barrier."

"And if I fail?" I asked in a whisper. It had only been a handful of days since Da died. I had no idea how to fight or shift, but I suddenly had a much larger issue to face.

An issue that I had to face alone.

Ísak pursed his lips. "Then I fear we may have another Great War on our hands."

CHAPTER
ELEVEN
BRYN

I barely slept that night—my racing thoughts refused to slow long enough for me to fall asleep.

I had struggled to sleep since the night my village was attacked. Every night, images stained in blood drifted behind my closed eyelids. I was haunted by the look in Da's eyes as he died. I knew that they weren't another nightmare—it wasn't anything like that made-up horror that I suffered back home.

I was trapped in my own memories.

My chambers consisted of two rooms divided by a heavy curtain that hung in the doorway. My bedroom was fairly simple, with my bunk built into one of the walls. Other than my bunk, the only pieces of furniture in my bedroom were a chair, a bookcase, and a few clothes chests of various sizes. I kept Ma's healing kit on top of one of the chests. A fireplace in my bedroom provided both heat and light. My living area had a couple of couches near another fireplace, as well as a few chairs. Another two bookcases lined one of the walls, and fur rugs softened the stone floors.

Last night, after Hákon had finally cleared me to begin training, Rúna helped me pick out an appropriate outfit. I knew how to dress for long runs in the elements, but I had no idea what to wear to learn how to fight.

As happy as I was that I could run again, that I could train, part of me wished that the pain that lingered from my injuries hadn't disappeared. It helped ground me. It reminded me of everything that happened. But it also reminded me that it was over and that I was safe now.

I made my way to the common room. Only Gil was there. He sat at the furthest seat at the table like he had since we arrived at the fortress. His eyes met mine as I entered, burning into the side of my head as I looked away to take my seat at the table.

Meats, fruits, and cheeses dominated the selections for breakfast. I filled my plate with some fruit as a servant filled my tankard with cold water. Pétur entered as I began to push the fruit around my plate with her fork. He took a seat beside me after he shared a terse nod with Gil.

"You have to eat," Pétur said. He began to fill his plate with meats and cheeses. "Georg's training is intense. Without any food in your body, you won't last twenty minutes."

"I'm not hungry," I said quietly. Gil's eyes landed on me again as I spoke.

Pétur shoved a piece of cheese in his mouth, not even bothering with a fork. "I don't particularly care if you are hungry or not. You have to eat." A piece of meat joined the cheese in his mouth.

I ate a forkful of food, taking my time to chew it. Pétur seemed appeased at my efforts and turned back to his plate. He ate with a ferocity I had seen in Fannar after a long day of work. I returned to pushing my food around on my plate.

"Eat," Gil said. "You have barely eaten anything since you got here. It would be a poor use of your parents' sacrifice if you do not take care of yourself."

My eyes burned at his words, and I had to blink several times to keep my tears contained. I gave him a nod that he only returned once I finished my plate. Óskar, with Yugar by his side, and Georg joined us as I finished. With Óskar's jokes and Yugar's antics, they had me laughing in no time—wherever that pair went, they seemed to bring a lightheartedness with them.

Rúna joined us as we made our way to the training room, and Gil tossed her two apples that she easily caught.

I studied Gil as we entered the training room. As much as he tried to keep himself separate, he didn't block us out. The relationship he shared with Rúna reminded me of mine with Fannar.

Gil also paid attention.

He noticed I hadn't eaten much since I got to the fortress. He knew that Rúna wasn't a morning person, so he brought her some food in case she didn't have a chance to eat.

As much as Gil portrayed otherwise, he cared.

He cared but still kept himself separate.

Maybe he wasn't as cold as I originally thought.

The training room was tall, with large wooden beams that spanned the width of the ceiling. Wooden dummies and targets hung from the ceiling, tied together with rope. The ground had five evenly spaced white circles painted on it. One wall had two doors and six racks of weapons against it. The room was brightly lit by an entire wall of windows.

Georg stopped at the edge of a white circle in the centre of the room. We gathered in front of him. "Tactically, it is essential for everyone here to understand each other's strengths and weaknesses. With that in mind, I want to start today with a demonstration of our abilities so Bryn can see them. Pétur, Rúna, and Gil will show their bloodrites; you will have plenty of time to see their fighting skills later." Gil's face was blank as he continued to watch Georg. "Since Óskar's bloodrite is hard to demonstrate in the fortress, he will show you his archery skills instead."

"What will you be showing?" I asked.

"I'll do a combination of both my bloodrites and weapons." Georg turned his attention to Pétur. "You're up first."

Georg headed towards the corner of the room, where several ropes were tied to the wall. The ropes continued up to the ceiling and tied the targets together.

Pétur made his way towards the windows, opening each before stopping a few feet in front of them. He rolled up each of his sleeves and focused on the targets that still hung from the ceiling.

I leaned over to Óskar, my eyes never leaving Pétur. "Why did he open all the windows?"

"Pétur's able to control the elements. Since using earth in this room could result in *its* destruction and using water or fire could result in *our* destruction, he can't use them right now," Óskar explained. "So air is his only choice."

Pétur nodded to Georg and settled into a slight crouch, his feet shoulder-width apart, his knees slightly bent.

Georg untied one of the ropes. A string of dummies swung from the ceiling.

The air started to race through the room. My braid whipped around my face, and the wind snagged against my clothes. Some dummies stopped midair as if they hit an invisible wall, falling to the ground with a clatter. Some split in two. Others had large holes blasted through the middle of them.

Pétur barely moved as he allowed the dummies to fall towards him. His eyes darted to each one before a surge of wind attacked them. The last of the targets hit the ground with a wooden clang. All the broken pieces of wood were swept to the side as if an invisible broom was at work.

"Gil, you're next," Georg's voice rang through the room.

Gil made his way to the furthest corner of the room from where we stood and turned towards Pétur. Gil nodded at him, but it wasn't much more than a jerk of his head.

The wind rushed through the room as it flung targets at Gil. The darkness seemed to gather around Gil. A slender tendril of darkness wrapped around a target and flung it at the wall.

The target shattered.

Gil continued to throw targets at the walls. Ten targets were picked up by the wind. They were all flung at Gil at once. He moulded the darkness into a solid wall that surged forwards to slam into the targets.

Gil panted, his eyes frantic. I could have sworn that they flashed the darkest of black.

"End it, Pétur," Rúna said quietly.

Pétur's wind picked up another ten targets. The targets surrounded Gil as they flew at him. Gil's growl rang throughout the room. He retracted the darkness inside of himself before he allowed it to burst back out. Ten razor-sharp tendrils speared clean through the centre of each of the targets.

"End it *now*," Rúna snarled.

Pétur ignored her and picked up more targets with his wind.

"Gil. You're done," Georg said. His voice left no room for argument. The targets fell to the ground with a clank at his words. "Go get some air."

Gil strode out of the room without a single look at the rest of them. His shoulders shook, his muscles so tensed that they could be seen through his shirt.

He was like a predator preparing to pounce on its prey.

"Rúna, if you would," Georg said as he nodded toward where Gil had stood before.

Rúna spun on her heel and stalked over to the weapons racks. She grabbed one of the whips and uncoiled it as she approached the corner. Rúna cracked the whip off the ground before she sent a vicious smirk towards Pétur. "Bring it on."

The wind once again raced through the room as Rúna settled into the same stance that Pétur used.

Light flickered along her whip until it was fully encased in a golden glow.

The whip was a blur of light as it flashed through the air, cracking against the wooden targets with a snap. The smell of burning wood filled the air as each target that fell to the ground had a scorch mark in the centre.

When she finished, Rúna lazily recoiled her whip before she put it back on the weapons rack.

Óskar heaved a sigh. "I suppose I'm next."

Yugar lounged at my feet as Óskar headed towards the weapons rack to gather a bow and quiver. He made his way toward a different corner of the room. This one was covered with stationary targets. The wall, surrounding floor, and ceiling were littered with them. The targets all varied in size from what looked like the size of my hand to the size of a coin.

He drew an arrow and nocked it. Óskar balanced his weight evenly across his body, his eyes focused on Georg.

With Georg's nod, he surged into motion. The thrum of the bow filled the room at a steady rhythm. His firing speed made me think that he wasn't bothering to aim, but a quick glance at the targets proved me wrong. Each one was speared with an arrow.

Right through the centre.

Óskar swept his arms out dramatically and dropped into a neat bow when he finished. A single one of Yugar's ears flipped up from where he still lay, his head pillowed on his paws. Apparently, Yugar wasn't impressed by Óskar's tricks.

"Perhaps you would feel better suited to performing on stage during the festivals rather than training and donning armour like the rest of us," Georg sighed.

"You wanted me to put on a show for Bryn, so that's what I did," Óskar smirked, his eyes sparkling with mischief.

"Perhaps you need a reminder that you are, in fact, a Verndari and not a stage performer," Georg said, causing Óskar to pale. "You can practice hand-to-hand combat with Gil when he returns."

The grin that Rúna sent Óskar was positively wicked.

"He should have known better than to tweak Georg's nose when he hasn't had to practice hand-to-hand combat in a while," Pétur said with a chuckle as he moved to stand beside me.

"Why is sparring with Gil such a punishment?" I asked.

"Gil is the best close combat fighter out of all of us, except for Georg. And while he may be lethal with his swords, he can pound someone into the dirt with just his fists."

I knelt down to scratch Yugar's ears. The dog rolled onto his back, lounging on the ground as I pet him. "Óskar won't get hurt, will he?"

"We fight to pin or disarm," Rúna explained with a smirk as she and Óskar joined us. "He won't get hurt. He'll definitely have some bruises, though, on his body and his ego."

Pétur tipped his head back as he laughed. Rúna chuckled alongside him.

"How am I supposed to trust you guys to have my back when you are clearly looking forward to my suffering?" Óskar asked as he flipped them off, his eyes twinkling in humour.

Rúna grinned. "Bryn's your partner. She's the one that really has to have your back. Pétur and I only need to protect your back when the situation calls for it."

Óskar opened his mouth to retort but didn't get the chance before Georg called for everyone's attention.

He stood in the centre of the room with a double-sided axe in each hand. Rúna and Óskar backed away from the circle, and I was quick to follow their lead. Georg settled into what I was beginning to realize was a fighting crouch before he nodded to Pétur.

The wind spread through the room and picked up dummies.

Twenty-five dummies surrounded Georg before they all flew in at once. Georg's axes flashed as he moved faster than humanly possible. Some dummies lost limbs and heads before they fell to the ground. Others were slammed away from him with such force that they shattered. In less than five minutes, all the dummies lay broken on the ground.

Georg wasn't even panting.

Georg returned his axes to the weapons rack before he turned to me. "Unlike the Verndari, my bloodrites of speed and strength are quite common. I learned early in my combat training that combining my fighting with my bloodrites is what makes them lethal."

Georg assigned Rúna and Pétur to hand-to-hand combat before he sent a young servant boy to get Gil. Gil didn't even glance in my direction when he returned to the hall. He just headed straight for a sparring circle where Óskar stood alone. Gil sent Rúna a single nod before he settled into a fighting crouch across from Óskar.

Georg led me to one of the weapons racks in the room. "The weapons that each of you train on are the weapons that your ancestors used. During the Great War, they were able to combine both their weapons and their bloodrites for the best tactical advantage."

"Has my family always used daggers?"

"Yes," Georg said. "It was a surprise to everyone that your ancestor chose to do so."

"How come?"

Georg leaned against the side of the weapons rack. "The original Verndari from your family was a high-ranking Jarl alongside Pétur's. After Pétur's ancestor chose the sword as his official weapon, without even considering the other suggestions that had been made, many people assumed yours would do the same. Or, at least, choose the war axe."

"Why?"

"At that time, only the highest-ranking Jarls could legally carry a sword alongside their axe. It was a point of pride for them all, but especially for Pétur's ancestor. When people allowed Gil's ancestor, an assassin before being recruited to fight in the war, to carry a pair of swords, there was some anger. Pétur's ancestor held on to that anger and refused to part from the sword as a matter of bruised pride."

I studied the daggers on the rack. "And my ancestor didn't feel the same?"

"No. He felt that if Gil's ancestor was willing to fight in the war, she deserved to fight with whatever she felt most comfortable with."

My eyes darted to look at Rúna and Óskar. "What about the other two Verndari? What were they before the war?"

Georg tipped his head towards Óskar. "The man in charge of the royal hounds. The bow was an extension of himself." His head tipped towards Rúna. "A daughter from a merchant family that used staffs and whips to protect their merchandise."

I flipped my braid over my shoulder. "Why did my ancestor choose daggers?"

"Your ancestor realized the brutal efficiency of combining shifting while wielding and throwing daggers. Ever since that discovery on the battlefield, your family has always trained to be lethal with a dagger." Georg crossed his arms over his chest. "My duty is to make that true for you as well."

He led me to one of the sparring circles close to the weapons rack. "In order to fight well with daggers, you must first fight well and defend well without them. So that's where we have to start."

CHAPTER
TWELVE
BRYN

When I asked around the fortress where I could find Fannar, many had no idea who I was talking about. It wasn't until I came across an older gentleman who wore leather armour under his cloak that someone finally had an answer for me. His short-cut hair was balding back from his face, and his shortly trimmed beard was as grey as the hair on his head.

"You want to find that new boy?" His voice was gruff as he spoke. "Right this way, lassie, I was heading that way myself."

I sped up to keep up with the man's fast strides. "How do you know Fannar?"

"He has spent much time with the Hersir since he arrived here."

Many of the people we passed didn't acknowledge our presence. Only the servants bothered to nod in respect as we passed.

"Who is the Hersir?" I asked. Georg had been filling my head with so many titles and positions I felt as though much of the information had vanished.

"The commander of the Royal Regiment is called the Hersir," the man said. He surveyed me out of the corner of his eye. "You would know him as Hákon."

The man led us out of the fortress into a yard filled with sparring rings and training dummies. Various people milled around the yard as they trained. Some fought within the circles, some practiced fighting drills against the dummies, while others simply ran laps.

"I didn't know there were training grounds outside," I said. I scanned the yard, searching for Fannar.

"That's because the Verndari usually trains in their personal training hall. They only really come outside occasionally," the man explained. He guided us effortlessly through the somewhat controlled chaos of the training field. "These are the training grounds of the Royal Regiment that we use year-round. If we are expected to fight in the rain or snow, then we should train in it as well."

The man led me towards a corner of the yard that was emptier than others. Fannar lifted a large rock over his head before placing it on the ground and did the whole thing again. Hákon leaned against the wall near him, his arms crossed over his chest.

"Hersir," the man said. Hákon turned towards them. "The lassie here was looking for the boy."

"I have a name, you know," Fannar huffed as he dropped the rock on the ground.

The man chuckled. "I know. You've got to earn it, though, same as everyone else. Until then, you're the boy to me."

"Thank you for bringing Bryn here, Lúdvík," Hákon said. He nodded towards a group of men and women lounging by one of the fighting circles. "Your line is waiting for you."

Lúdvík nodded his head towards Hákon. He made his way

toward the fighting circle as he called out, "Hope you're all ready, lovelies. We have something fun in store for today."

"The last time you claimed we were doing something fun, my muscles ached for days," one of the men around the circle called back.

Lúdvík's laugh rang through the training field.

I turned towards Hákon. "His line?"

"The Royal Regiment is a large fighting force with over three hundred warriors. I decided to divide them into lines of twenty warriors, one of whom was appointed sergeant of the group. That," Hákon nodded in the direction that Lúdvík went, "was Sergeant Lúdvík who leads line two."

"I had no idea."

I watched as Lúdvík joined his line. The men and women joked around with each other as they settled into their places for whatever drill they were about to do.

"There's a lot of things we don't know here," Fannar said, bumping his shoulder against mine. "Better get used to it."

I worried my lip. "Are we still going to the shipyard? We don't have to if you are too busy here."

"If I push Fannar too hard, too fast, it will do more harm than good. Regardless of how much potential he has shown so far," Hákon pushed off the wall and made his way towards them. His gloved hand ran through his hair. "Taking a break to go to the shipyard would do you both good. I have to work on drills with the lines I often fight alongside. I'll send someone to guide you to the shipyard."

Hákon spoke briefly to a servant girl nearby before he made his way across the yard. No one even bothered to nod their head as he passed. They seemed to treat him differently in the training grounds than they did in the city.

Hákon joined Lúdvík's line and drew his sword from his belt.

He nodded once towards the woman across from him before they met in a clash of steel.

Fannar rested his arm on my shoulders and began to lead us out of the yard. "Just give me a few minutes to wash up, and then we can go." He guided us down hallways that I hadn't explored yet. I hadn't had the chance to. Just like I hadn't had the time to visit Fannar or Ma to see if they were doing okay.

We came to a stop in front of a heavy wooden door.

"I've been staying with Ma in the extra rooms attached to hers," he said.

"I didn't know," I said as Fannar opened the door. "I had no idea you were training with the Royal Regiment."

"Hákon met with me the day after we arrived here and drilled me pretty good. He said it would be a waste for him to train me to simply be a guard when in the drills, I showed the potential for so much more." Fannar smiled at me. "We haven't had much time to talk since we got here. We've both been busy with things that were too important to ignore."

"I still feel that I should have spent more time with you."

"Bryn," Fannar sighed as his hands squeezed my shoulders gently. "What you and I are doing cannot be avoided. You will be out there fighting those monsters, and if you skip the training that would keep you alive just to spend time with me, I don't think I could ever forgive myself. Give me a couple of months, and I may even be out there fighting with you."

I swallowed thickly. "What?"

"Well, it's too soon to tell for sure, but Hákon says I have a natural talent for fighting. Once I'm trained up a bit, he says that either he or his sister could use me in the field," Fannar said, completely oblivious to the panic that had begun to weigh down my chest. He gave me a small smile.

Fannar made his way into his rooms and pulled the curtain to completely cover the doorway. My eyes had just begun to sweep through the room when a knock sounded on the door. I opened the door with a smile, assuming that Hákon had sent Óskar or Rúna to guide us.

I froze as I realized who stood on the other side of the door.

Gier and Gil stood there, both with cloaks over their shoulders. Gil stood with his arms crossed, his clothes finely made but simple. His eyes studied me for a moment before his jaw clenched.

"You weren't expecting us," he sighed.

Gier was a silent guide as he led us through the winding streets of Goldhelm towards the shipyards. Gil walked just behind me; my body was painfully aware of exactly where he was.

Fannar nudged his arm against mine and nodded toward the warships on the horizon. "I knew that there would be more ships than we were used to, but gods, I didn't expect this."

My fingers twitched towards my back as I instinctually searched for the medical supplies I used to carry to the shipyard. My hand fell uselessly by my side after finding no pack on my back. I hadn't bothered to bring it with the healers from the fortress so close by. "Neither did I."

The warships were taller than the average longship I was accustomed to seeing. It was taller to account for a floor below deck that the longship didn't have. Long oars, that needed three men instead of two, powered the ships forward. The large, vibrant sails formed a rainbow on the water. Reds, oranges, purples and every colour in between. The ends of the ships were intricately carved with monsters from legends.

Warship after warship arrived at the dock, and gangplanks slammed down. As soon as the planks were secure healers rushed aboard the ships. The returning raiders began carrying their loot off the boats once the healers were safely on deck.

Gier lingered at the entrance to the shipyard with a raider from one of the first ships that docked. Their heads were bent together as they spoke. The raider painted an intimidating figure in his armour. His brown hair was tangled from days at sea, but his face was cleanly shaven. A still-healing pink scar stood out against his eyebrow. The raider handed Gier a parchment that he quickly tucked into his shirt.

Fannar and I began to weave further onto the docks with Gil on our heels. The raiders' armour was slashed, and their furs were singed, but many they passed had large smiles.

A successful raider returning home for the winter, their battle lust sated for the time being.

My eyes widened as I searched the raiders. These weren't the small, underfed boys who went on raids in order to provide for their families. These were warriors—large, trained, and hungry for glory. The best of the raiders that only answered to the King Commander. They sailed where he told them to sail to inspire fear and awe in his enemies. Everyone knew that they also got to increase their wealth and earn glory through the raids as well.

"It's enough to make a man want to return to the days when he was able to hide behind his mother's skirts," Fannar murmured in my ear.

"I remember going to the shipyard with Ma and having to treat almost everyone we knew," I said quietly. "They had no training before they went out on the ships, but it was the only way to provide for their families. They didn't return smiling—they returned haggard and on the brink of death. Were their lives less valuable because they didn't come from the family of a Warlord or a Jarl?"

Fannar threw Gil a worried look and gently tugged me onto an empty dock. Gil lingered at the entrance, leaving the dock deserted as everyone gave him a wide berth. "Bryn. You can't say things like that. You are one of *the* warriors of Drysden now. You can't risk anyone hearing those thoughts. It's too dangerous."

"Not yet, I'm not. And there's no guarantee that I ever will be."

"You made Da a promise," Fannar's voice was tense. "Don't break it now that he's been burned."

My eyes drifted towards the closest warship. Two raiders carried off a body-shaped bundle wrapped in cloth from the ship. As they passed down the dock, each person bowed their head for a moment, honouring the dead.

"Every time I close my eyes, I see that night over and over again. It's only a matter of time before it breaks me," I said quietly.

"It won't." Fannar wrapped an arm around my shoulder and tucked me close to his side. "We won't let it."

I ONCE AGAIN FOUND MYSELF SITTING ACROSS FROM GEORG IN THE meeting room.

"Before we can go any further into your training, you need to have a good understanding of how bloodrites work," Georg said. "How much do you know already?"

"Very little, practically nothing," I answered. There had never really been a reason for me to learn more. I never knew that I had a bloodrite, so why would I have cared?

Georg shifted in his chair and braced his hands in front of him on the table. "Almost every person is born with a bloodrite, but not all have enough power to use it. For many, their bloodrite is hidden, never able to be used. Some only have enough power to do small tricks with it. Others, like you and I, have enough power to wield it at will."

"I didn't know that I had a bloodrite until the attack. Why didn't it show itself before then?"

"There are two ways to awaken a bloodrite. The first is most commonly used in families like the Verndari or the King Commander. From the age of four, when most peoples' power has stabilized enough to control a bloodrite, there are strenuous training regimens to safely awaken the person's bloodrite. That is the preferred method."

I swallowed. "And the second way?"

"If a person finds themselves in a position where they are experiencing particularly strong emotions, such as terror, the bloodrite may awaken in response." Georg ran a hand over his head. "I assume you were forced to awaken your bloodrite this way because your family never sought the proper training to awaken it themselves. Most likely to avoid revealing their location to us."

"How are bloodrites supposed to work?" I asked. "How am I able to shift?"

"The power force inside of you intertwines your bloodrite with something else. In your case, your bloodrite is intertwined with the most essential parts of your body. Through this connection, you are able to shift your body into something else. In the case of Pétur, his bloodrite is intertwined with the elements around him. If there is no fire around him to connect with, then he isn't able to manipulate fire until there is. Does that make sense?"

"Yes," I said as I pushed my hair out of my face. "Are we able to use our bloodrite whenever we want?"

"Not exactly. Think of the power inside of you as your stamina. If you run for an hour, your stamina needs time to recover before you can run for another hour. The same is true for your power. You can only use your bloodrite so much before you need a break."

I sat up straighter in my seat. "How much is too much?"

"That's impossible to answer. Certain things you do with your bloodrite will take more power than others, and it's impossible to know what your limit is until you hit it."

I rested my elbows on the table. "You mentioned that almost everyone is born with a bloodrite. What happens to the people that are born without one?"

"The people born without a bloodrite are often exiled, ostracized, or even killed," Georg said.

"Why?"

"Without a bloodrite, the power within them is restless and untethered. It seeks stability by finding a bloodrite. The power is so unstable that it is able to steal a bloodrite from another person through touch. But the greater the power within a person, the more bloodrites it needs to stabilize it. We call it the Hunger."

I clenched my fingers into a fist to hide their shaking. "What happens to the person that loses their bloodrite? Do they get the Hunger as well?"

"No. The bloodrite within a person stabilizes their power within the first few years after they are born. It is why we can't awaken a bloodrite until we are four years old—that is when our power fully stabilizes. If someone loses their bloodrite after their fourth birthday, they cannot develop the Hunger because their power is already stabilized."

"How do I gain control of my bloodrite?"

"You've already awoken it, so we don't need to worry about the training regime. What you need to do now is find whatever triggers it within you and learn to harness it. You need to learn to tame the untameable."

CHAPTER

THIRTEEN

BRYN

I was dragged from my sleep as something hammered on the door to my room. The first rays of sunshine hadn't even begun to pierce through the clouds.

I rolled out of my bunk, the furs falling to the ground. I squinted my eyes in the darkness as I swung open the door to see Georg, his fist still raised to knock again.

"Get dressed." His voice was rough with sleep.

"Why? There's no way it's time for training already," I rubbed the sleep from my eyes as I realized that he was already dressed for the day.

"A war council has been called." Georg's face was grim. "We're needed in the war chamber. Be ready in five minutes."

I shut the door before I stumbled to my clothes chest. I pulled on a loose white shirt and a pair of leather pants that I stuffed into my calf-high boots. I laced a tight leather vest over my shirt before I joined everyone in the entranceway. I immediately regretted not grabbing a cloak as I shivered.

"Let's go," Georg said.

As we headed for the doors, Gil pulled a spare cloak from

the wall and handed it to me. He didn't say a word as he followed Georg into the fortress. I slung the knee-length cloak over my shoulders, pulling it close to ward off the morning chill.

The halls were empty, as even the servants were still asleep in their beds. It took us no time to reach the war chamber.

It was not an inviting room.

There were no windows, causing large shadows made by the fireplace to dance around the room. A large round table stood in the centre of the room with maps and figurines adorning its surface while more maps covered the walls. Lanterns were hung on the walls, and candles brightened the table.

Ísak was already seated at the table along with some other people that I didn't recognize. Ottó sat at the table as well. His face darkened when his eyes met mine. Gier was flanked at the table by the younger woman from the library and a woman who seemed to be in her thirties.

We filed into our seats as we waited for the Commanding Family to arrive. Everyone around the table stood as the King Commander led his family into the room and only re-took our seats once the family had taken their spots around the table.

"What we discuss today will not leave this room," the King Commander said, his voice strong as he left no room for argument. "You will not like the consequences."

"Why is the girl masquerading as a Verndari here?" Ottó asked.

My cheeks warmed.

"That *girl* is not masquerading as anything," Georg said as he leaned forward in his seat. "Not only is it her right by blood, but it is also the right awarded to her by the King Commander. He said that Bryn is to serve all the duties expected of a Verndari until the winner of the trials is officially appointed."

Ottó's nostrils flared as his lip pulled back over his teeth. "Be that as it may, by awarding the girl advantages such as this, she has an unfair edge over Emilía."

"We are in the war chamber, Jarl Ottó. This does not provide an advantage to anyone," Gil growled. His words ripped from his throat as though he had no hope of stopping them.

"I wouldn't expect you to understand. Suffering and pain often cause people to go insane." Ottó sent Gil a vicious smile. "Tell me, have you had to pay a visit to mommy recently?"

"You *dare*—" Rúna snarled.

The King Commander raised a hand and leaned forward in his seat. "Enough. Your daughter has agreed to this arrangement. I suggest that you do not push me on this."

"It's funny that you should bring up the importance of an even footing for Bryn and Emilía. Surely Emilía's experience, both at court and in training, would put her at an advantage regardless of whether or not she is in this meeting," Rúna said. "Unless, of course, you are a subpar trainer, and you believe that she does not properly conduct herself."

Óskar hid a smirk behind his hand.

"Ridiculous. Although most of the court has come to expect a certain level of absurdity from certain members of the Verndari," Ottó snarled as he turned to Óskar. "Shame that the lack of skill we have seen in your fighting and bloodrite isn't the only place that the Verndari are pathetic."

"Óskar's skills have passed every test we have required of him. Not only are your claims of inadequacy completely unfounded, they are also incorrect. I would suggest that you get your facts straight the next time you decide to attack someone more important to this country than you are, Jarl Ottó," Ragna spoke with the confidence of someone who was used to people listening to what she said.

She was a leader. She was powerful.

And she knew it.

"I said *enough*," the King Commander barked. "If you are done with your squabbles, I would like to focus on why we have gathered today.

Ragna raised her chin and set her jaw. "We have kept the events surrounding the discovery of Jarl Brynja a secret for as long as we could, but the time has come when we can no longer do so. The night she awakened her bloodrite, she did so to protect her family from the Skolli that attacked her village."

The two women Gier was sitting beside showed no surprise.

Ottó seemed to notice the younger woman's lack of reaction as his jaw clenched. "You should have told me."

"I'm sorry, father," she said quietly as her eyes darted to Ragna for a moment. "But I was under orders not to tell anyone." Ottó's face turned a concerning shade of purple, a vein in his neck bulging. The two women must also be members of the Striking Shadows.

"How is it possible for them to be back?" asked one of the people that I didn't recognize.

"We don't know yet. All we know is that it is happening and that we need a plan to combat it," Baldur said, shocking me. After how he treated me at my would-be appointment, I assumed he was awful. What he just said was actually quite reasonable. "I say we should just send out the royal regiment to hunt down the beasts. Make them actually earn their pay for once."

Nope. There it was. He discussed sending out people to fight as though he was sending them to go and buy bread.

What a dick.

Hákon shook his head, crossing his arms over his chest. "If we send out the Royal Regiment with no real plan, all we will achieve is countless unnecessary deaths. I refuse to send out my troops when I cannot look them in the eyes and tell them that they have a chance at survival. Not when we still have other options."

"Who would you propose we send out for slaughter instead, brother dearest?"

"I don't *propose* that we slaughter anyone. I suggest we develop a plan where the slaughter of our own people isn't necessary."

"Why convene the war council now?" Georg asked as he leaned forward in his chair.

"Two more attacks have occurred since then," Ragna said. She shifted through the papers in front of her. "I've also had reports that people have experienced nightmares in areas around the attacks. That means that the Ógn are back as well."

"Is there a pattern to the attacks? Any way to predict where they might hit next?"

"No, nothing links the two attacks together. The only similarity is that the victims have rudimentary defences. Still, there is no indication as to how they are chosen. With the number of small settlements, towns, merchant caravans, and travellers in Drysden, there is no way to predict where they will strike next," Gier explained as he passed some parchment to Ragna. "Every attack occurs during the night. The only known survivors are Brynja, her mother, and her friend."

"If they are striking in small groups, it would be best to send the Verndari after them. Smaller groups travel faster. Not to mention they will be more useful outside the fortress," Sigrún suggested as she twirled a piece of hair around her finger.

"You have a point. There is no way that the Royal Regiment would be able to move with the speed needed to respond. However, I do not want the Verndari riding about the country with so little information," the Queen said. She tapped her fingers slowly against the table.

I studied the table in front of me. There had to be an answer. Something we could do. We needed smaller groups, but they also needed to be capable of dealing with the threat. None of the current fighting forces that I was aware of, at least, fit that description. What we needed was something new.

"Response teams," I said suddenly. The King Commander and the Queen studied me. "We could form smaller response teams that can move faster yet still have the skills to combat the Skolli and the Ógn."

Silence followed.

"That could work," Hákon finally said. "We could include a line of soldiers from the Royal Regiment. If we keep them with the comrades they train with daily, they would have a better chance of survival."

"We could add some bloodrite users and healers to further aid them," the King Commander added.

"If we add a member from the Striking Shadows, I would have a direct link with the teams for information. With the added intelligence, I may be able to put together a better way of predicting where the next attacks will happen," Ragna interlaced her fingers together and braced her arms on the table in front of her. "It would also be the quickest way for them to contact us should the need arise."

"Who will lead these teams then?" Baldur's voice grated on my nerves.

"The sergeant in charge of each line. They are used to giving commands in both battle and peace."

The King Commander nodded before he turned towards Georg. "I want the Verndari ready to move at a moment's notice should a larger attack occur."

"Of course, Commander." Georg bowed his head. "I will ensure we are prepared."

"Very well. You may go," the King Commander said. Everyone began to make their way out of the room. "Jarl Ottó." Everyone froze. My eyes darted to the other people in the room. No one was surprised, but everyone seemed to be holding their breath.

Ottó tensed before turning back to the table. "Yes?"

"I would suggest that you not try to alter an agreement with your King Commander to suit your own purposes. The next time you try and force the Commanding Family to cave to fit your needs you will not like the result. Am I clear?"

"As crystal."

The King Commander stood from his chair and began to sweep out of the room. He paused by Ottó and leant close to him. "No matter how much you wish otherwise, I am still your King Commander. You do not want to see what will happen if you do not learn your place."

When we left the room, the hallways were filled with people going about their day. A heavy feeling pushed down on my chest as my thoughts raced.

More attacks. Two more attacks where everyone was killed.

I choked down the nauseous feeling in my stomach. We had come so close to not surviving that night. Da *hadn't* survived.

I had come so close to losing them.

I broke away from the rest of the Verndari, desperate to see Fannar or Ma. My hands shook as I tore through the hallways.

Óscar called out behind me, but I ignored him. I let myself into Ma's set of rooms without bothering to knock. A quick peek into Fannar's room showed that he wasn't there. I braced myself before I entered Ma's bedroom.

The curtains were pulled back from the windows, allowing the dreary light of the rainy season to seep into the room. Ma lay on her side in the bed as she stared blankly at the wall.

I made my way to stand in her line of sight, but Ma didn't so much as blink.

"Ma." My voice shook as I sunk to my knees beside the bed. "Ma, I need you to look at me."

I needed to hear Ma's voice. I needed my family.

"Please, Ma. *Please.*" My voice broke as I pleaded with her.

Ma continued to stare blankly beyond me. A tear slipped down my cheek.

"Bryn," Óskar's voice made me jump. I hadn't realized that he had followed me into the room. His almost silent steps crossed the room towards me. "She just needs some time."

"But I need her," my voice broke. "I need her to tell me that everything is going to be okay. I can't do this on my own. I *can't.*"

Óskar knelt down beside me. "No matter how it feels, you are not alone. You have us, Hákon, and your friend from home." He pulled me to my feet and led me out of the room. "You can lean on us—you can trust us."

CHAPTER
FOURTEEN
BRYN

The next day, Georg changed our training routine. Which, I was quick to learn, was never a good thing. As Georg led us outside of the fortress, Óskar grumbled from my side. The people on the grounds sent us strange looks. Lúdvík mentioned that the Verndari rarely trained outside their wing, but I didn't realize how true that fact was until I noticed all the stares.

It made me crave the safety and comfort of our wing. I hadn't noticed how I had settled into the wing until I began to long for it. Once we reached the gates, Georg broke into a jog. Rúna hissed complaints under her breath.

"Three laps of the walls." Georg's words carried over his shoulder. "The last one to finish has to clean the training room after we are finished today."

We all picked up our speed. I lengthened my stride and easily picked up my pace.

This I could do.

This was familiar, and after so long at the fortress without a good run, it was like a soothing balm to my nerves.

It was freedom. It was comfort. It reminded me of Da in a way that didn't feel like my heart was shattering all over again.

By the end of the first lap, I was comfortably in the lead. My red braid streamed behind me as a beacon for the others. Yugar ran beside me, easily able to keep up with my pace.

I was waiting for the others at the gates as they finished.

I felt *alive* again.

I sent Georg a grin; if not for this, I didn't know when I would have started to run again. I fell back to walk back with Óskar as Georg led the way back into the fortress. Yugar jogged up to Óskar, his tongue hanging out of his mouth with a large canine smile on his face.

"Bloody traitor," Óskar said, but how he scratched Yugar's ears took away any venom from his words. "At the very least, you don't have to look so happy about Georg's newest form of torture for us."

"You should get used to it. We will run every morning from now on," Georg called over his shoulder. Óskar groaned as he tilted his head back to stare at the sky. I wasn't sure what he was doing, but if he was asking for help from the gods, I suspected they had much bigger things to worry about.

When we reached the training hall, Georg pointed me toward one of the sparring circles. "I've been drilling you on the basic hand-to-hand techniques to build up your muscle memory. But drills will only do so much. You must spar as well." He turned towards Óskar. "I want you to face Bryn in hand-to-hand combat. If she demonstrates an understanding of the basic moves, I will begin her training with the daggers."

I took my place in the circle and started to loosen my muscles. The others stood on the sidelines as Óskar joined me and began his own stretches.

"A surprise run and hand-to-hand combat," Óskar muttered. "Could today get any better?"

I snickered at his words before I took my spot across from him in the circle.

Óskar settled into a fighting crouch. His knees were slightly bent, with one foot in front of the other. His hands were in fists up by his shoulders. "Arms up, Bryn. You need to protect your face and your core."

I quickly settled into my fighting crouch, but I knew it wasn't as sure as Óskar's. I was flat-footed instead of on the balls of my feet. My muscles were tensed instead of loose.

Óskar launched himself at me just as I brought my hands up. His first punch was at my core. I dropped my arms to block it.

I sent a punch towards him before I jumped back to avoid a kick aimed at my side. I had little time to regain my balance before I dropped to the floor to avoid another kick.

While on the ground, I hooked a leg around one of Óskar's. I forced him down to the floor. I pushed him onto his back as my knees pinned his legs, and my hands found his shoulders.

"I win," I grinned down at Óskar as I tried to catch my breath.

Óskar's eyebrows raised. "How so?"

"I have you pinned."

"Are you sure?" Óskar took advantage of my confusion and surged upwards. I toppled off of him. I yelled as I hit the ground and found myself pinned by Óskar. He laughed.

"One thing to remember," he said, "if you are fighting hand to hand, never try to pin someone much bigger, and dare I say stronger, than you. It won't end well."

I let out a huff. "Great. Thanks. I'll keep that in mind." Óskar laughed. He climbed off of me and offered me a hand up.

"Good," Georg called out. "Go again. Tomorrow, we will start on the daggers."

We entered the meeting room to find it completely transformed. The walls were covered with sketches of a Skolli's body. Large front and back views were on the table, the corners crinkled and creased from use.

I froze in the doorway. A Skolli stood in the corner of the room. I scanned it, my body tense. My muscles loosened as I realized the Skolli was attached to a metal stand. I made my way towards the table. As I got closer, the stitches that held the Skolli's neck together were easy to see.

I took my seat between Óskar and Gil with hands that shook.

"There is no shame in a healthy amount of fear," Ísak said from his seat at the head of the table. "The only time you should ever be afraid of your fear is when you allow it to cripple you."

I had nothing to say to that. I wasn't just scared—that I could deal with.

I was haunted.

"We've already had lessons about Skolli and Ógn," Pétur said. He rested his elbow on the table and propped his face against his fist. "It's a mandatory part of our training."

Ísak tucked a piece of hair that escaped from his horsetail behind his ear. "With the return of the Skolli and Ógn, the King Commander has ordered a review. That's what we will do, especially considering that Bryn hasn't learned any of this yet."

"Arguably, out of all of us, Bryn is the one that probably *doesn't* need to sit through this lesson," Óskar said. I sent him a nasty glare. It had been luck that I survived. I would need more than that if I had to face those monsters again.

"Strategically, it is best if we ensure we all have the same knowledge," Georg's voice was not that of the father figure he was when we weren't training. It was the voice of a soldier, one that promised trouble for whoever decided to oppose him.

Ísak nodded. "Precisely. As I'm sure Georg has told many of you, knowing who you are fighting is half the battle. You use this knowledge to exploit your enemies' weaknesses and account for their strengths."

Everyone was silent as we waited for Ísak to continue.

"The Skolli are large creatures with thick, almost armour-like, protection over most of their bodies. Their wings allow them to not only attack from the ground but also from the sky." Ísak's hands drifted over the sketches before him as he spoke. "Not to mention the long talons and claws they wield as a raider may wield an axe—with absolute lethal force. When you are fighting a Skolli, it is important to remember that not only are they bigger than you, but they are also faster and stronger." Ísak's eyes left the sketches to look at me. "Unless, of course, you are somebody who is able to utilize their bloodrite to shift your body to develop some of their traits. Giving yourself the legs of a Skolli would allow you more power and speed when moving. Wings, claws, and talons also would allow you to fight on a more even footing."

I shifted in my seat, my eyes focused on my fingers as they picked at an invisible thread on my shirt. "I've only shifted once. I can't control it yet. It's probably a bad idea for my plans to revolve around it."

Georg scratched his chin, his eyebrows furrowed. "Perhaps. But that was in a life-or-death situation. You may not be able to shift at will yet, but I have no doubt that if you, or others you care about, were at risk, you would be able to shift."

"I suppose." I crossed my arms tightly over my chest. "I still think I need another plan. Just in case."

"Very well. We shall focus on their weaknesses instead."

"Thank you." My words were soft.

Ísak stood from his seat and pulled the Skolli closer to the table. My heart raced. I gripped the arms of my chair to hide the fact that my hands shook. Gil's eyes burned into the side of my head. He shifted his chair so that his cloak just barely brushed against my shoulder.

"There are three spots on a Skolli that are not covered with their thick natural armour. The eyes," Ísak said as his finger tapped on the jet-black glass beads that had replaced the Skolli's eyes when it was stuffed. Gil's cloak shifted as he flinched. No one else seemed to notice except for Rúna, who rested her hand on his knee for the shortest of seconds. I doubted I would have noticed if Gil wasn't sitting so close.

"The wings," Ísak continued. His finger moved to the wings stretched out and attached to metal poles to hold them in place. "And the back of the knee."

"The neck—" my voice cracked. I cleared my throat. "The neck is another weak spot."

Georg's brows were furrowed as Ísak investigated the Skolli's neck. "Is that why it is sewn here? I assumed it was from the stuffing."

I nodded.

"How can you be sure?" Georg stood up and joined Ísak at the Skolli.

"That's how I killed them." Pétur's lips pursed at my words. "I ripped out their throats." No one spoke for several moments. Eventually, uncomfortable with the prolonged silence, I changed the subject. "You mentioned teaching us about the Ógn as well, but I don't see any pictures of them."

Ísak sat back down at the table. "We don't have any pictures of them. We only have a general idea of what their true form looks like. Roughly the size of a full-grown man whose head and hands are covered with shadows. The only distinct feature you can see is their long, curved claws."

"Their true form?" Gil asked with a frown.

Ísak sighed and steepled his fingers together. "The issue is that they create, and feed on, feelings of fear and desperation. In the Great War, they often took on the appearance of someone their opponent loved."

"That's *awful*," Rúna breathed as her hand covered her mouth.

"Everything has a weakness," Georg said as he retook his seat. "What about the Ógn?"

"They don't wear any armour. If you stab them through the heart, you will kill them, just like a man," Ísak said.

Pétur stared out the window. "So they are more vulnerable than us. When we are wearing armour, at least." His fingers tapped against the table. "Are they easier to fight than the Skolli?"

"No," Georg said after he shared a long look with Gil. "When you fight a Skolli, the monster is right in front of you. You can see the evil you are fighting. When you fight an Ógn, you see your father. Your wife. Your daughter. Your comrade." Gil stared down at the table, his hands clenched in tight fists. "You are no longer fighting a monster. You feel like you are the monster."

∼

"THE FIRST THING TO UNDERSTAND IS THAT YOU HAVE DIFFERENT daggers for different purposes," Georg said. We stood in front of my weapons rack. "A throwing dagger is not going to be as good in close combat but will work in a pinch. Does that make sense?"

"Essentially use them for their intended purpose unless you are out of choices, and in that case, a blade is a blade?" I asked.

Georg rolled his eyes and plucked two daggers off of the rack. "Not the most eloquent of explanations, but the nature of it was true." He passed one of the daggers to me. "The first building stone is your grip. How you hold the dagger when you are fighting and how you hold it when you throw it."

"How do you know so much about daggers?" I asked as Georg wrapped my hand around the dagger in the proper hold. "I've only ever seen you use a war axe or your bare hands."

"In preparation for the Trainer's Tournament, I trained with various weapons to show that I had the versatility I would need to train you all. After winning the tournament and being named the new trainer, I continued to study the core weapons of the Verndari."

He had me repeat the grip over and over again. Georg passed me a weapons belt to practice the grip after I had to draw my weapon. When I could repeat the grip enough times for him to be satisfied, he led us over to the side. A target hung on the wall, and a whole tray of daggers was beside it.

"We are going to focus on two main skills with your daggers for the foreseeable future. The first is close combat fighting, which is tied into your hand-to-hand combat training. The second is throwing. We'll start with throwing first."

Georg passed me one of the daggers from the tray. He

wrapped my fingers around it in the proper grip before he made me repeat it myself.

Georg took another dagger from the tray and stood across from the target. He spun it in his hand before he wrapped his fingers around the hilt. He threw the dagger at the target.

It spun, end over end, before embedding itself in the target's centre.

Georg grabbed a second dagger from the tray. He repeated his actions slowly as he explained each step to me. The dagger landed in the target right beside the first.

"Your turn. Try to copy what I just did. I'll correct your form from there," Georg said.

It took me a second longer than Georg to find the proper grip. I drew it back and threw it. The dagger spun end over end, but it wobbled in the air like a bird that had just learned how to fly. It hit the target hilt first and bounced off. I swore.

"Well, there are a few things to work on there," Georg said.

"Yeah," I grumbled. "Like making sure, you know, it actually stays in the target."

"That will come with time. Grab another dagger."

I lost count of how many times I threw the daggers. Georg corrected my form and grip more often than he let me try to throw without guidance. Each time, the dagger hit the target hilt first or missed entirely. It wasn't until my last throw that the dagger actually stuck in the target.

It was in the outermost ring of the target, but it stuck.

That was something I could work with.

FIFTEEN

BRYN

I spent the next week repeating basic dagger drills, over and over again, with Georg. We didn't have enough time to train me in depth. Instead, Georg focused on the most important attacks, blocks, and sequences. The muscle memory from the constant drills should kick in when in a fight.

When we entered the training hall, Georg did not wait for us in the centre of the room like usual. Instead, he stood beside the weapons racks as he inspected one of Gil's swords.

"In the past week, Bryn has become reliable with her basic use of daggers," Georg said. "Today we spar."

Pétur grinned. "What's on the docket for today, then? Solo or pairs?"

"Both. Bryn and Óskar will face off against Gil and Rúna. Afterwards, you and I will spar." Georg said before he turned to Rúna. "Help Bryn with her sparring gear; we will meet in the circle when you are ready."

Rúna nodded, dragging me to our changing room. With a "We're wearing red today!" tossed over her shoulder, she led me into the room.

The changing room was fairly bare, with all the furniture along the walls. A raised cot was closest to the door, with shelves of medical supplies over it. The cot was stained red in places, causing my stomach to churn uncomfortably.

Two chairs, designed for efficiency, not comfort, were on the other two walls. Each one had a table beside it holding two shirts and a neatly folded pair of pants. A pair of boots were tucked underneath. On the other side of the chairs was a wooden stand holding a set of leather sparring armour.

I quickly pulled on the blue shirt and pants from the table before I laced up my boots tightly. The boots had sheaths for my daggers. I braided my hair back from my face as I waited for Rúna to show me how to put on the rest of the gear.

"When there's an emergency, focus on protecting your core and throat. Everything else is a bonus if you have time," Rúna said. "When it's just a spar, I always start at the bottom and work my way to the top since I can take my time."

Rúna gestured for me to turn around before she helped me tie on the gear. The guards for my shins and thighs wrapped all around my leg but still allowed me lots of movement. Each of the thigh guards had slits for daggers.

A belt was settled onto my hips with two sheaths for daggers. The chest protector had thick straps that rested on my shoulders, curving elegantly around my curves before lacing in the front. Similar guards were added to both my forearms and my biceps. The last piece was a wide piece of leather tied around my neck to protect me from a rogue blade.

"Just give me a second to get ready, then we can head out together," Rúna said. Our armour was similar but seemed to be tailored to our skills.

"Are you ready yet?" Óskar called.

Rúna rolled her eyes, leading the way out of the room. "Just because they pull on their sparring gear in less than two minutes doesn't mean we have to."

Rúna made her way towards her weapons rack. She strapped her whip to her belt before she split her staff in two and strapped it to her back.

We went to my rack next, and Rúna helped me strap on and sheath all of my daggers. Rúna left me to slip on the last couple of daggers as she left to join the guys in the centre of the room.

"There you are. Did you lose Bryn?" Óskar asked.

"I didn't *lose* anyone," Rúna said.

"I'm right here," I called, tucking a dagger into the sheath on my thigh as I came around to join the others. "No need to go looking."

"Damn," Pétur whistled.

My face warmed as Gil cuffed him over his head in response.

Rúna propped a fist on her hip as she quirked an eyebrow, a small smirk playing on her face. "Why didn't I get that reaction when I came out in my leathers?"

"We've seen you in your leathers enough times to become desensitized to it. We've never seen Bryn in hers, so it will take a while for her appearance to lose its effect on us."

"Yeah, well, you're all arses," Rúna said as she flipped the end of her horsetail over her shoulder. She joined Gil in the circle and began to stretch out her arms. "Really, if you are more concerned about how a warrior looks in her armour instead of realizing the threat that she poses, then you deserve whatever arse kicking you receive. You guys are just a bunch of pigs."

Gil quirked an eyebrow at her. "I had nothing to do with it."

"That's because you're a big softy, Gil."

Did Rúna not see the same Gil that I did? He cared; that much was obvious, but calling him a big softy?

I would believe that when I saw it.

Georg cleared his throat and pulled our attention back to him. His arms were crossed as his sparkling eyes darted to each of them. "If you are done making fools of yourselves, I would like to get training started for the day."

I took a deep breath to steady my nerves before I followed Óskar into the circle. The points of Óskar's arrows were padded by a bit of cloth.

Gil drew the two swords from his belt and settled into his fighting crouch. I pulled two daggers from my belt. I would have to take on Gil because Óskar didn't fight in close combat like I did.

"Begin," Georg said.

Gil launched himself at me, his swords a flash of light. My daggers met them with a loud clash. Gil was faster than me. He was bigger and stronger. But I knew that what I lacked in size and power, I gained in agility. His training couldn't match the conditioning Da put me through.

I blocked his strikes—but each blow prevented me from my own attack. My body settled into the core movements drilled into my head over the past week.

My attacks became faster.

They became harder.

Gil hooked his blade around one of my daggers, easily wrenching it from my grasp. I dropped to the ground and rolled away as he advanced on me. I sprung up onto a knee, fishing one of the small daggers from my boot. I threw the knife at Gil, forcing him to dodge it. He knocked it down with his sword. I knew that he wouldn't risk Rúna getting hit.

Gil dropped his sword and sank to a knee. His jaw

clenched. Darkness began to gather around him like a cloak.

The darkness rolled and crashed like a wave as it rushed towards me.

I didn't have time to attack. I didn't even have time to look at him. My entire focus was needed to avoid the waves.

I risked a glance at him, and our eyes locked. I stumbled.

His eyes were jet black, with no whites or vivid green left.

I drew two blades from my thigh and threw one at him. The darkness surged up and hardened. It formed a wall between him and the dagger. I tried to attack him from the side. He swung the wall of darkness between the two of us.

The wall hit me hard. It surged against me and pushed me out of the circle. The darkness seeped back into Gil as soon as it had done its job. I hit the ground hard, rolling a few times before I came to a stop. I let out a pained groan.

"Gil and Rúna have won the match. Bryn has left the circle," Georg said. I lifted my head from the ground as Óskar hurried over.

Óskar's eye was blackened, his lip bloodied, and his eyebrow cut. "Are you okay?" His voice was frantic.

"I'm okay, just sore and probably incredibly bruised," I laid a hand on his arm. "I just had a rather unpleasant run-in with Gil's darkness. It was like a stone wall."

Óskar cast a worried look over his shoulder towards the circle. "Let's get you up. Hákon should probably take a look at you, too, just to be sure." He eased me to my feet. Pétur joined us, wrapping my arm around his shoulder to help support my weight. The voices of the others rang through the room.

Pétur shared a long look with Óskar before he eased out from under me and rejoined the others.

We had almost reached the door when a loud snarl whipped through the room.

"Watch out!" Georg yelled.

Óskar pulled me to the floor before he covered my body with his. I turned my head towards the circle as a harsh wall of darkness slammed into us, forcing us to tumble into a wall.

We hit hard.

Pétur and Georg scrambled to restrain Gil while Rúna tried to calm him down. They started to force Gil out of the room when it became obvious that their efforts were in vain. Rúna followed closely behind them. Gil sent one last look of pure hatred towards me, his muscles bulging with his effort to get to me before they were gone.

I trembled in Óskar's arms.

I couldn't figure Gil out.

I thought that he cared much more than he let on, but he just attacked us with our backs turned.

"Come on," Óskar said gently. "Let's get you up."

"Why—" My voice broke. I cleared my throat before I tried again. "Why would he do that?"

"It's not my story to tell."

"Did I do something? Did I offend him or—"

Óskar laid me on the cot in the dressing room, interrupting me as he did. "You have done nothing wrong." I knotted my hands in my lap. "I need you to trust me when I say you did not cause this."

"I trust you. Will he tell me what happened? Why did he do what he did?"

"Eventually, he will, I'm sure."

I leaned my head on Óskar's shoulder as he sat beside me. "I just want to understand."

"Right now, the best way to help him is to give him space. Give him some time to process what happened. He will come to you when he's ready."

CHAPTER
SIXTEEN
GIL

Georg and Pétur forced me into my rooms before binding me to a chair with rope. I could feel Rúna's hands on my face, but her words were muffled. I snarled, pulling against my binds.

"Fight it, Gil. Come back," Rúna pleaded, but I knew it wouldn't work. It never did.

"Just leave me alone. I have no use, no desire, for someone who fails almost everything they have ever done," I growled.

"I have *never* failed you." Her voice was quiet but fierce.

Georg and Pétur cinched the ropes tight around me. "You may not have failed me, but you have failed someone else. Someone that you swore to always protect."

Rúna brushed the hair out of her eyes before turning to the others. "Go," she told them softly. "I'm fine here."

Georg patted her shoulder before they left the room and shut the door behind them.

Rúna pulled a chair in front of me and sat down with a sigh. "Be careful of what you say next, Gil."

I screamed inside my head. Pounded fists against my mind

trying to prevent what I knew was going to happen, but lacking any kind of control.

I was trapped.

Trapped inside the shell of a monster, unable to do anything to protect Rúna from the pain I knew I was about to inflict. "Didn't you promise to always be there for your little brother? That you would sacrifice yourself to ensure he was never harmed?" My face - the monster's face - sneered. "Where were you then when he needed you? When you were his only hope, but *you failed him and let him die.*"

"I can see that you are too far gone for talking to help you. Rúna stood, clearing her throat. "I know you're still in there, Gil. I know that you didn't mean what you said. When you are back, we can talk about it, okay?"

I had no choice but to remain a prisoner of my own mind as I continued to growl and snarl at Rúna. I didn't know how long it took for me to slump in the chair, exhausted.

Once again in control of myself.

My breathing was ragged as I tried to come to terms with the fact that I had lost myself.

Again.

"How are you feeling?" I swallowed thickly, unable to answer Rúna's question. Her eyes searched mine before softening at whatever she saw in them. "Is it alright if I untie the ropes now?"

"No." My voice broke. "Could you leave them on for a little longer?"

"Of course. Let me know when you are ready."

We sat in silence for several minutes before I finally let Rúna take off the ropes binding me to the chair. "I'm sorry."

Rúna brushed away a tear that had run down my cheek

before giving me a watery smile. "You have nothing to be sorry for. That wasn't you talking."

"I was still there for the whole thing. It was me, Ru. *Me.*" My vision became blurry as my voice broke again. I shuddered and sank to the floor. I wrapped my arms tightly around myself as if that could keep me from breaking. "I'm the monster. I'm a monster."

Rúna knelt down beside me and put her hand against my cheek. Against my better judgment, I leaned into her as my eyes slid closed. "It wasn't *you,* Gil. You forget that I know you." My eyes snapped open to find her eyes on me. "You are not a monster."

I let my eyes slide closed again.

For now, at least, I could take comfort in the fact that Rúna, who was almost like another sister to me, didn't think I was a monster.

But how long would that last?

I AVOIDED THE OTHER VERNDARI FOR THE REST OF THE DAY BY HAVING lunch and dinner sent to my rooms. The next day, I made sure that I was at breakfast as soon as it started so that I would be long gone by the time that Bryn made her way down to eat.

But I knew that my isolation would only be allowed for so long before Georg forced me to go to dinner. He was adamant that we all eat dinner together whenever possible. His way to keep us close or perhaps to make us feel a little less alone when we occupied a very lonely role. Either way, I knew it wouldn't take long for Georg to have enough of my hiding.

Which meant that I had to attend dinner that night. I sat in the seat furthest from Bryn, but Georg couldn't complain since I was there.

I kept my eyes focused on my food even as the conversation flowed around me. Rúna spoke quietly to me, and I responded with murmurs that were never loud enough for anyone else to hear.

Dessert was being served when a maid came to the door. "Sorry to intrude, but someone at the wing's entrance is requesting to see Jarl Rúna."

My eyes slid from the maid to Rúna and back again.

"Please inform them that I am unavailable for the rest of the night," Rúna said before she dug into her cake with gusto. Only a very stupid person would come between Rúna and her food.

Rúna was plain nasty when she is hungry.

"Jarl Rúna, I really think that you should meet with them."

Rúna paused with her fork in the air before she turned towards her. My eyes narrowed as I studied the woman in the doorway.

Rúna raised an eyebrow. "I will see them tomorrow," she said.

The maid swallowed before she curtsied and left the room. Only once Rúna returned to her food did I return to mine. I only had about two bites left when a door slammed.

Loud voices echoed through the halls.

"What the hell?" Pétur asked as he climbed to his feet and turned towards the door. I stood from my seat, my hands clenched by my side.

It wasn't long before the door slammed open, and the maid scurried in with Baldur right behind her. A piece of parchment was clenched in his fist.

The maid wrung her hands in her skirt. "I'm so sorry, Jarl Rúna. I tried to—"

"—Oh, shut the fuck up," Baldur interrupted her with a sneer. "I require Rúna's presence, and I require it now. I will not be told to leave again."

"What do you want?" Rúna dropped her fork to her plate after a wistful glance at her cake.

"Is that any way to speak to the Commanding Son?"

Rúna took a deep breath as she crossed her arms. "I'm sorry. What the hell do you want, *Commanding Son?*"

"I want to speak with you," Baldur said. His lip curled as his eyes slid across the room. "Alone."

Rúna pat my shoulder before she followed Baldur out of the room.

"I take it that's not normal?" Bryn asked. My eyes met hers for the first time that night, my chest tightening before my focus drifted back to the door that Rúna had just disappeared through.

Georg shook his head. "No. It's not."

SEVENTEEN

BRYN

"Jarl Brynja!" The all-too-familiar sound of someone banging on the door filled my still-dark room. "Jarl Brynja!"

I stumbled to the door in my nightclothes, the embers of my fire providing the dimmest of light to guide my way. I jerked open the door. "What?"

A maid stood at my door. "Prince Hákon is here. He's demanding to see everyone. They are in the common rooms." She didn't even wait for an answer before she continued down the hallway, no doubt to wake someone else.

My stomach sank as I wrapped a blanket around my shoulders. I shoved my feet into the closest pair of shoes I could find. My stomach rolled, threatening to rebel, as I made my way into the common rooms.

Georg stood in front of the fire in loose cotton pants and no shirt. Hákon was beside him, fully dressed in colours that clashed. He must have just pulled on the first things that he could find. Gil and Óskar took the time to pull on a shirt while Pétur arrived in the now very wrinkled clothes that he had worn at dinner. Rúna stumbled through the door just after me with a blanket wrapped around her shoulders and dark circles under her eyes.

"Tonight, there was a Skolli attack at the fortified logging town of Hazelpeak. It's too big for the response team to handle by themselves," Hákon said. Pétur grimaced as he tucked his hands into his pockets. "This isn't like the other attacks. This time, there are survivors that will need protection while Hazelpeak rebuilds its defences."

"When do we leave?" Georg asked, bracing himself against the table in front of him.

"The Skolli fled the scene just before the response team arrived. Hazelpeak should be safe until nightfall. If you leave within the hour and ride hard—" Hákon nodded towards Óskar, "—you should be there by dusk."

"How bad is it?"

"So far, over ten deaths have been reported, but we suspect that the number will be climbing shortly," Hákon said as Pétur paled. I clenched my hands in fists to hide their trembling. "Other than that, we don't know much. They could need help defending the town or even with healing or a search for survivors."

Georg nodded his head. "What do you want us to do? If you want Óskar to speed up our travels, we can't take much with us. Just our saddlebags and perhaps a few tents strapped to the back of the horses."

"We're sending another response team out after you leave. They'll have all the supplies Hazelpeak needs, so they will have to travel slower. We need you there for the few days they will take to arrive. Once they are there, you are to return here." Hákon scrubbed his eyes, yawning. "Hazelpeak needs the security and support you can provide."

"Alright. We'll be ready to leave within the hour. Are we to be riding in our official gear?"

I couldn't remember the last time the Verndari were sent on a mission in their official gear. It had been at least a decade.

Hákon turned towards the window. "We will see you in the courtyard in an hour. If there's going to be an official send-off, it only makes sense that you wear the official gear."

It had been even longer since the Verndari had been sent out with an official send-off. It was saved for war and times of great danger. For the King Commander to be issuing one now would send a big message to the realm.

Rúna dragged me out of the room by the arm. "Go. Pack everything you may need. Prepare for the worst-case scenario —those always hit when you think you are safe." We took off at a run towards our rooms, our blankets streaming behind us like sails caught in the wind.

I scrambled around my room as I gathered everything I thought that I might need. A few sets of clothes were stuffed into one saddlebag, along with the brush for my teeth, my hair combs, and the leather bands I used to tie my hair back. I hesitated before I packed my healing kit from home into my other saddlebag as a knock sounded.

Georg didn't wait for me to grant him entry before he came in with two bundles under his arms. The first, he tossed beside my saddlebags.

"A bedroll," he said with a nod towards the bundle. He handed me the second bundle. "Your uniform. Fill all the slots in your gear with daggers and pack extra in your saddlebags. Don't worry about food or tents; people are preparing them for us as we speak."

Georg left the room with very little fuss, no doubt to pack his own bags.

Or, at the very least, to get dressed.

The leg and arm guards were similar to the ones we used for sparring, but these were made from a thicker, harder leather reinforced with metal rings. The chest protector moulded to the curves of my body, clinging to me tightly while a large metal piece in the shape of my family's crest covered my heart and a rigid collar protected my neck.

It was just high enough to keep me from getting my throat slit.

A long piece of black fur attached to my shoulders and hung behind me like a cloak. The last item I pulled on were gloves with added padding on my palm and thin metal strips over my knuckles.

I slung my saddlebags over my shoulder, grabbed my bedroll, and headed towards our armoury. I slid a dagger into each boot sheath before strapping two larger ones on my thighs. Four fit on my belt, as well as six thin daggers over my ribs. The last two went on the underside of my forearms. I packed as many extras as I could into my saddle bags.

I looked up as Pétur joined me in the room. He looked as though he hadn't slept. His eyes flowed up and down my body before he sent me a small smile. "You're positively bristling with steel," he said as he turned towards his own weapons rack. "If I didn't know better, I would assume you were a pin cushion."

"You couldn't think of anything more intimidating than a pin cushion?" I needed to find a way to cope with my nerves and needed to do so quickly. Maybe humour would do the trick.

Pétur grabbed two extra swords and took a deep breath. He turned to face me again as his face showed the smallest quirk of his lips. "What would you prefer? A porcupine? A hedgehog?" He held the door open for me before he took up a place by my side.

"I think you need to work on your jokes," I joked. Pétur pursed his lips and tensed beside me as we entered the grounds.

The servants, who were in the middle of their morning duties, stopped to stare at us. Some of those with higher rankings followed us as we made our way to where Gil and Georg had already gathered.

Pétur taught me how to attach my saddle bags to my horse before he attached his own to his mount. Óskar headed towards me as his horse followed behind him without a lead. He wrapped his hands around my foot and gave me a slight boost to get into the saddle.

It was slightly embarrassing for him to have to help me, but I had to admit it was for the best. This was my first time mounting my horse in all of my gear. Accepting help was better than making a fool of myself in front of the crowds that gathered in the courtyard.

Óskar gracefully mounted his own horse and settled into his position beside me. The rest of the Verndari formed their lines around us. Georg and Pétur positioned themselves in front as Gil and Rúna settled in the back.

I leaned towards Óskar. "What are we waiting for?"

"If we are officially being deployed into the field, we need formal permission to depart. I'm guessing we wouldn't bother in emergency situations where we can't spare the time, but I don't know," Óskar shifted the reins of his horse into one hand. "I've never been in this situation before."

The entire courtyard came to attention as the Queen and her sons exited the castle. Hákon and Baldur were a step behind their mother, flanking her sides. She led them straight to where we were waiting.

As they reached the horses, Ottó stormed out of the fortress with Emilía right behind him. "Ready my daughter's mount," he snapped at one of the stable hands.

"No," the Queen said as she set her shoulders. "The King Commander never requested that Lady Emilía join the Verndari on this mission. She is to stay here."

"I thought that was simply an oversight, Your Majesty." Ottó's eyes slid over us before they landed on me. His lip curled. "You don't mean to tell me that the King Commander would send out that worthless girl rather than my daughter?"

Hákon crossed his arms. "The game you are playing is rather dangerous, Jarl Ottó. My father does not like people, presuming they know better than he does."

"If Emilía were to accompany the Verndari, she would only put them at risk," Ragna joined her family and seamlessly supported her brother. "She hasn't trained with them and has no bloodrite that she can wield. Bryn is the Verndari's biggest asset because she is the only one here who has been in a situation like this before."

"So, really, Emilía would be about as helpful as a festering wound and as desirable as a pile of dung in this situation," Óskar leaned forward and ran a hand over his horse's neck. "No offence intended, Jarl Ottó."

Georg's lips twitched before he schooled his features into a neutral expression. "I apologize for Óskar's inappropriate words, Jarl Ottó. However, I must ask you to back away so we can prepare for our departure. If you do not comply, I'm afraid we will have to involve the guards."

Ottó's face pinched before he stormed out of the courtyard with a flushed Emilía close behind him.

The Queen led Georg and Ragna away to speak discreetly with Gier. Baldur headed towards Rúna without sparing the rest of us a glance.

"I wish to speak with you," he said in the same tone he used when talking to his servants.

"Then speak," Rúna said. Her voice was frigid. Hákon's eyebrows rose as he came to join Óskar and me.

"I wish to speak to you alone," Baldur said. Rúna crossed her arms over her chest from her place atop her horse. Baldur growled. "Now."

Rúna dismounted and allowed him to lead her to the other side of the courtyard. "I don't think I have ever seen him willingly talk to any of you before," Hákon said.

"He came to see her a few days ago in our wing. He pulled her out of dinner and everything," Óskar said quietly.

Across the courtyard, Baldur held on to Rúna's arms and bent slightly so his face was close to hers. Rúna's body was rigid, her hands in fists by her sides.

"Is she alright?" Hákon's quiet voice was almost drowned out by the sound of hoofs on stone as Gil's horse shifted. Baldur began to lead Rúna back towards them with her hand tucked neatly into the crook of his arm.

Óskar shrugged his shoulders. "I hope so."

Baldur smirked at me. "I guess we all get to see if the hopeful Verndari will survive her second dance with the Skolli." He moved closer to me. "My money is on her being ripped apart within five minutes."

Pétur and Óskar both growled. "Leave it," I ordered.

"You are truly sadistic," Rúna said. She wielded her words like they were her whip as she lashed out at Baldur. She gripped Gil's forearm tightly, his eyes alight with anger. "What gives you the right to say such things to her when she is the one willing to risk her life, and you are not."

"Need I remind you that I am the Commanding Son, and as such, I will not tolerate your behaviour." Baldur cocked his head. "Or perhaps you simply need a reminder."

"I need no reminder of my place in the kingdom, *Commanding Son*. But perhaps you need to remember who you rely on to maintain *yours*." Rúna's words dripped with venom. She mounted her horse without giving Baldur a chance to retort.

The Queen and Georg rejoined us. The Queen came to stand with her sons, but her focus was on the rest of us. "Other than what you were told already, we know nothing. The response team hasn't had the opportunity to send another message. We are sending you out there practically blind." Her eyes landed on each of us. "Keep your eyes open and protect each other. Do not die on me."

"We'll do our best, Your Majesty," Georg said as he bowed his head.

Her smile was soft. "I have no doubt that you will."

The Queen and her sons made their way to the stairs that led to the top of the walls surrounding the fortress. She paused once she reached a landing in the middle of the staircase. Hákon and Baldur flanked her the same way they had as they entered the courtyard. Hákon raised a horn to his lips, ignoring the glare that Baldur sent him.

It looked quite old. The white curve of the horn was scorched and slightly battered. Everyone fell silent as the sound of the horn rang through the courtyard.

"Strike hard, strike fast. May the gods guide you." The unusual silence allowed the Queen's words to carry.

Georg nudged his horse forward and led us towards the

gate. Georg and Pétur's horses walked across the stones. Once they were about five horse lengths ahead, Óskar bumped me with his arm before he guided his horse into a walk. I followed his lead as I tried to contain my fear. A few moments later, another set of hoofbeats meant that Gil and Rúna followed us.

As Georg and Pétur reached the Queen, they bowed their heads. "Strike hard, strike fast." Their voices were confident. With the Queen's nod, they continued through the gate.

I swallowed thickly and flexed my hands around my horse's reins. Fannar arrived in the courtyard with red cheeks. His shoulders lifted as he panted. He raised his hand in farewell. I raised my own. There was no time for anything else.

Once we reached the Queen, we bowed our heads. "Strike hard, strike fast." My voice was quieter than Óskar's.

Hákon flashed me a smile as the Queen nodded at us.

Once we were all clear of the courtyard, Georg motioned for a trot before he signalled for us to gallop. A third signal and Óskar's power surged the horses forward.

EIGHTEEN

BRYN

The sun had just begun to set when we arrived at Hazelpeak. It was in ruins. The town, or what was left of it, could be seen over the ring of the scorched stone remains of the walls. Many of the buildings had missing walls and roofs. Smoke rose from the still-smouldering houses.

"Our first priority is to find the response team and discover what they have managed to get done so far," Georg said softly. "After that, we're to help wherever we can."

Georg led us into Hazelpeak through gates that hung from their hinges. The townspeople we passed were all covered in soot, and their clothing was ripped. Many of them had bandages wrapped around some part of their body. When Georg dismounted from his horse to talk to one of the townspeople, murmurs began to spread throughout the village. A man pointed Georg further into the town before they clasped hands, and the man continued on his way.

Georg remounted his horse. "The command station has been set up in one of the stores in the marketplace." Georg led us to the only store that had people going in and out of it.

"Óskar, ask the horses to stay around here. They can roam, but we need them nearby in case there is another attack."

Óskar nodded. We all dismounted but held on to the reins until he nodded again.

Georg was the first to drop his reins and head into the shop as we followed behind him. There was a constant flow of the townspeople in their ripped clothes and the recovery team in their own dirty uniforms within the store.

A table stood in the middle of the space covered in what looked like hastily drawn maps of Hazelpeak and the lands around it. Other stacks of parchment were shoved off to the sides as two heads were bent over the maps.

The store had been converted into a commander's office.

One of the heads bent over the parchment turned towards us as we stopped by the table. His long, blond, scraggly hair was braided and knotted away from his face. His beard appeared to be separated in two as if he had tugged at it with his hands. His body seemed to loosen at the sight of us as he nudged the person beside him. The man beside him had the same dark skin as Georg, and his close-cropped hair and beard were as dark as coal. His face spread into a tired grin as he came around the table to shake Georg's hand.

He turned towards the rest of us and ran his hand through his dark hair. "By the gods, am I happy to see you," The man said before he turned towards me. "The name's Fridrík, and that's Agnar. Haven't had the pleasure of meeting you yet. Been out in the field a lot more than I'm at the fortress lately."

"It will make our night a lot easier with all of you here," Agnar said with a nod.

Georg gestured back towards the door. "We've seen some of the physical damage. How bad is the rest?"

Fridrík shook his head, his lips pursed. "Bad. From what

we've been able to gather so far, it looks like seventeen were killed directly by the Skolli," he said. My legs felt like they were going to give out. I locked my knees, desperate to stay on my feet. "Another forty-two have died as a result—by fire, injuries, or the like. Everyone was injured in some way in the attack, and dozens may not make it through the night." I whimpered as Pétur's shoulders slumped.

Fifty-nine people were dead.

That was the best-case scenario.

"Strategically, we are in a dangerous situation. Our respite during the day was filled with healing and trying to make a plan for tonight. The townsfolk are in no state to defend themselves, and my men may not be enough to defend Hazelpeak should the Skolli return tonight. With you all here, it should ease the situation," Agnar turned back to the map and began to trace his fingers over it. "With so many of the buildings damaged, we had to designate various parts of the village for new purposes."

We drew close to the table. Certain sections of the map were outlined in coloured wax. They used the colours as markers like we always did with our medical supplies. Agnar tapped the four green markings that were spread around the wall. "These are the least damaged buildings along the outskirts of the town. We've made them into quarters for my men."

"The townspeople didn't fight you on it?" Rúna asked.

"No. They all felt safer knowing that there would be some protection surrounding them with their walls destroyed."

"But they were just attacked by the Skolli last night. There should be no way that they will be attacked again tonight."

Agnar crossed his arms as Fridrík shook his head. "You have no way of knowing that for sure," Fridrík said.

Rúna pursed her lips and turned away as Agnar pointed out two larger buildings outlined in yellow in the centre of the village. "We're using these as makeshift healing centres. Hazel-peak had a small, basic one, but it was lost in the attack." His finger landed on an orange building near the yellow markings. "We've also set up a triage centre in case of any future attacks. Some of our men are still there treating the wounded."

"We've found several stable buildings and have converted them into housing for the townspeople. However, we also ensured there was a large communal dining hall for them to get their food from," Fridrík said, his own fingers pointing out several buildings marked with brown and a larger one marked with blue.

Georg tapped on a building marked red on the map. "I'm assuming this is where we are now," Georg said. Agnar nodded. Georg moved to a building marked with black on the map. "What's here?"

"The dead," Fridrík said softly. "We need to examine the bodies to see if we can learn anything that I can send back to the Chieftain. There also hasn't been time to properly burn them."

Pétur ran a hand through his hair. "What can we do to help?"

ONE OF THE SOLDIERS FROM THE RESPONSE TEAM SHOWED US THE rooms we would be staying in. Rúna and I were in a small room on the third level of the building. It looked to be an old storage closet. Once we had both rolled out our bedrolls, there was barely any room left for our saddlebags.

Rúna curled up in her bedroll as night fell, her staff and

whip within reach. I tossed and turned, but sleep wouldn't come. After an hour of trying, I gave up. I pulled my uniform back on and strapped on my weapons belt.

I paced along what was left of Hazelpeak's walls for the rest of the night. I caught glimpses of Gil and Georg doing the same. Yugar made his own rounds, meaning Óskar wouldn't have been far behind.

There were no attacks that night to the relief of everyone in Hazelpeak.

As dawn began to bloom on the horizon, I finally allowed myself a few brief hours of sleep. By the time I woke, Rúna's bedroll was empty. A quick glance at the sun showed that it was midmorning at the earliest.

I made my way to the makeshift dining hall to find it mostly empty. Most of the townspeople must have already eaten and gotten started on their work for the day. I sat alone as I ate before I headed to the command centre in the centre of the town.

I arrived at the same time as Pétur, who had the same dark smudges under his eyes that I knew I must have as well. Inside the building, Georg leaned against a table with his arms crossed over his chest. He was dressed in the uniform he had worn the day before, but his furs were on the table beside him.

Gil's face was pale, causing the dark circles under his eyes to stand out. Rúna had a wicked smirk on her face as she bantered back and forth with Óskar.

"Chieftain sent notice that we should be able to expect the replacement recovery team and supplies the day after tomorrow," Fridrík said as he ran his fingers over his dark beard. "I'm going to be heading back to the fortress to report as soon as they arrive, while Agnar and the rest of the team will follow a day or two behind me. A smooth transition is the least we can do for the townsfolk after everything they have been through."

"I've drawn up some sign-up lists. The people here are proud and want to do their part to help rebuild their home." Agnar laid out several pieces of parchment on the table. "Feel free to sign up where you will be of the most help."

Pétur was quick to sign up to rebuild the walls surrounding the village. His bloodrite would ease their workload considerably. Óskar signed up for the search and rescue outside the town, while Rúna signed up for the one inside the walls.

I scanned the lists for where I would be the most helpful. I was out of my depth as most of the lists were for tasks that I very rarely, if ever, had to do before. I paused as I came across a list at the bottom of the pile with no names written.

Pyre building.

I hesitated for only a second before I wrote my name at the top. Once I finished, Gil took the list from me and added his name as well.

I turned to him, shocked. Gil ignored me.

Once everyone added their names to the lists, Agnar posted them in front of the command centre so that the townspeople had a chance to add their own names.

A quarter of an hour later, Gil and I reached the grounds where Agnar wanted the pyres to be built. It was a small distance from Hazelpeak but still close enough to be safe. The town's burning circle had been ruined in the attack. Even if it wasn't destroyed it would have been too small for all the burnings that would take place.

We waited another quarter of an hour for any people who wanted to join us.

But no one did. No one else was going to help.

Perhaps it was still too fresh for them to face the thought of burning their loved ones.

My eyes lingered on Gil as I handed him a shovel. We had to clear the ground to ensure the fire didn't travel where it wasn't meant to as the pyres burned.

We worked in silence for several moments before I had enough. I knew Óskar told me to be patient, but I couldn't pretend to ignore what was happening anymore.

"Why won't you come near me?" I asked. Gil stopped shovelling and turned to face me. "Did I do something that has made you feel the need to avoid me like this?"

Gil turned away from me as he stabbed the shovel into the ground. "No."

"Why do you refuse to talk to me? I've noticed that you tend to stand apart from us, which is fine, but you barely look at me anymore."

"I haven't spoken to you much since we arrived at the fortress."

"I'm well aware of that fact. But I also know your behaviour has changed since then, and I just want to know why."

Gil roughly threw the dirt that he cleared to the side. "Have you forgotten what happened when we sparred?"

"I remember it, but I don't understand why it happened," I propped a hand on my hip.

Gil turned his face away from mine. "I would prefer if we did not speak of it."

"I have things that I would prefer to never speak of again." I pushed a flyaway curl behind my ear as Gil paused his digging to look at me. "But there are times when I am forced to because certain people deserve to know what happened. I would like to think that I deserve to know why one of the people that I will be fighting alongside attacked me when my back was turned." I looked him in the eyes. "I am not going to judge you for your actions. I just want to know what happened and why you are treating me differently than the others."

His throat bobbed as he swallowed. "You do deserve a reason, and I will give you one." Gil tilted his head back to study the sky. "Just give me a little more time."

I spent several moments studying his face. "Will you stop pushing me away?" Gil nodded his head. "Then take all the time you need."

It took us most of the day to clear the ground. Tomorrow, we will focus on building the pyres. Agnar took us through the building where the dead lay. To build the pyres properly, we would need to know what size to make them.

Countless bodies lay in the building. Some were covered in blankets, others with jackets or bolts of cloth. My legs were like lead as I made my way through the building with Gil by my side, a silent but steady presence.

As we reached one small bundle, I froze. My legs felt too heavy to move.

The little bundle, wrapped in a tiny quilt, was small enough that I could have cradled it in my arms.

My vision swam as I stumbled backwards. I had to get out.

I ran out of the building as the doors slammed behind me. My hands knotted in my hair as I stood in the middle of the street, panting. Voices from the dining hall floated down the abandoned street.

It must be dinner time. No wonder the street was so empty.

"Bryn," Gil said softly, but it still made me jump.

I cleared my throat harshly. "Yeah?"

"How can I help?"

I spun to face him and dropped my hands from my hair. "What?"

"I don't know you well enough to know what you need right now. I need you to tell me how to make this better for you," Gil's hands flapped uselessly by his side before he tucked them into his pockets.

"I don't think anything you could do would make this better. Did you see the little—" My voice broke.

"I did. I understand why you ran."

"How are you dealing with this? How do you not run?"

Gil studied me for a long moment. "I have seen a monster before, Bryn. I have seen the horrors that they leave behind."

"I have too," I whispered. "And it was just as horrible this time."

"How did you handle it?"

I let out a humourless chuckle. "I had no choice. I needed to heal Ma."

We stood in silence for several moments. "It is honourable to care for others. Sometimes healing or rebuilding is the best way for us to recover." Gil shuffled his feet awkwardly before his green eyes met mine. "I am sure the healing centre would be grateful for our help."

"You would go with me?"

"I would. Every healer needs an assistant."

We made our way back toward the building we were staying in. If we were going to do this, I would need my healing kit. I was sure they would be grateful for the extra supplies.

Gil fell into step beside me. He kept a careful difference between us, but he was choosing to join me when he didn't have to.

"What happened to keeping your distance?" I asked.

"We all have our ways of coping. That is mine," Gil said, his eyes focused on a point down the road and not on me. "You asked me to stop. This is me trying."

"Thank you," I said softly.

When we arrived at the building where we were staying, Gil raised his eyebrows but didn't say anything. He waited outside as I grabbed my saddlebag and rejoined him outside. We made our way to the healing centre.

A harried-looking man met them at the door. "What's wrong? I can't spot any injuries on you," he said tiredly.

"We're not injured. We're here to help," I said with a small smile at the man.

The man studied us for a moment. "In that case, a couple of kids could use your help. They're scared, and nothing we have said to them has helped. They won't even let us clean their cuts."

"Where are the children?"

"Over there in the corner." The man pointed. "Do you need any supplies?"

I shook my head. "No. I've got my own here." I lifted up my saddlebag.

The man left us with a nod.

We began to weave through the various beds toward the corner the man had pointed to. In the corner, there were two beds that were pushed together, one along each wall. Two kids sat about as far as they could get from each other. They both shared the same brown hair and blue eyes. The girl looked a little younger than the boy did.

The girl had her arms wrapped around her legs as she sobbed. The boy sent us a look of hopelessness, his eyes wide.

I sent the boy a soft smile as I knelt down by the little girl.

"Are you alright? Are you hurt anywhere?" I asked. The girl nodded her head. There was a long cut on her arm, but there didn't appear to be any others. "My name is Bryn. Do you want to tell me yours?"

"Lily," she hiccupped.

"Well, Lily, my friend is going to grab a bowl of water and a cloth so we can clean you up. Then we'll be able to see your cut a bit better, okay?"

The little girl nodded as the tears still ran down her cheek. The boy shifted to the edge of the bed, closer to his sister. Gil handed me the water and cloth before he took a seat beside the boy.

I dipped the cloth in the water and wrung it out. As I brought the cloth closer to Lily, she flinched away. "This must be really scary for you," I said. "But I can't help you until I can see what's wrong. Can you be brave for me?"

"Okay," Lily said softly. Her tears seemed to slow.

I started with her face and gently washed away the dirt and grime that had clung to her face from the tears. After the dried blood was washed away from Lily's arms, I was relieved that there was only one cut. I studied her for a minute; there was too much blood on her for it to all be from the cut.

"Can you tell me who was hurt, Lily?" I asked. "I don't think this blood was all from you."

"It's Ma's. One of those monsters hurt her, but she wouldn't get up to keep running," Lily whispered. A knot settled in the pit of my stomach. I shook my head to try and chase away the images of my own parents being attacked by the Skolli. "It was just like my scary dream from the night before."

"What happened?" Gil asked softly.

"It slashed her with its claws." The boy's voice was

threaded with grief. "There was so much blood, and she couldn't breathe."

I forced myself to focus on Lily instead of the memories that ran through my head. "She stopped running to protect you. It was to give you time to run, Lily."

"No!" Lily cried. Her voice was full of anguish. "I tried to stay! I wanted to help her! But Finn didn't let me. He made us leave her."

"She said to protect Lily and stay safe," the boy—Finn—murmured. He leaned towards his sister, and his hand reached for hers. "I did everything I could."

"I hate you! It's your fault that Ma is gone!" Lily growled. Finn recoiled from her as if she had struck him.

I couldn't let them be torn apart. They had already lost too much. "I lost my Da, he's gone, and he's never coming back," I said in a rush. Lily's wide eyes snapped to meet mine. "Two of those monsters attacked my family. My Da died to save me like your ma did." I took Lily's hands in mine and squeezed them gently. "It hurts, doesn't it? More than anything you've ever felt."

Lily pulled one of her hands free and rested it over her heart. "It hurts here."

"Now imagine how Finn feels. He lost his ma, and he's probably really scared that he is going to lose his sister too," I explained.

"He made me leave Ma," Lily's hand clutched at her shirt.

"Finn *protected* you because he loves you. Don't push him away because of that; he did nothing wrong."

Lily nodded hesitantly. Finn rushed forward to pull her into a hug. The siblings sat together as I tended to them. Gil pulled each item I asked for out of my healing kit, a steady, silent presence by my side. My shoulders were lighter as Finn led Lily out of the healing centre.

We made our way back towards the building where we were staying once we had gathered up my supplies.

"Where did you learn how to do that?" Gil asked.

"My Ma. She was the closest thing we had to a healer in Ebonwell. She taught me how to heal from when I was little. My Da was the one that was really good at talking to kids. I got that part from him."

"I am happy that you were able to learn from them."

I smiled at him. "I'm sure you were able to learn plenty from your parents too."

"I learned plenty," Gil bit out before he clenched his jaw. "None of it was like that."

CHAPTER
NINETEEN
BRYN

It took Gil and I most of the next day to build all the pyres needed for that night's burning. We left the townspeople to place their loved ones on the pyres and prepare them for their journey. Gil made his way to find Rúna as I headed to the dining hall to help the cooks prepare the evening meal.

Only Georg and I had passable cooking skills. The others only knew the basics, and even then, there was a strong chance that it wouldn't turn out well, at least according to Georg.

Georg and I were helping the cooks with dinner when Fridrík found us. He burst through the doors, causing the few townspeople in the building to startle. Georg handed me the spoon he was using to stir the stew before he followed Fridrík outside without a word.

I turned my attention to the stew as I tried to ignore the nerves that fluttered in my stomach. There was no denying that Fridrík was in a rush. The fact that he needed Georg for whatever reason—no. I couldn't work myself up like this.

Being in a place that was attacked so recently had put me on edge. That's all.

The door opened again to reveal Pétur. He slid quietly into the room and joined me at the stew pot. "What's going on? I saw Fridrík leave here with Georg quick behind him," he whispered. His eyes slid over the other people in the room.

"I don't know," I said as I stirred. "You don't think there was another attack?"

"No. There couldn't have been."

I tilted my head to the side. "How can you be certain?"

"I can't be, I suppose," Pétur turned his head away to survey the people around us. "It's just one of those gut feelings."

The doors opened once again to reveal Gil. He headed straight for us, not sparing a glance at the others in the hall. "We've got orders. Straight from the fortress," Gil said. My knuckles whitened around the wooden spoon. "We're to return as soon as possible. We leave in a quarter of an hour."

"It's almost dinner. There's no way we would make it back before dark. We would have to spend the night in the field with no protection. We will be vulnerable," Pétur said.

"Georg has a plan for that." Gil's voice strengthened. There was no way this would remain only a Verndari matter for much longer, so there was no point in being secretive. "The response team with the extra supplies is due to arrive shortly before dusk." He turned for the door. "We're to meet at the gate."

Once I handed off my cooking duties it didn't take long for me to ready myself to leave. I changed back into my uniform and ensured that my daggers filled all the available sheaths. I gathered up my saddle bags that I hadn't bothered to unpack.

By the time I reached the gate, Georg and Gil were already there. Several of the young people from Hazelpeak stood with pride as they held the reins of our horses. I joined Gil slightly off to the side as Georg moved aside to talk with Fridrík and Agnar.

I began to secure my things to my horse. "Still no new information?" I asked.

"Only that this return is political and not combat-based," Gil said softly. There were too many little ears around us for him to speak any louder. The knot in my stomach loosened.

It wasn't long before the others joined us. While Óskar loped over to us with a sense of ease, the same could not be said for Rúna and Pétur. Rúna's face was set in a scowl while Pétur's was pinched.

Georg left his conversation with Fridrík and Agnar with a nod. He surveyed the townspeople that gathered around us before he gestured off to the side with a grim look. "Mount up."

Once everyone was settled on their horse, the children dispersed into the crowd that surrounded us. Some joined what looked like their families, while others stood off to the sides on their own. I could see Lily and Finn together with some of the other children.

Georg gestured for us to form a circle. "We got direct orders to return to the fortress as soon as possible. Ottó has decided that with us gone, there is an opportunity to sway the fractured court to his side." Georg kept his voice low to ensure that he was not overheard.

"What's the plan?" Óskar asked as he stroked a hand down his horse's neck. "Even with my bloodrite, there is no way we would be able to return before dark."

"We ride without your aid to the forest not far from here. We will camp there for the night. With the trees for cover and no fire to give away our location, we should be safe from attack. Come first light, we ride hard for the fortress. I want to be there by midmorning," Georg nodded to Óskar. "We save your bloodrite tonight just in case. Tomorrow, you will get us there as soon as possible."

Georg gestured for us to assume our positions. Once everyone was in place, he kneed his horse into a trot. When we were all clear of the village, we settled into a gallop.

We rode hard until we reached the forest. We slowed when we entered to ensure that none of the horses were needlessly injured.

We rode in silence for several moments before Óskar finally broke the silence. "What are we going to do about Ottó's spew?"

Rúna sighed and flicked the end of her horsetail over her shoulder. "Really? Out of all the possible words you could have chosen you went with spew?"

"Seemed like the appropriate choice. Spew's vile and unwanted. So is Ottó."

"Regardless of Óskar's word choice, it is a valid question," Pétur rested his hands on his saddle. "It's a delicate situation. We play our cards too fast, and everything goes to shit. If we play our cards too slow, everything still goes to shit. When we return to the fortress, we will be walking on a sword edge. One wrong move, and we're fucked."

Georg rubbed his chin. "We can't let on that we know of his actions. If it comes to light that Hákon and Ragna favour us over him, it could cause more problems for Bryn when she has to face Emilía."

"How do we know he is acting alone? What if he is just the loudest voice of the dissent?" Gil asked. His voice was measured as though he carefully selected each word before he spoke.

"So there's the possibility that even more people want me to fail," I groaned. "That's what I needed to hear."

Óskar nudged her with his leg. "Well, technically, Ottó is trying to discredit all of us—"

"That's true, but Bryn is the only one that has the possibility of being eliminated from the equation," Pétur cut off Óskar. "She has the greatest chance of failing. Naturally, they will target her more than the rest of us."

I tucked a rogue curl behind my ear. "It's really encouraging to know that you have such faith in me."

"It has nothing to do with faith. The political and military power that comes with the appointment of a Verndari is almost impenetrable. Once they are officially appointed, only the most extreme of circumstances will allow for their removal," Pétur said. I watched the lengthening shadows around me instead of responding.

"We should set up camp for the night at the next clearing we come across. It's too dangerous to travel this path at night," Georg said.

By the time we reached the clearing, the sun had set behind the trees so that only the smallest patches of light remained. It didn't take long for Georg to assign us tasks, and the camp quickly took shape.

When only the barest amount of light was left, we gathered around the dying fire we had used to cook our food. I took a seat between Óskar and Gil. I wrapped an arm around my leg as I made myself comfortable.

"Who's going to tell the scary story?" Óskar asked as he

leaned back on his arms and stretched out his legs.

"Who needs a scary story when I think everyone would agree that we are living one? If you insist on a story, can it not be scary?" Rúna proposed, crossing her legs under her.

Óskar groaned. "Come on. We're sitting around a dying fire in the middle of a forest. It has to be at least a little creepy."

"There's the story of the Spirit Sword of Graythorn," Pétur said. He sat across the fire from me. The light from the fire cast long shadows across his face. "That should be creepy enough for Óskar."

"What's so special about this sword?" I asked.

"It's not a sword. It's the nickname of one of the legendary warriors of Drysden. Einar of Graythorn."

Óskar turned to me with raised eyebrows. "Don't tell me you've never heard the name before."

"Sorry to disappoint you, but I've really never heard of him," I shrugged.

"Einar of Graythorn was one of the strongest warriors of the realm. Technically, he was only supposed to be a Warlord, but the King Commander elevated him to a Jarl for his abilities and successes in combat," Georg explained. He ran a sharpening stone over the edge of his war axe. "The connection between him and his war axe was almost magical. Some believed it might even be an undiscovered bloodrite. Regardless of what might have caused the connection, he was given the nickname of the Spirit Sword of Graythorn."

"One day, the town of Graythorn was attacked. It was the middle of the night, so they were able to kill many people in their beds before the alarm was raised," Pétur added.

My eyes were wide. "Why were they attacked? Who attacked them?"

"They were attacked by a monster," Gil said sharply. "A monster that didn't care about the destruction they caused."

I paused for a moment. "Was it a Skolli?"

"No."

"There was terror when the alarm horn was blown," Pétur said. "In order to give his family and people time to escape, the Spirit Sword stood alone against the monster. His wife led the townspeople into the mountains near the town, carrying their sons in her arms. The sons were barely a year apart. One of them was only a few months old."

I swallowed thickly. "What happened to Einar?"

"He died," Gil said through clenched teeth. "His body lay across the road into the Graythorn as the town was set ablaze."

"The charred stone ruins of Graypeak still stand as a memorial to the Spirit Sword," Óskar added.

I pulled my legs up to my chest and wrapped my arms around them. "What about the people that fled?"

"Most of them made it to Goldhelm. They had to travel across the entire realm in winter, so some didn't make it," Rúna said from her spot on the other side of Gil.

"Did his family make it?"

"His wife and oldest son did. The youngest was lost on the way," Georg said softly. "His wife and son still live in Goldhelm." He cleared his throat. "It's getting late. Even though we should be safe here, we are going to rotate the watch. Óskar will take the first shift. Then Rúna, Pétur, myself, Gil, then Bryn." Georg's eyes landed on each of us in the rapidly dimming light. "Keep your eyes and ears open. Have your weapons with you."

Gil and Georg were the first to leave for their tents. I made my way to the tent I was to share with Rúna as the others lingered around the last scraps of the fire a little longer.

I quickly shucked off my armour and left my weapons belt beside my pillow. I curled up in my bedroll in just my loose shirt and leggings.

It took a little while for me to fall asleep with the sounds of the forest around me.

They no longer sounded like home.

CHAPTER
TWENTY

BRYN

It was still dark when I was jolted from my sleep. I blinked the sleep out of my eyes and searched for Rúna in the dark.

Her bedroll hadn't been slept in.

I scrunched my eyebrows as I searched for what woke me up. Pétur shouted from outside of the tent. I scrambled out of my bedroll. I paused just long enough to shove my feet in my boots and strap on my weapons belt before I threw myself out of the tent.

The fire that raged in the fire pit illuminated the clearing as numerous Skolli descended on our camp.

I had to fight every instinct that told me to flee and every part of me that desperately wanted to freeze. I couldn't let that happen. I had failed that night in the village, but maybe tonight would be different.

Tonight *had* to be different.

I forced myself to palm two daggers from my belt before I tried to fight my way to Óskar's side. He was my partner—we would face this better as a pair. Rúna and Gil fought back to back as Pétur and Georg fought side by side.

A Skolli spiralled down from the sky and landed hard in front of me. My daggers flashed as I went straight for its throat, slicing through its veins and thick skin.

Even with my eyes turned away, I knew that the Skolli's blood had sprayed from its cut.

Its burning wetness seared my face and neck.

I spun to find Óskar in the chaos that surrounded me. The rhythmic snap of his bow drew my attention to where he fought from the outskirts of the camp. Óskar turned to focus on a Skolli that was targeting Rúna and Gil.

He didn't notice the Skolli that approached him from behind. My blood ran cold. Fear and fury rushed through my body as I was pulled back to that night.

Ma being struck down. Da bleeding out in the grass. I brutally pushed the thoughts down. I had already decided this night was going to end differently.

My legs started to burn. My feet ripped through my boots as my legs tore through my pants. A quick glance down made my head spin. I had shifted to give myself the legs of a Skolli.

I didn't give myself time to think as I launched towards the Skolli. With the added speed and strength the legs gave me, I slammed into the Skolli before it reached Óskar.

Óskar yelled, but my focus was on the Skolli. We rolled with claws and daggers flashing.

Its claws slashed my ribs as I struggled to gain any advantage over it. My teeth burned, and I instinctively lunged for the Skolli's neck.

I ripped out its throat with my fangs.

I spat out the chunk of thick skin in my mouth and shoved the body off of me.

I stood to find Óskar staring at me. With the Skolli legs, I was a good head taller than him. His eyes widened as they travelled down my body before the sounds of the battle once again gained his attention.

Óskar turned back to the battle, an arrow already nocked on his bow. "I'll get some wolves to protect our backs so we can fight side by side." He fired. The arrow pierced through Skolli's eye. He turned slightly towards me with a small smirk on his face. "Glad to see you can fight, Talon. We might have been in trouble otherwise."

"For some reason, I feel like we are in trouble regardless." My words slurred together. I wasn't used to talking with my fangs.

I launched myself at the closest Skolli.

My fangs and daggers were both weapons that I used to wreak havoc on the Skolli. The legs allowed me to put more force behind my blows and more speed behind my attacks. Some of my daggers stuck in the dead Skolli I faced, while others lodged themselves in their throats when I threw them.

I cursed when I noticed I only had one left.

Three Skolli approached me. Their attack was an ongoing onslaught.

My head jerked around as it became hard to see. I hadn't noticed that the Skolli were slowly driving me away from the campsite until the trees blocked the light of the fire. All I had left was the light from the full moon overhead.

The Skolli attacked and forced me to become more defensive. I struggled to block their strikes. With a lucky slash of my dagger, I managed to kill one of the Skolli, but my dagger got stuck in the corpse.

My only choice was to drop it.

I desperately tried to come up with a plan as I stared down two Skolli with no daggers left.

I fled deeper into the forest with a strangled cry. I needed to buy some time. I needed to think. I needed to plan.

The branches that whipped past me cut into my face and arms. I raced into another clearing. As I turned to see the Skolli chasing me, I stumbled. The Skolli took advantage of my off-balance state and charged me.

It slashed me across my already hurt ribs.

I screamed in pain and twisted to swipe my claws across the Skolli's eyes.

"Shit!" I cried as I pressed a hand against my ribs. My other hand tore a chunk off of my shirt. I kept a close eye on the remaining Skolli as I tied the fabric around my ribs blindly. I risked a glance down to ensure I covered the wound well enough, and I froze.

My body and hands were covered in the black blood of the Skolli and my own red blood.

My breath came in short, quick bursts as the edges of my vision blurred. I barely felt the burning in my legs and teeth as they returned to normal. My heart felt like it would beat out of my chest. My mind raced. I was forced into a painful loop of images of my last time seeing this much blood.

Da's death.

His body covered in the same awful mix of red and black.

I fell to my knees, my arms wrapped tightly around my body, shaking as I tried to will down the tears that threatened to come. There was nothing that I could do. The heavy footfalls of the Skolli came closer, but I couldn't bring myself to move.

I couldn't bring myself to fight back.

I bowed my head, and my vision blurred with tears. There was nothing left to do. I was paralyzed, left to await my own death at the hands of the Skolli. I could see its feet as it came closer to me. I closed my eyes as the tears started to roll down my face.

"*BRYN!*" Gil's voice roared through the clearing. The sound of him crashing through the forest caused my eyes to open.

A sob escaped me.

My vision darkened further as my body flopped onto the ground. I looked up to see the Skolli above me. Its claws slashed down towards me.

"Gil," I whispered. I turned my face towards the Skolli's feet, unable to watch my death approach. "I'm sorry."

The Skolli fell into my vision with a loud crash. My eyes searched its body. A sharp point of darkness retreated from it.

I rolled painfully to my back and studied the stars above me. Gil's face blocked the stars as he bent over me.

The edges were blurry, but it was *him*.

His face was pale in fear as his eyes flashed from his normal green to black and back again. "*Bryn*," he breathed. Gil quickly scooped me up into his arms. I rested my head on his chest.

His heartbeat raced.

"You saved me." My voice broke.

"Of course I did." His voice was softer than I had ever heard it. He took off at a run as I whimpered in pain. The blackness edged closer as my head lolled against his chest. "I need you to stay awake for me. Fight it, Bryn. I need you to fight it."

"I'm so tired."

His arms tightened around me. "I know you are, but you have to be stronger than it. You hear me, Bryn?"

I nodded slowly against his chest as I focused on the sound of his heartbeat. My head lolled again as I tried to fight back the darkness that clouded my vision.

"Don't you die on me, Bryn. Am I clear? *Do not die on me.*"

My hand clenched onto his shirt as the sounds around us got louder. "ÓSKAR!" Gil's voice thundered through the air as we came to a stop. Crashing sounded around us. "You need to take her to Hákon now. It's her only chance."

"She's bleeding too much." I couldn't tell who was speaking. "She won't make it."

"It's her only chance," Gil growled.

I squeezed my eyes shut before opening them again. "My bags," my words were weak.

"Grab her bags!" Gil yelled.

"I don't think now is the time—" Was that Rúna?

Gil cut her off. "It has her healing kit."

Footsteps rushed off as I was lowered to the ground. I tried to tighten my hold on Gil, but my muscles barely listened to me. He propped my head up against his leg before his hand held onto mine tightly. Even in my near-delusional state, I could tell that Gil was tense.

"How did you know about the healing kit?" I was pretty sure that was Óskar.

"Does that matter?"

I tilted my head to the side as Rúna ran up to the group with my saddlebags in her hands. "I've got bandages here and what must be skin thread and a needle," Rúna's words were frantic. "But I don't know what's in the jars."

Óskar's head popped into my line of sight. "I need you to tell us what to use, Talon. You need to focus." Focus? How was I meant to focus when I could barely keep my eyes open?

But I knew this.

I healed numerous people healed even more with the help of Ma.

"Blue ink." I rasped. "Blue cleans."

My ripped shirt was lifted to the top of my rib cage. The

cream from the tin was cool at first, but it began to burn as the bubbles cleaned my wound. I squeezed Gil's hand as I whimpered.

"What's next, Bryn?" Óskar's face reappeared, but it seemed blurrier than the last time.

My eyes began to close before a rough shake made me open them again.

What was next?

"Black. Black helps slow bleeding," I said.

Something was smoothed onto the wound before a sharp pinch caused me to shout. It was followed by another and another. I cried out each time as tears raced down my face. Someone brushed them away, but my vision was too blurry to see who it was.

"Óskar, as soon as she is bandaged, you have to get her to the fortress. The rest of us will follow behind as soon as we can," Georg said.

Something was wrapped around my ribs—that must be the bandage. Someone pulled my shirt back down. My vision swam as I was lifted up. I was settled sideways across someone's legs and what must have been a saddle. Warm arms wrapped around me as we launched forward.

The jarring motion of the horse's gallop caused me to cry out again.

"Come on, Talon, be strong." That had to be Óskar. He was the only one who called me that. His voice grew fainter as the darkness spread across my vision. "Don't let this be the end."

CHAPTER
TWENTY-ONE
BRYN

I struggled to open my eyes. It took me a few moments to realize I was at the fortress. Fannar sat in a chair by my side, his head pillowed on his arms on the edge of my bunk.

I shifted, hissing in pain. I pressed a hand to my ribs, where bandages were wrapped tightly around me.

"*Bryn,*" Fannar said gruffly. He stared at me tiredly from where his head still rested on his arms. I sent him a sad smile. He jumped up from his seat. "Here, let me help." Fannar fluffed up the pillows behind my head before he helped me sit. His hands tightened around me briefly as I let out another pained hiss.

I tried to speak, but it came out as a raspy croak. Fannar poured me a tankard of water and tipped it to my lips. He let go once it was clear that I wouldn't drop it, waiting for me to finish before he refilled it and took his seat again.

"How long was I asleep?" I asked.

"Three days," Fannar said. "I was with Hákon when Óskar brought you back. We could hear him yelling from the training grounds, and the guard that came to get Hákon was so pale that I was sure that someone died."

I shifted painfully to one side of the bunk and patted the spot beside me. Fannar didn't hesitate to climb up beside me. I leaned my head against his shoulder. "What happened next?"

"When we reached you, the first thing I noticed was the blood. You had soaked through the bandages over your ribs. It covered Óskar's clothes. You were so pale, Bryn, and he was panicking." He cleared his throat. "We got you in here, and Hákon started healing you. It was touch and go for a while. Even with the crude healing that someone did, you were still in really rough shape."

"Have you been with me the whole time?"

Fannar sent me a pained smile. "I was kicked out when Hákon was healing you. He wouldn't let anyone in here as he healed you. Óskar and I waited in the hall. He didn't even bother to change out of his bloodied clothes. We have been alternating who sits with you since."

"You didn't have to stay with me."

"Of course I did. You're my sister, and I thought you were going to die. There was no way that you were going to be left alone until I knew that you were going to be okay."

We sat in a comfortable silence for a while. Fannar tipped his head to rest on top of mine.

"How is everyone else? Was anyone else hurt?" I asked.

"Most of them only had minor injuries and are already well on their way to being fully healed," Fannar eased out of the bunk carefully.

"You don't have to go."

Fannar smiled at me. "I know, but I also promised to let them know if you woke up while I was with you. Besides, I should probably go check on Ma."

"How is she?"

"She's the same as when you left," he said softly. "I tell myself it's better than her being worse."

Fannar gently kissed the top of my head before he walked out of my room. I leaned back against my pillows as I finished my water. My eyes fluttered shut as I waited.

I woke to the sound of someone entering my room. A few seconds later, Óskar's head popped around the curtain. I raised an eyebrow.

"I was just checking that you were still awake," he said.

"I think that three days of sleep is more than enough. I probably won't need more until later today," I joked.

Óskar shook his head, glaring at me. "That's not funny, Bryn." He pulled back the curtain and made his way into my room, flopping in the chair beside my bed. "You look better."

I quirked an eyebrow. "If I look as hurt as I feel, then I suspect you are lying. Fannar told me I looked bad, but if this is better, I couldn't imagine how I looked before." Óskar's face was grim. "I wanted to thank you."

"Why would you want to thank me?"

"You got me back here. You saved my life."

Óskar scoffed before clenching his jaw. "Don't thank me. It's because of me that you are like this."

"No," I leaned forward, reaching for his hand. I did my best to hide my pain, but his narrowed eyes told me that I wasn't successful. "This isn't your fault, Óskar."

"I failed you. I told you the wolves would protect our backs, but they fought against what I wanted. They abandoned us part of the way through the fight. It left you vulnerable."

"I don't blame you for that."

Óskar shook his head. "I blame myself. I wanted to protect

you like you were protecting me. That's what we are meant to do."

I searched his face for a moment. "Are you talking about when I shifted?" He nodded. "It's no secret that I don't know how to control my shifting yet. In the forest, when I saw Skolli approaching you from behind, I was terrified. I had already seen Skolli destroy the people I care about and couldn't—I *wouldn't*—let that happen to you, too. You've become a part of my ramshackle family."

"You saved me with only a few weeks of training. I've trained my whole life, and I still failed you."

"*No.* Do you know how that Skolli was able to get behind you?" He shook his head. "A Skolli was attacking Rúna and Gil from their blind spot. You were protecting them. Do not beat yourself up over the fact that the wolves left us. You were still able to help me. *You* were the one who was able to get me to focus long enough to tell you how to keep me alive. *You* were the one that got me back to the fortress in time." I squeezed his hand. "Try not to blame yourself when you have *absolutely nothing* to be sorry about."

Óskar was silent for a few moments. "I'll try." His hand squeezed mine. "A part of your family, huh?"

"You've quickly become like another adoptive brother to me," I explained hesitantly before adding, "If that's alright."

"I won't say no to another sister. That is, as long as you don't see the need to torment me like my sister does."

I chuckled, ignoring the sharp pain in my ribs. "I promise to limit my tormenting to once or twice a week just for you." Óskar tipped his head back as he laughed.

A knock on the door drew our attention. Óskar ducked back behind the curtain to answer it. Murmured voices floated into the room, but I couldn't tell what was being said. Georg, Pétur and Gil followed him back into the room.

Óskar opened the curtains to reveal the setting sun as Georg and Pétur stopped at the end of my bunk. Gil took the chair beside me, causing Óskar to shrug his shoulders and sit on the edge of my bunk. He took my now-empty tankard from my hand and placed it on a small table.

"Where's Rúna?" I asked. Georg and Gil exchanged a long look. "What's going on? Fannar said that everyone was okay."

"She's fine," Pétur said as he sent me a smile. "There's nothing wrong with her. She just isn't here."

I felt my shoulders loosen in relief. "She isn't here?"

"Rúna has been spending the majority of her time with Baldur since we returned." Georg ran a hand over his bald head. "We only see her at training and some meals."

"You gave us quite a scare there," Peter said. "Glad to see you're still kicking around. All that steel came in handy, did it?"

"We know you need your rest, but we wanted to see for ourselves that you were okay." Georg smiled at me. "If you need anything, let us know. Hákon should be coming to check on your wounds tomorrow."

Georg and Pétur made their way out of the room. I could tell that something was bothering Gil; his eyes hadn't once left his hands to look at me. I sighed. I had a bad feeling that I knew what it was about. "Why don't you go wash up, Óskar?"

Óskar tilted his head to the side and pursed his lips. "You just woke up. Fannar and I don't want you to be alone."

"I'll be fine. Gil's here with me," I said. "Honestly, go have something to eat and wash up. The chair will still be here for you when you come back."

His eyes searched mine before he sighed and stood from the bed. "Alright, fine. Half an hour and I'll be back."

"An hour." I sent him a cheeky smile.

"Three-quarters of an hour." Óskar quirked an eyebrow as he challenged me to try and up the time anymore. I nodded in agreement, and he left the room.

Gil and I sat in heavy silence.

Eventually, the words burst from Gil. "Why did you give up?" I looked away from him as if that would allow me to avoid answering the question. "When I found you, you were lying on the ground, not even trying to protect yourself."

"I froze," I whispered. "When I looked down and saw the mixture of my red blood and the black blood of the Skolli, it brought me back to the night that Da died. I was frozen. I couldn't fight back." I cleared my throat and turned my attention towards the window. "I'm useless."

"You are not useless. The only way I found you was by following the bodies of the Skolli that you left behind," Gil said. "You were barely conscious when you told us how to heal you. None of us would have known what to do."

"What use is a Verndari if they freeze at the sight of blood?" I asked as I closed my eyes. "It might be better for everyone if I just stepped aside and let Emilía become the Verndari instead."

"No." Gil's voice was harsh.

My chin quivered. "But there's something *wrong* with me. That night, the Skolli attacked my village. Something inside of me broke, and I don't know how to fix it." My voice cracked as I wiped away a tear. "I don't know how to fix *me*."

"Something may have splintered that night," Gil finally said. "Something may have bruised or tarnished. But you are not broken, and you do not need to be fixed." His eyes searched mine for a long time. "Sometimes people who face combat return war-scarred."

"Of course they do. I have a scar from that night in my village."

"I don't mean physically." Gil leaned forward in the chair and braced his arms against his knees. "Some can't sleep without reliving what they experienced. Others panic. Some struggle to return to their normal life. A few can be triggered and sent into a flashback of what happened."

I stared at my fingers that were interlaced in my lap. "You think that I'm war-scarred?"

"I do," Gil said. "Why didn't you ask for help?"

"How could I have?" My voice rose as my eyes met Gil's momentarily before I turned away again. "Who would I have asked? Rúna? She's too busy with Baldur these days. She didn't even sleep in the tent the night of the attack. Óskar? What would he have understood about what I am going through?" I pulled at my hair anxiously. "Fannar? I don't see him nearly as much as I used to because of our training. Ma doesn't even look at me anymore, let alone speak to me. You? You were too busy lashing out at me and then pushing me away. You only just stopped. How could any of you fix what is wrong with me?"

"There is *nothing* wrong with you. You can and will get through this." Gil dragged a hand down his face before his hands clenched tightly around the armrests of the chair. "How much do you know about how my family's bloodrite works?"

My brows furrowed. "What does that have to do with any of this?"

"It has everything to do with this."

"Alright," I said, interlacing my fingers again as I took a moment to calm down. "I don't know much about it. All I know from my lessons is that it works like mine. Our blood-rites allow us to manipulate something."

Gil sighed and fiddled with a loose string on his shirt.

"Exactly. But where your bloodrite manipulates your body to become something else, mine manipulates any darkness inside me. The darkness I wield is a direct manifestation of what is inside of me."

"How does that relate to you lashing out and pushing us away?" My voice was gentle as I watched Gil carefully.

"When I use my bloodrite, it feeds on and magnifies the darkness inside me. The darkness becomes more powerful than any light I have inside, and the longer I use my powers, the deeper it is able to sink its claws into me." Gil's jaw clenched. "When that happens, the darkness takes control. I know what is happening, but I am not able to stop any of it."

I sucked in a breath. "That's awful."

Gil let out a humourless laugh. "Historically, my family has only been good for so long. We can only use our bloodrites a limited amount before the darkness gains complete control. There's a wing underneath the fortress reserved for those in my family who have given in to the monster inside them. That way, we can't hurt anyone else."

"I'm so sorry." The man in front of me looked broken. Defeated. "But I would like to think it will be different for you." Gil was focused on his hands. "I remember when you found me in the forest." His head snapped up to meet mine. "I could see your eyes flashing to black and back again. I could see you fighting the darkness in order to save me."

His eyes lit with hope. "I was able to gain some semblance of control over the monster long enough to save you."

"Everything I have been told about bloodrites revolves around determination. While emotion may play a part, determination is ultimately stronger."

"Yes." Gil sent a sad smile in my direction. "I don't understand how that applies to this situation, though."

"You were able to keep control over the monster because you were determined to help me, right?" Gil nodded, his brows furrowed. "It seems everyone has always treated your family as something to be used and locked away rather than focusing on learning how to control the darkness. Maybe your determination just has to be stronger than that of the monster to remain in control."

Gil considered my words for several moments before he ran a hand through his hair. "That could be true, but I would need to use my bloodrite more to test your theory. I already pushed you all away to protect you. What else would I need to lose to do this?"

"Maybe I could help. I could help you train. Last time, you were focused on me long enough that it helped you regain control. If that doesn't work, I could just lock you in the room until you calm down."

"That could work." He leaned closer to me. "But only if you are sure."

"I'm sure." I smiled at him. "I just ask one thing. Will you help me overcome my inner demons, too?" Gil reached forwards, fingers twitching as though he wanted to reach out to me, but he held back. "I'll help you control the darkness, and you'll help me heal from that night in my village. We can do this. Together."

Gil nodded, a small smile on his face. "Together."

CHAPTER
TWENTY-TWO
BRYN

I spent time with Fannar and Óskar as they maintained their constant presence by my side. Still, at night, I found myself wide awake even as my daily companion slept.

Things from the attack began to replay themselves in my head on a loop. There was something here that I needed to know. I had missed something.

The third morning, it finally clicked.

I could *see* that night.

It should have been pitch black, but the fire allowed me to see. There was a fire after Georg said that there shouldn't be one—that it would give away our location. But, someone that was in the forest that night had re-lit it.

The attack was intentional.

The second Hákon finally cleared me to leave my bunk, I ran towards the common rooms, ignoring Hákon's calls to take it easy.

I didn't have time to take it easy.

I skidded into the room, gaining both Georg and Gil's attention. It was too early for any of the others to be up. Óskar had gone back to bed as soon as Hákon had cleared me.

"Where can I find Ísak?" I asked out of breath. After three days in bed, my body was already going soft.

Georg arched a brow. "He has rooms near the library, but if there's something I could help you with instead—"

"No. It has to be him," I said before I turned and ran out of the room, managing to slow down as I entered the main part of the fortress so that I didn't draw attention to myself. Once I reached the library, I asked a servant to point me where I could find Ísak.

I banged on his door until Ísak finally answered it. His hair hung lankly down his back instead of his regular braided horsetail.

"Brynja?"

"We need to talk," I said. "Now." I didn't wait for him to answer as I made my way into the library, heading straight for the stained bookcase and waiting for him to join me. I turned my head as I pricked my finger, allowing the blood to drip onto the shelves.

I stormed into the hidden room, pacing as I waited for him to close the door. "What didn't you tell me?"

"I beg your pardon?" Ísak took the seat that was furthest from me.

"The traitors. You didn't tell me the whole story, did you?"

"When did you realize?"

I growled under my breath as anger surged through my body. "This morning. The Skolli were lured to the forest to attack us, and the only reason that would happen would be if one of the Verndari was a traitor, like you mentioned."

"You're quite clever," Ísak tapped his fingers on the table. "I assumed you wouldn't realize for another moon at the earliest."

I slammed my hands down on the table. "Why did you hide it from me? I deserved to know!"

"I needed you to have a clear mind. If you began building relationships with the other Verndari, this could have clouded your judgment. You would have seen things that weren't there or second-guessed every thought you had about them."

"Or, perhaps, I would have been more prepared for something to happen. Like, I don't know, maybe *an ambush in the forest*," I hissed. "I almost died because you wanted to handle this your own way. You put this on my shoulders, which means that I get a say. Tell me everything that I need to know."

Ísak studied me for several moments before he let out a sigh and crossed his arms. "The barrier was tied to two of the strongest bloodlines in the realm—one was a Verndari, the other was a member of the Commanding Family."

"*What?*" I felt as though all the air had been knocked out of my lungs.

"I said—"

"—I heard what you said." I sank into a chair, suddenly exhausted. Going up against a Verndari and their family would be hard enough. Going up against the Commanding Family as well? I couldn't do that on my own. I needed help, but who could I go to? "I don't even know what to think or who to trust."

"I've always thought trusting your instincts is the best way to go," Ísak said. "Perhaps that would be a good place to start."

～

Even though Hákon finally allowed me to get out of my bunk, it took another four days before he cleared me to train. I attended all the sessions that Georg held to create tactics for the next time we faced the Skolli. Now that we had all fought them, we could create better plans.

Those four days that I couldn't spend training were hard. Made even worse by the fact that I couldn't go on any runs until he cleared me for training.

To distract myself from my frustrations, I spent three of the four days holed up in the secret room in the library. I needed to find something—*anything*—that could point me towards who the possible traitors were.

But there was nothing.

The Verndari and the King Commander had carefully chosen the details they recorded involving the barrier. There were no names listed. No distinguishing factors and no reference to bloodrites.

As each day ended, I felt myself becoming more desperate. I was going to break under the weight of this task. I couldn't do this alone, but if I told the wrong person, then everything could go to shit.

I didn't want to think of what would happen if this got out. Death would probably be the best-case scenario. I didn't want to consider what the worst-case scenario would be.

Finally, something clicked. I couldn't trust anyone whose bloodline could be traced back to the Great War. That was too much of a risk. But someone who was only recently introduced to the Verndari? That was someone I could trust. There was no way that his family could be tied to the barrier.

The first morning I was cleared to train, Georg refused to let me do much. He let me run so I didn't lose my mind, but nothing else. Regardless, I lingered in the training hall long after the others left the room. The only person left was Georg. He ran a sharpening stone over one of Gil's swords.

"Can I talk to you?" I asked. "In private?"

Georg raised a brow. "We're the only two in here. Is that not private?"

"Is there anywhere else we could go? Somewhere where it is less likely that we would be overheard?"

Georg stared at me for a long moment before he put the sword back on the rack. "We can go to my office."

He led me down to a small room tucked away on the first floor of our wing. The room was barely large enough for the limited amount of furniture that Georg had in there. A desk, a pair of chairs, and a bookcase left just enough room to walk around. Georg shut the door and sat in the chair behind the desk. He gestured for me to take a seat in front of it.

"I didn't know you had an office," I said.

"It's mainly for ensuring the upkeep of the Verndari, which you don't have to worry about," Georg explained. "Commissioning more weapons or armour, requesting more dummies or sharpening stones—those sort of things. But I doubt that it was that which you wanted to talk to me about."

There was no way to ease into the conversation that I had to have with him, but I didn't want to just come out and say that one of the people he was closest to was a traitor.

"When you came to the fortress, did Ísak tutor you too?"

"Yes, he did. Rúna's grandfather wanted to ensure I knew as much as possible before the Trainer Tournament started."

I shifted in my chair. "What did he teach you?"

"Everything I would not have grown up knowing. He went over the different councils and fighting groups. We covered all the families in powerful alliances and anything considered important for the position." Georg crossed his arms over his chest.

I had been hoping that he had more lessons in the Great War. "Did Ísak ever teach you about our—" I searched for the right word "—history?"

"Not until I won the tournament. It's too dangerous to share Verndari secrets without a permanent connection to the position."

"So he told you about everything? He told you about the Great War, the detainment of the overthrown Commanding Family, the formation of the Verndari?"

Georg leaned forward in his seat. "What do you mean the *detainment* of the Commanding Family? Were they not killed?"

It didn't take long for me to explain everything to him. I had to stop partway through as he swore. Loudly. I cleared my throat. "Not to make matters worse, but I think the traitor is already starting to make their move."

"Explain." Georg's voice wasn't harsh, but it was certainly strict.

"Emilía and Ottó are trying to undercut my position. The Skolli attacked us after the fire was relit. They aren't bothering to hide the escalating attacks when they were careful about not being caught for hundreds of years. They don't seem to care anymore, which can only mean one thing."

"They are confident that there will be a future—a not-so-distant future—where there is no need for them to hide anymore." Georg ran a hand over his head. "They are going to be making their move soon. It's the only logical explanation. For them to succeed, they would need the help of a member of the Commanding Family. They would have to be certain of it."

I nodded my head. "There's two traitors and the only people I can be certain of are you and I."

"Do you have any suspicions of who they may be?"

I took a moment to consider everything before I answered. "I don't know who the traitors are, but I know who I want to trust."

"Who is that?"

"I trust Óskar and Gil. I want to trust Hákon." I tucked a curl behind my ear. "I want to be able to trust Ragna as well, but I don't know her well enough."

We were silent for several moments before Georg sighed. "We need to narrow down our options. We need to be sure that they deserve your trust."

"How do you plan to do that?"

Georg grabbed a piece of parchment from the top of a stack on his desk and studied it. He was quiet for several moments as he read. "The Crepuscule, and the annual tournament associated with it, is coming up. We are all expected to compete. Knowing Ottó, he wouldn't let Emilía pass up the chance to compete against you. If she were to beat you, it would only further the agenda he is trying to push."

"It would show that she is more skilled than me. That she deserves the position more than I do."

"Exactly. I would assume that he is working alongside the traitor because weakening the Verndari would help them both. If I were him, I would have the traitor inform me of what event you decided to compete in."

I nodded. "Then he could enter Emilía in alongside me. But how do we plan for that? I have to choose an event regardless."

"I think you should do the agility course, but when we gather to select our events, we will say you are entering a different one. We will only tell the people that we trust the truth. Then we will see which event Emilía is enrolled in," Georg leaned back in his seat. "Who are we going to tell?"

I considered my choices for several moments before I decided to go with my gut. "I want to tell Óskar and Gil the truth. I think we should let Hákon know, too."

"Alright," Georg nodded. "I will tell Hákon because I have to inform the Commanding Family of our event choices. It'll be up to you to tell Óskar and Gil."

"I can do that," I said. I stood from my chair and made my way towards the door.

I had just rested my hand on the handle when Georg spoke again. "Bryn," I turned to look at him. "You don't have to handle this alone anymore. Thank you for trusting me."

Óskar and I walked through the fortress side by side while Yugar trotted ahead. Ottó hadn't continued his public rallying against us since our return.

Regardless of the fact that Ottó was forced back into the shadows for his campaigning, Georg wanted to try to regain control. It was a delicate situation since we couldn't let on that we had been tipped off. Georg figured that if we made our presence stronger around the fortress, it would help curb his arguments. It was the most subtle option we had.

Which meant that we now took turns strolling through the hallways and grounds of the fortress each day. Today was Óskar and I's turn.

Fannar waved to us as he walked by with Hákon and Lúdvík. They seemed to be heading towards the training grounds, so I simply waved back and let them be.

Baldur and Rúna lounged on the benches in the large entry

hall. Baldur had one arm curled over Rúna's shoulders as she sat with her arms crossed. Various Warlords were gathered around them, their laughter loud enough to ring through the hall. The raider from the shipyards leaned back against the wall beside the middle-aged woman from the Striking Shadows on the war council. Their heads were tilted together to be heard over the merriment of Baldur's gathering. From the grins on their faces, I guessed that they were catching up rather than discussing anything serious.

I smiled at Rúna as we passed by.

Rúna showed no sign that she even saw me. She certainly didn't smile back.

We made our way outside. We just barely caught a glimpse of Gier as his horse galloped through the gates. Ragna and Svanna stood in the shadows nearby. Svanna's head rested on her shoulder. Svanna said something that caused a small smile to bloom on Ragna's tired face.

We made a circuit of the walls, smiling and greeting the soldiers. I tried my best to learn all of their names. I may fight by their side one day—I may have to *lead* them one day. The least I could do was learn their names.

We passed Pétur on our way down the walls. He stood in front of Sigrún, who sat on the edge of one of the steps. In Pétur's hand spun a small water cyclone as Sigrún clapped and laughed with glee. Her dark hair drifted across her face from the wind, but she didn't seem to care.

"That's going to come back to bite him in the arse," Óskar muttered once we had passed by.

"Why? What's wrong with what they are doing?"

"Nothing if they are just friends. But if either of them are hoping for more," he drew his thumb across his neck. "The

King Commander has decreed that Sigrún will marry the Commanding Son of our closest neighbour once she turns twenty. He doesn't take well to people going against his wishes."

TWENTY-THREE

A week later, we're back in the war chamber once again. I hated this room and everything it stood for. We had been gathering more frequently with the attacks, and every time we gathered here, it was to discuss more death and destruction.

The meeting was held shortly after dawn when most residents of the fortress were still in their beds. We couldn't risk anyone knowing what was happening.

"The Skolli attacks are becoming more frequent. Several of them have been increasingly more intense. Last night, we lost a small village completely. It was burnt to the ground. There were no survivors," Ragna said, her voice devoid of emotion.

She looked as though she hadn't slept. Dark circles had taken up residence under her eyes. All our information relied on whatever the response teams managed to send to her. I half expected to see her shoulders slumped from the weight.

"I sent out one of my agents to see what they can find, but based on the reports I've received, it is pretty safe to say that they won't find anything good," Ragna continued.

"Send out the Verndari, send out the Royal Regiment, I don't care. But perhaps we should do something rather than sitting around twiddling our thumbs?" Baldur asked in a tone that made my blood boil.

He discussed sending out warriors to risk their lives as if they were simply pieces in a game he wanted done quickly. A game where he didn't care if he lost almost all of his pieces.

"We can't," the Queen said. Baldur huffed. "The Verndari have to be here until the trials are over; we can't send them out if they aren't at their full strength. As for the Royal Regiment, there is no way we could mobilize such a large fighting force without a more concise idea of where the Skolli are going to strike next."

Ragna rubbed her forehead. "All the reports I've gotten from the Recovery Teams suggest that they aren't planning to return to the fortress between attacks. All eight teams are already in the field rather than having four in reserve. I'm currently forming teams that can travel to the response teams to replenish their supplies."

"I want the Verndari ready to move as soon as the trials are over," the King Commander demanded. "If we keep dividing up our forces, then we will be weakened. We would be open to attack. That cannot be allowed to happen."

"Yes, Commander," Georg said as he bowed his head. "Perhaps you should start stockpiling supplies as well."

Sigrún turned to Georg. "You think there's going to be a war."

"It certainly feels that way. I would rather we be prepared for a war that never happens than be surprised should one arise."

"I'll start preparing the regiment," Hákon said before he leaned back in his seat. "I'll ensure they have the training they need for a war. But I will need more warriors. I can't fight a war with just the Royal Regiment. It would be a slaughter."

"You also have the Verndari," Baldur smirked. "Who could ever forget about them?"

Hákon clenched his jaw. "Regardless of how skilled they are, I will still need more than *six people* to fight a war."

Ragna shuffled the parchments in front of her. "I need to know what Jarls and Warlords we can count on for support. For supplies, yes, but also for numbers. I need to know who we can trust to support us."

"After the trials, we'll send the Verndari out, along with your agents." The King Commander stroked his beard. "They will not only help us respond against the attacks but also pay visits to the Jarls and Warlords of the realm. And, should it come down to it, they can begin to recruit the public for additional support."

"If that's the case, I would suggest keeping Egill here," Baldur smirked at me. "It would be a shame if he was the reason that they didn't side with us. After all, most people wouldn't want to fight alongside a monster."

My body tensed as I wiped any emotion from my face. I refused to show anyone, especially such a vile person as Baldur, that his words had hit the mark. Bryn's eyes were burning into my face as Rúna was staring intently at the table.

"Gil isn't the monster in this room," Bryn said, her voice soft but laced with steel.

My eyes darted to Bryn. It had always been Rúna who defended me. My chest warmed at the thought that she would do that for me.

Ottó grabbed onto Pétur's arm and whispered heatedly into his ear.

Probably another complaint about Bryn.

Baldur's face turned red. "How dare you? By the end of the trials, you will be nothing more than dirt under my shoes."

"Watch it," Óskar growled.

I could take people hissing insults at me - I had been dealing with it my whole life.

But gods be damned, I would not let them do that to Bryn.

I stood from my seat and slammed my hands on the table. "She is far more powerful than you. You don't even have a bloodrite," I growled. "She is worth far more than you. Watch your fucking tongue."

Georg rested a hand on my shoulder. "If we are done here, then I believe it is best to leave."

"I agree," the King Commander said. We began to file out of the room when he spoke again. "I would suggest you keep a tighter leash on your Verndari, Georg. I may not be as understanding of another such outburst in the future."

Georg bowed deeply. "Yes, Commander."

We left the room in a rush, and Rúna did not follow us.

Bryn wrapped her hand around my forearm and pulled me back so we fell in step next to Pétur. "What did Ottó want?" Bryn asked.

Pétur glanced around the hallway before he spoke quietly. "He wanted me to remind you to know your place."

"And were you going to?"

Pétur looked at Bryn sideways. "No. I simply agreed to his words so that he didn't lose it. So much around us is already going to shit, and I couldn't deal with another outburst on top of it all."

Pétur caught up to Óskar while Bryn pulled me towards the entrance to the fortress. "Where are we going?" I asked.

"We are going to go buy some herbs and jars. Then I am going to teach you how to make the medical salves and ointments," Bryn looked at me. "I meant what I said, Gil. You are not a monster. The easiest way to show that to others is to teach you how to heal them."

IT TOOK A WHILE FOR US TO FIND EVERYTHING THAT BRYN WANTED. I tended to avoid the city more often than not, and I struggled to help her find what she was looking for.

Eventually, we had everything we needed, and we each carried a large basket of supplies back to the fortress. Instead of returning to the Verndari wing, Bryn led me towards the residential wing of the fortress.

"Where are we going?" I asked.

"To my family's rooms." Bryn glanced at me for a second before she turned her attention back to the hallway. "You opened up to me about your family. It only seems fair that I do the same."

I shifted the basket to my other hand as we stopped in front of the door to her family's rooms. "It was not a transaction. You don't have to repay me with your own story."

"I know. I want to," Bryn murmured as she reached for the handle. "I want to start letting people in. My walls have been built so high since the attack on my village, and I want to tear them down. I *need* to tear them down to move on."

Bryn pushed open the door. She let me enter first before she shut it behind us. The sitting room was empty, and it was eerily quiet. The curtain separating one of the rooms was pulled back, revealing an open bedchamber. The curtain to another room was shut tight.

I stood in the middle of the room, the basket still in my

arms. "It's rather quiet," I said. "Is your family normally like this?"

"We never used to be," Bryn placed her basket on the table. "But now? It's silent unless Fannar or I are here."

"Why?" I placed my basket beside hers.

"You'll see," Bryn made her way towards the shut curtain. She paused in front of it, the fabric clutched in her fist.

My footsteps rang through the silent room as I stopped by her side. I stood there for a moment, debating with myself before I rested a hand on her shoulder.

I gave her the softest of squeezes.

"Does anyone know what is behind this curtain?" I asked with a soft voice.

"Hákon and Óskar do."

"You do not have to show me if you are not ready."

Bryn swallowed thickly and shook her head. "No. I want to show you. It's just hard for me to see her like this."

She pulled open the curtain to a bedchamber where a woman was drifting around the room mindlessly. She wore a loose dress and had her hair braided loosely down her back.

"Hi, Ma," Bryn said as she made her way into the room. Her mother wandered to the window, where she took a seat in the chair that was there. "I've brought someone for you to meet. I'm going to teach him how to make some of our ointments."

She didn't answer. Her eyes didn't even leave the window.

Bryn knelt by her mother's chair as I slowly joined her. "This is Gil. He's one of the Verndari."

"Good tidings, ma'am." I knelt down beside Bryn, careful to keep my distance from her.

Still no answer.

"It's been a while since we made our ointments, but I still remember everything by heart," Bryn spoke quickly as if she was desperate to fill the silence. "I never thought I would miss those hours we spent chopping and crushing herbs, but I do. I'm happy that I get to teach someone else your recipes, Ma."

Nothing.

"Well." Bryn stood up. "We will just be in the other room if you want to join us. I'm sure Gil could use any insight you could give him. I was never as good at healing as you are."

Bryn led me back into the sitting room and drew the curtain behind us. She began to set up everything we would need for what we were making. Bryn had decided to teach me how to make the things that I was most likely to use; burn soothers, numbing cream, and cleansing balm. I could heal most basic injuries with those three. We could focus on anything more unique, like knockout tea, another day.

"How long has she been like that?" I finally asked.

"Since she woke up after the attack on our village," Bryn said before she let out a humourless laugh. "She's actually better than she was then. I've never seen her willingly move around like that."

I studied her for a moment. "Thank you."

"For what?"

"For trusting me with that. I know how hard it is to see your parent as a shell of who they are."

Bryn looked up from the herbs that she was setting out on the table. "You do?"

"I do. My mother was soft, and she was kind. Then, the darkness consumed her. Now whenever I see her, she is there, but she's not really *there*."

Bryn smiled sadly at me before waving me over to her side as she turned back to the table.

Maybe if I was able to help people, they would see more than a monster when they looked at me.

TWENTY-FOUR

BRYN

That morning I agreed to meet Gil so that we could begin to work on our training. We decided it would be best to use one of the unused rooms in our wing. It was tucked away by our common room, too big to be a storage room and too small to be of any use to the entire group.

With the trials quickly approaching and the number of attacks climbing, we needed to work on controlling my blood-rite. I also needed to focus on overcoming my fear of blood — if I froze again, I may not survive. Thankfully, Georg had decided that while all the Verndari needed to be aware of my fear, they were not to tell anyone else. We needed to understand my weakness, not announce it.

Gil was already in the room when I got there. He leaned against the wall with his arms crossed over his chest. I sent him a small smile that he returned with a nod. The room was small; there wasn't even a fireplace for heat. Light streamed in through the windows, and a pile of furs had been dragged in.

The door swung open behind me as I made my way across the room.

Óskar entered with Yugar by his side. Óskar didn't bother to close the door as he headed towards the pile of furs and flopped down on them. I shook my head and shut the door myself.

I turned back towards Óskar. "What are you doing here?"

"That's not very polite, Talon," Óskar tucked his arm behind his head. His other hand scratched between Yugar's ears. "You're going to make me feel unwanted if you keep talking like that."

"I asked him to be here," Gil said. Our eyes met. "I needed a way to make sure that the blood could be eliminated quickly if you reacted badly to it."

I raised my eyebrows. "What does that have to do with Óskar being here?"

Óskar rolled over onto his side and propped his head up on his hand. "See, this is what I mean. You're going to hurt my feelings if you keep saying that kind of thing."

I rolled my eyes, my mouth quirking up despite the nerves that had tied my stomach up in knots.

"Óskar is going to cover his arms in blood. That way, he can leave quickly if we need him to." Gil crossed his arms over his chest. "But first, we will try and trigger your bloodrite."

I scrunched my nose and turned back towards Óskar. "How's that supposed to happen? Do I have to cut you to ribbons with my daggers until you're covered in blood?"

"As delightfully horrific as that sounds, I have to decline your very gracious offer," Óskar shook his head. "Gil sent me to the kitchens this morning to gather a jar of blood from whatever they were slaughtering for dinner."

I swallowed thickly as Óskar held up a jar. Blood ran thick along its walls. "Alright."

Gil pushed off the wall and made his way over towards me. "Sparring first. As long as you are comfortable."

"I'm comfortable with that," I said as I sat on the floor and started loosening my muscles. "I don't think I will be able to control my bloodrite."

Gil joined me on the floor and helped stretch my legs. "What makes you say that?"

"The only connection between all the times I've shifted is my fear." I smiled at him. "And as much as you try to deny it, I'm not scared of you. Or your darkness."

"You can't rely on fear. You need to find something stronger to rely on instead."

We sparred for almost twenty minutes, and I was right. I didn't shift once. I didn't even start to shift.

I spent most of the time dodging Gil's attacks, but a couple times, I braved the darkness to attack him head on. One time, I forced Gil to the floor, climbing on top of him to pin him. His darkness slammed into me, and I tumbled onto the ground. Gil rolled on top of me and pinned me under his body to win the spar.

My eyes locked on his as they became pitch black. They reverted back to their normal green and back again. I gently freed my arms from his and rested my hands on his cheeks.

"*Stay with me*," I whispered.

Gil's throat bobbed before he rested his forehead on mine. I watched as the black eyes remained for less and less time until it was just his vivid green left.

After a moment, Gil cleared his throat and climbed to his feet. He reached down a hand to help me up and rested his large hands on my shoulders. Gil gently turned me away from where Óskar now stood. He shared a nod with Óskar over my shoulder before he turned his attention back to me. "Are you alright?"

My heart beat faster at the clink of the jar as Óskar unscrewed the lid. "I don't know," I whispered.

"I know I am probably not your first choice, but," he cleared his throat, "I am here." His words were awkward, but it was more comfort than I thought he would be capable of so soon after he had to use his darkness.

I nodded my head and sent him a hesitant smile. "I know. Thank you."

Yugar came to sit at my feet. "Whenever you're ready, Bryn," Óskar said, making my heart race.

"Turn around when you are ready. He has covered his arms in the blood. Focus on something else before you look there," Gil suggested. I nodded before I blew out a breath.

I turned around, my eyes fixed on the ceiling. I took a deep breath to steady myself. I let my eyes rest on Óskar's face first. His eyes showed his worry, but he still sent me a smile. I swallowed thickly and slowly traced my eyes down his body until they landed on his arms.

My breath froze in my lungs as my mind went blank. My heart pounded in my chest, but everything else seemed so far away. So distant. As if it were hidden within the thickest of fogs.

I started to shake and dimly registered the muted sting on my knees from the floor. It took me a minute to realize that someone's arms were wrapped around me. That I was being lifted off the ground and into someone's lap.

I blew out a shaky breath.

"I am here." Gil's words slowly filtered into my awareness. "I am here." Slowly, my body stopped shaking and I was able to breathe easier. The fog around me dissipated enough that I could hear Gil's heartbeat under my ear. "Are you alright?"

"Yeah," I said softly. "I didn't get trapped in memories."

Gil eventually rested his head atop mine. "Perhaps that is only a result of mixing our blood with the blood of the Skolli."

"Maybe." I let out a harsh laugh as I stood up. "I know overcoming it on the first shot wasn't likely, but I stupidly allowed myself to hope."

"That is one of your greatest strengths. Perhaps it's even your most important one."

"How could hope ever be enough?"

Gil stood to meet me. He raised his arms slowly, hesitating, before he wrapped his arms around me and held me close to his chest. "Hope is stronger than almost anything else. After all, no one could head off to war without the hope of survival. They need that hope of a better tomorrow." His voice rumbled in his chest. His heart raced under my ear. "That is part of our job. We need to be that hope."

"What about our hope? How do we find that?"

"I cannot answer that for you," Gil said softly. "You must answer that for yourself. Find your hope, Bryn, and you will find your strength."

I RAN THROUGH THE GROUNDS THAT SURROUNDED THE FORTRESS. A light rain signalled the approach of another storm. Yugar trotted by my side, his tongue lolling out of his mouth. He had become my new running partner, and I found myself relaxing in his canine companionship.

The loud clash of wooden weapons rang through the courtyards as I made my way through the gate. Emilía and

Ottó sparred in the centre of the courtyard as a small crowd watched on. In Emilía's hands were a pair of wooden daggers, while Ottó wielded two wooden axes. I took a spot among the crowd.

Emilía was skilled; I had to give her that much, but she was also reckless. She didn't have to risk getting slashed when she fought with wooden weapons. Emilía took chances that she would never get away with if they fought with real weapons. It was why Georg insisted that we trained with steel. It was dulled, but the point still stood.

Ottó barked at Emilía each time she got hit by his axe after she took a risk. But that didn't stop her from doing it again.

The crowd dispersed as they finished their spar. Only a few people still lingered in the courtyard. Pétur sat near the entrance to the Verndari wing as he read what looked to be a letter. Rúna walked by on Baldur's arm as his friends followed along behind them. Ragna, Gier, and Svanna sat off to the side as they played a game of cards.

Emilía sent me a vicious smirk. "Enjoy the show?"

"Not particularly, no," I said. There were many things that I wished I could say to Emilía, but I would bite my tongue.

"Intimidated already, then?"

I forgot every idea of restraint.

"No," I said. "That was sloppy and unrefined. You'll probably want to work a little harder on that."

"Who do you think you are?" Emilía asked with a glare. "You shouldn't even be here. You don't *deserve* to be here."

"I may be new here, but at least I fight with steel rather than wood. Even I know that wooden weapons are reserved for children's toys."

Emilía sneered as she leaned in close to my face. "I would

be careful how you speak to me. I would hate for something to happen to you."

"I'd like to see you try," I said, holding my ground. There was no way that I was going to back down from Emilía. If she wanted to take my position in the Verndari, then I was going to make her earn it.

Emilía stared me down for a few more seconds before she stormed away.

"Good for you," Ragna said as she stopped beside me. Her shirt and pants flattered her larger figure, and the front pieces of her hair were pulled back from her face by a small knot on the back of her head. "Emilía underestimated you. She didn't expect you to stand up to her like that."

"Who won the hand?" I asked.

"I did," Gier said as he and Svanna joined us. "They rarely beat me at cards."

"Dice is a different story, though. He always loses at that," Svanna said with a grin.

Gier crossed his arms. "She wasn't asking about dice. She was asking about cards. Therefore, my statement is much more relevant than yours."

Svanna rolled her eyes with a chuckle. Clearly, she had spent enough time around Gier to be used to his rather abrasive personality. "I'm sorry about my sister," Svanna sent me a small smile.

"What she does is not your fault. You don't have to apologize," I said.

"I know I don't, but someone should. Father has her wrapped so tightly around his finger he might as well be holding her puppet strings. It doesn't surprise me that she does whatever he wants."

I studied Svanna for a moment. She looked a lot like Emilía, that's true, but there were subtle differences between them. Like the fact that Svanna's mouth was often quirked in a smile rather than a sneer like her sister. "What about you? Do you do whatever he wants as well?"

"No," Svanna said. She glanced towards Ragna before she looked back at me. "But it's complicated. It's hard to forge your own path when someone tries to keep you chained up."

TWENTY-FIVE

BRYN

At breakfast, Georg announced that we would be selecting our events for the tournament after we finished our training for the day, kickstarting the nerves in my stomach.

My distraction made it easier for Pétur to pin me. So easy that he pinned me three times in a row. Incredibly frustrated with myself, I fuelled my movements with all my fury at letting him beat me so easily.

I pinned him the next two times.

After we finished training, Georg led us to one of the small meeting rooms in the wing. He stood in front of the large chalkboard on one of the walls. "As we all know, the Crepuscule is approaching and, with it, the annual tournament. The list of events for the tournament has arrived."

My eyebrows scrunched together. Georg had mentioned the tournament when we created our plan, but I had been so nervous that I hadn't asked any of the questions I had. "What is the tournament?" I asked.

"Did you village folk never celebrate the end of the longest night of the year?" Pétur leaned back in his chair.

"Of course we did. It wasn't anything too fancy, though. Just a nicer dinner and time with close family. Perhaps exchanging gifts or tokens if there is the money for it."

Georg nodded. "That's the case in many small villages. Larger cities and towns will often hold festivals. But here? Here, the tournament is the biggest festivity other than the weeklong festival held in the city."

"On the day of the longest night of the year, a tournament is held where people may compete to show how strong the country's warriors are. However, in our case, it's mandatory participation," Óskar said as he braced his arms on the table. "It's like we're a bunch of prized ponies for the Commanding Family to show off."

"Don't speak for me. I'd certainly be a stallion. None of that pony shit," Pétur said with a smirk to Óskar before Georg clipped him behind the head.

"Regardless of what four-legged animal you may be—" Georg glared at Pétur and Óskar "—our event selections must be submitted today."

Gil shifted in his chair. "How many events are there this year?" he asked.

"Eight. There are events for bloodrites, swordsmanship, hand to hand combat, archery, staff fighting, horsemanship, agility, and two-on-two combat." Georg wrote each event on the chalkboard before he took a seat at the table. "Who would like to select first?"

"Seeing as none of you can shoot to save your life, saving you, almighty Georg," Óskar bowed mockingly towards Georg from his chair, "I'll compete in the archery competition." He smirked as Georg nodded his agreement. Óskar stood and added his name to the chalkboard beside where Georg had written archery.

"Add me for the bloodrite event," Pétur said.

Óskar didn't bother to wait for Georg's approval before he added Pétur's name to the board. We all knew that Pétur was arguably the best with his bloodrite out of all of us.

Georg turned to Gil. "I would like to enter myself for hand-to-hand combat unless you would rather compete in it."

Gil shook his head. "No, I would prefer the swordsmanship."

Óskar wrote both of their names down beside their respective events.

Georg sent me a subtle nod. "I believe that Bryn should compete in the horsemanship event. It's the best choice for her because she doesn't have the same amount of training as the rest of you. Depending on her opponent, she could be eaten alive in the combat-based events."

I nodded in agreement. Óskar narrowed his eyes at me but thankfully remained silent as he wrote my name on the board. I knew that Óskar was going to be the toughest sell—he knew how much I loved to run.

"I want to do staff fighting. It makes the most sense for me. It's one of my weapons, after all," Rúna said. It was the first time that I had heard Rúna speak that day. She only spoke to Georg and Gil during training.

"The Commanding Family announced their events this morning," Georg said. Óskar hesitated at the board when Georg didn't agree with her choice right away. "Hákon and Sigrún are competing in the two-on-two combat. Ragna's slated to do the agility course. Baldur has entered in the staff fighting."

"Why would that matter? I want to compete in the event." Rúna's words were sharp.

Gil rubbed his neck. "You told me that the Crepuscule was going to be the first time you would officially be seen on Baldur's arm. Baldur will not be happy when you inevitably try to best him publicly in the event."

"My priority is to show that I am a worthy partner, not to be some well-trained dog for the Commanding Son to show off." Rúna stood. "I'm a member of the Verndari first and foremost, which I think Baldur needs a reminder of. Put me down for staff fighting. Now, if you'll excuse me, I'm late for my morning commitments."

No one spoke for several moments, allowing the chalk's scratch and Rúna's distant footsteps to fill the air.

"Well, this is bound to be interesting," Óskar said as he placed the chalk on the small table near the board.

Pétur stood from his chair. "The kindling has certainly been laid, and I don't think we will want to be anywhere near it when it catches."

I GALLOPED THROUGH THE FIELDS, ÓSKAR AND FANNAR CLOSE BEHIND me. I leaned forward over my horse as we tore through the grass. I shifted my position as we approached a log that was set up. I settled my weight and braced myself for the jump. But the jump never came. Instead, my horse reared up on her hind legs, and I had to scramble to stay in the saddle.

Óskar and Fannar stopped beside me as my horse finally calmed enough to have all four hooves on the ground. Fannar snickered as I glared at him. "Not one word," I growled.

"How about more than one word?" Óskar asked. "You

know you were supposed to go over the log, not almost fall off your horse, right?"

I tapped my fingers on my leg for several moments as I watched Óskar with narrowed eyes. "I can tell Georg that you want to work on your hand-to-hand sparring some more."

"You wouldn't."

My grin was positively feral. "Try me."

"Fine. I won't give you a hard time about it. But you do need to be able to jump that log. Jumps are always a part of the horsemanship competition."

This was it. I had to tell them now before I backed out of it. Fannar would support me unconditionally, just like I would if he were in my shoes. It was Óskar that I was worried about.

"I'm actually entered in the agility course," I said with what I hoped was a casual shrug. "Georg and I thought that it was best."

"It certainly makes more sense than the horsemanship if you ask me," Fannar said.

Óskar shifted the reins in his hands. "Why did you say that you were going to do the horsemanship then?"

I realized that I really should have prepared an answer to this question. I couldn't tell them I wanted to hide what event I was competing in from Emilía. If they knew that, they just wouldn't tell Emilía that I changed events. No—I needed something believable and close to the truth that wouldn't give away what we were trying to do.

"I didn't know much about the tournament, so I thought it was best to trust what Georg suggested." That was true. "But we talked about it last night and realized that the agility course was probably better. Georg is going to let Hákon know about the switch." Also true. "I just figured it was easier to keep the switch quiet since it didn't matter too much in the grand scheme of things." Not quite true, but close enough.

"Fair enough. Why did you still have us helping you train today, then?"

"I'm going to need to learn how to do it eventually. Might as well be now," I said.

We spent the next hour running through the small jumping course that Óskar had set up. Fannar flew through it with an ease that took me by surprise. I never expected that would be something that he would be training in, but it made sense. The Royal Regiment was expected to be able to ride just as I was.

Hákon rode up to us on his own horse. "When I was told I was going to find you out here, I didn't expect this."

"They're teaching me how to ride," I said. "I can handle the basics, but anything involving jumps is still a little too much for me."

"It takes practice; don't let yourself get too worked up about it," Hákon turned towards Fannar. "I need you at the fortress. It's time."

Fannar nodded. "I'll be right there."

"It's time for what?" I asked.

"It's nothing to worry about, Bryn," Fannar said as his horse stopped right beside mine and grabbed my hand. "I'm going to do my best to be there for the tournament, but if I don't see you before, good luck. You'll do great. You've been running your whole life. I'm sure it will pay off now."

"Thank you," I said before Fannar rode off to the fortress with Hákon.

Óskar's horse shifted impatiently, its hooves scratching against the ground. "Just because Fannar left doesn't mean you get out of this that easily. Run the course again and have a more solid position for your jumps. I will not hide my laughter if you fall on your ass."

I didn't get a chance to retort as Óskar urged my horse into a trot, then a gallop with his bloodrite.

THE FESTIVAL IN GOLDHELM STARTED THREE DAYS BEFORE THE Crepuscule and continued for three days afterwards. The Crepuscule was a holiday dating back to the Great War's end. Skolli and Ógn only attacked in the dark, making the longest night of the year the most dangerous. After the war, the longest night of the year became a holiday. The Crepuscule was a celebration of surviving the deadliest night of the year.

On the first day of the festival, I strolled through the streets of Goldhelm with Gil by my side. I took everything in with wide eyes. The streets were strung with garlands and banners. New vendors were set up in the markets that sold everything from candied apples to little flags and ribbons. People sang in crowds on the edges of the streets while little kids ran around with rosy cheeks and stained lips from their treats.

Gil agreed to join me while I shopped for gifts for the Crepuscule. He seemed reluctant but painfully aware of the fact that he had his own shopping that he had to do. I knew that it wasn't the shopping itself that bothered him. What bothered him was the big crowds and the looks that people sent him.

When I told him about my entry into the agility event, he simply nodded his head—no questions asked. However, I really should have expected him to respond in a way that used the least amount of words. That tended to be his style.

Gil pulled me into a clothing shop I knew was one of

Rúna's favourites. He bought a beautiful dress in a deep red colour that I had no doubt was for her. I pulled him into a weapons shop, where I bought Fannar a boot knife.

We took turns dragging each other into stores as we slowly whittled down our shopping lists for the Crepuscule. Gil's last choice was a small armour shop. He studied two beautiful leather sets but ultimately went with one reinforced with metal strips shaped like feathers.

"Who's that for?" I asked. "I would guess Rúna, but I'm pretty sure that the dress is for her."

"It is for my sister Klara," Gil said as he readjusted the baskets and bundles in his arms. "She didn't inherit our family's bloodrite, so she is not eligible to be a Verndari. She is a fierce warrior, though, and I have no doubt that she'll fight alongside me if this gets any worse. I know she will find this beautiful, but I also hope it will protect her."

I smiled softly at him. "I understand how you feel. That's why I got Fannar a boot knife. I know he will appreciate it, but it will also make me feel better about him fighting."

"My other sister is not a fighter. She knows how to defend herself, but she is more of a healer. She would appreciate those medical ointments rather than a fancy piece of armour."

"Is that what you were planning to give her?" I asked softly.

Gil looked at me out of the corner of my eye. "If that was alright with you. I was planning on making them myself."

I reached for his hand. He allowed me to hold his hand, even if he didn't wrap his fingers around mine. "I think that sounds wonderful."

TWENTY-SIX

BRYN

I joined the rest of the Verndari in the common room. I was in the leather armour I wore to Hazelpeak, or what looked like it. My hair was pulled back in tight braids that only allowed a few rogue curls to escape. I wasn't as heavily armed as the last time I wore this armour. I only had a pair of daggers on my belt, one in each of my boots, and one on the inside of my arms.

Gil had a pair of swords sheathed across on his back as well as two on his belt. Both Pétur and Georg carried no weapons, but Georg's knuckles were wrapped in cloth. Rúna carried her staff, no whip to be seen, and Óskar had his bow in hand with his quiver on his back.

"As you all know, today is the tournament," Georg surveyed each of us. "Each of us has prepared for this and is ready to compete. However, those of you in combat events must keep in mind that many of the people we will face want to see if they can best us. They want to claim that they have beaten a Verndari. Keep your head up and be prepared for everything."

Georg turned to where I stood close to Óskar. "Both of you are competing in non-combative events, but that does not mean you can allow your guard to slip. Am I clear?" Georg asked.

"Crystal. Although, technically, all I have to do is make sure I shoot straight," Óskar grinned.

Georg's eyes narrowed on Óskar, but he didn't have the chance to say anything as loud bells rang throughout the fortress. "It's time," he said.

He led us through the fortress to the tournament grounds set up outside. The large grounds behind the fortress had been transformed. Large wooden stands lined the outside with designated sections barred off. The designated sections were filled with chairs rather than benches and were reserved for the most important groups attending. A sparring circle was set up in the centre with archery targets in the distance.

The crowd stared as we entered the field and took our place in our assigned seating. We were close to the box reserved for the Commanding Family. Everyone stood and bowed as the Commanding Family arrived. The King Commander and the Queen were dressed as spectators, while Hákon and his siblings were dressed in leather armour like us. The King Commander nodded to a man who stood in the centre of the tournament grounds.

"Welcome to the Crepuscule Tournament," the man said, causing the crowd to roar. "Will the competitors in hand-to-hand combat please take their places in the ring?"

The cheers only got louder when Georg stood from our box and made his way down.

The man blew a horn once both fighters had taken their place in the ring. Regardless of Georg's strength and speed, his opponent was able to keep up with his fierce fighting skills. He was able to land a few solid hits on Georg that caused me to wince, but Georg was the obvious winner after he pinned his opponent to the ground.

When the man called for the competitors for the horsemanship event, both Gier and Emilía stood from their seats. Emilía eyes found mine as I made no move to join them. Emilía's face reddened as she leaned down to hastily whisper in Ottó's ear before she mounted her horse.

A knot in my chest loosened. Gil, Óskar, and Hákon all knew that I was competing in the agility event instead. But Emilía didn't. I shared a look with Georg, who gave me a barely discernible nod.

We could trust them.

Large pieces of mirrored glass were rolled out into the centre of the grounds. The King Commander stood from his seat and extended his arm towards them. One of the pieces was filled with an image of Gier, while the other featured Emilía. I had heard rumours of the King Commander's ability to display images, but I had never seen it happen before.

Emilía performed strongly. There was no denying the fact that she rode well, but she still came second to Gier. He was always assigned to Striking Shadows fieldwork that needed to be done quickly. Based on how well he rode, I could see why.

Next came the swordsmanship event. Once again, when Gil stood from our box, the cheers of the crowd simply got louder. He approached the ring with an air of confidence, fully aware of his skill with his swords. Yet, when he reached the ring and began sizing up his opponent, a spike of fear settled in my stomach. He was facing the large raider from the shipyards. I swallowed anxiously as Gil drew the swords from his belt and settled into his fighting stance.

Gil launched himself at his opponent, his swords a blur.

The raider was bigger, but he did not have Gil's speed and grace. Gil slashed and stabbed, spun and jumped, as the man managed to block all of his strikes. He managed to cut the man in the arm, but Gil got cut on the cheek in the process.

Eventually, Gil managed to gain the upper hand as the raider began to tire. Both of them managed to get cut or scratched several more times before Gil won the fight, one of his swords pointed at his opponent's neck while the other rested against the back of it.

Once Gil returned to our box, he sat beside me as Óskar made his way down to the grounds. My healing instincts kicked in as my fingers and eyes danced over his skin, trying to assess his injuries. Gil's hand wrapped around one of my own to stop me.

His eyebrows were scrunched. "They are all shallow," he said quietly.

"I was so worried, and then he got your cheek and—" Gil squeezed my hand as he cut me off.

"I'm alright." He let go of my hand and rested his arms on the edges of his seat. His attention turned towards the ring before his eyes swung back to me again. "You were worried about me?"

"Of course I was." My eyes drifted to the ring as the crowd roared around me. I watched as Óskar made his way towards the targets that were set up.

I hesitated before I rested my hand atop Gil's. After a moment, he turned his hand over and allowed me to interlock our fingers. Svanna joined Óskar in front of the targets with a small smile on her face.

At the horn, they began to shoot. The first one to finish was the winner, but to move on to the next target, it had to be a perfect shot. Óskar started to gain a lead on Svanna when she barely missed the target's center on two shots. Three targets later, he won; however, Svanna didn't seem too upset about it as she sent him a smile before she made her way back to her spot beside Gier.

I stiffened as Baldur stood from his seat when Rúna started towards the ring. The crowd was the loudest it had been all day. Baldur quickly caught up to Rúna and whispered something in her ear as they entered the circle. Rúna swung her staff as she took her spot.

When the horn sounded, Baldur lazily propped his staff against the ground and leaned against it. "Dearest Rúna, just back out of the fight. We all know that you have no desire to actually fight me."

Rúna settled into her fighting crouch. "As a Verndari, it is my duty to never back down from a fight. Especially not to soothe the Commanding Son's ego," she said. Gil groaned and closed his eyes for a moment. I sucked in a breath as Baldur glared at Rúna.

"Have it your way then," Baldur said as he launched himself at Rúna.

His staff slashed through the air to hit hers with a loud crack. The fight quickly became the most aggressive of the day. The power and speed behind the staffs made most of the crowd wince whenever they made contact.

Rúna managed to hit Baldur in the ribs, and he grunted in pain. She shifted her staff to sweep his legs out from under him. He jumped over her attack and brought his staff down on her collarbone. Hard.

Her pained scream cut through the stands as she fell to her knees.

The crowd was completely silent.

Gil tensed in his seat as his hands fisted on the armrests.

Baldur's staff slashed at Rúna from the side. He hit her ribs hard enough to knock her to the ground. His face took on a sadistic gleam as he swung the staff down on her cheekbone.

Rúna screamed again.

His staff turned into a blur as he brought it down hard upon any part of her body that he could reach as Rúna continued to scream and flinch in pain.

Gil rushed towards the ring, the rest of us close behind him. Georg overtook him as he used his bloodrite to rush ahead. Georg, Gil, and Pétur formed a wall between Baldur and Rúna. I dropped to my knees by Rúna with Óskar by my side. Hákon's gloved hands were already on Rúna's body, his healing bloodrite appearing as blue lightning under her skin.

"Enough," Georg said harshly.

"How dare you interfere with the fight?" Baldur growled, his voice shaking with rage.

"You have no right to beat her like this. The fight is over." Gil's voice quivered as he tried to suppress his fury.

"I have no right?! I am the Commanding Son! If anyone has the right, it would be me!"

"No," the King Commander's voice rang through the air. "The rules of the tournament are clear. The fight ends as soon as one is unable to continue. Leave the ring."

Baldur let out a snarl before he stormed away.

"There's not much I can do for her right now. Both of us have to remain here until the tournament is over," Hákon said softly. "I won't have enough time to heal her before Bryn and I have to compete in our events." His hands drifted over many of the places Baldur struck Rúna, and his blue lightning followed their path. Rúna whimpered. "I'm going to try and numb some of the pain. The most we can do is keep her comfortable until

216

the tournament is over. I'll meet you all in her rooms as soon as I can to heal her."

Gil picked Rúna up and made his way back to our box. I made to follow him, but Óskar grabbed my wrist. "Your event is next."

He led me over to a massive eagle that was taller than both of us. A girl slightly younger than Óskar was leading Ragna to another eagle close by. Óskar helped me onto the eagle before he climbed on behind me. "The agility course starts outside the fortress walls, so the first person back in the tournament grounds is the winner."

I tried not to pull any of the eagle's feathers as it launched into the air. "Who is with Ragna?"

"My sister. She began taking the other competitors one by one to give us more time with Rúna."

The eagle flew in a long arc around the fortress before it looped back towards the forest. "Will the King Commander be using the mirrors like he did for the horsemanship event?"

"Yeah. They are set up throughout the course so the crowd can see them. When you start to hear the cheers, you'll know that you are close to the end."

The tangles of nerves in my stomach tightened into knots. I had to win. Or, at the very least, I had to beat everyone but Ragna.

It was my first public showing as a Verndari, and I could not fail.

The eagle slowly descended to where the other competitors were gathered. Once my feet were safely back on the ground, Óskar left with a smile. His sister stayed behind but didn't bother to dismount as Ragna made her way over to join them.

"You're too far to hear the horn to start, so watch for the

fire. That will be your signal," his sister said. Her eagle took off. "Be ready," she shouted back over her shoulder.

The four competitors settled into a line that faced back towards the fortress. Ragna gave me a nod as we ended up side by side in the middle of the line. A fire plume erupted in the distance. I surged forwards and settled into a fast run.

One of the girls at the end fell with a cry. A large rock struck her hard in the chest. I pushed myself faster and began to weave as I ran.

Ahead, four bridges were tied up, their front ends lifted above the ground. Out of nowhere, a series of knives were thrown towards me, so I pulled two daggers from my belt, blocking the blades as I ran. When I was within range, I threw one of my daggers, cleanly slicing through the rope. The front of the bridge fell with a thud, allowing me to charge across.

A river coursed ahead, the current forming small, white-capped waves. I quickly re-sheathed my dagger as I neared the river. I didn't hesitate as I dove into it; the frigid water bit at my hands and face as I swam hard against the current. I could feel my muscles aching, but years of running with Da had prepared me for this.

I climbed out of the water, stumbling as I settled back into a run. The winter air numbed my frozen body further.

In the distance, four ropes swung in the breeze. As I reached them, the ground began to crumble away beneath my feet. I jumped at the ropes. My force allowed me to swing across to land on solid ground. Someone fell with a cry. A quick glance to the side showed only Ragna and I were left.

We were side by side as we raced for long bridges up ahead. As we got close, two people stepped out of the trees to block our paths. I drew two daggers from their place on my forearms as my eyes scanned the man who blocked my bridge.

He stood confidently with an axe in his hand. The man had to be at least a head taller than me and twice my size. Speed would be my greatest advantage in the fight, so I leapt at the man with a small cry. Startled, the man stumbled back a step before he attacked me. We traded several blows as the sounds of Ragna's fight rang across the field. I finally managed to get the man off balance. I swept his legs out from under him and pinned him with a dagger to his throat.

"Go," he whispered.

I took off across the bridge.

Ragna was already halfway across her own bridge, taking her first lead since the race started. As I reached the end, there were faint cheers from the tournament grounds. A wide-open stretch of the field leads up to the walls of the fortress. I pushed myself harder and settled into a full-out sprint.

I slowly started to gain on Ragna.

By the time we reached the base of the walls, we were once again neck and neck.

The walls had been adjusted for the tournament. The sides were rough and uneven rather than smooth. I started to scale them, the rocks cutting into my hands. The cheers from the crowd were thunderous as I climbed.

I reached the top at the same time as Ragna.

The wall had been widened and dismantled.

The now twenty-five-foot distance was mostly empty, with only scattered sections remaining. I took off at a run across the parapet, jumping from section to section towards the ropes that hung at the end. As I neared the edge, I could finally see the crowd. Georg and Óskar were on their feet, cheering.

We reached the end at the same time. As I made the jump towards the rope, my foot slipped.

I fell from the wall.

Some of the Verndari charged towards me, but they would never make it in time. Fear flooded my body as I started to panic.

A sudden burning in my legs alerted me to what was happening. I quickly turned in the air so I was right side up. I slammed into the ground; my now Skolli-shaped legs absorbed the impact, allowing me to stay on my feet.

The crowd erupted.

Óskar was quick to pull me into a hug once he reached me as Georg squeezed my shoulder. Gil hung back a little but sent me a small smile when I looked his way. As the fear left my body, my legs burned as they returned to normal, exhaustion flooding me.

The man who had been announcing the events stepped forward. "As Princess Ragna's feet were the first to touch the ground, she has been declared the winner." The crowd cheered. I allowed myself a moment to relax and laid my head on Óskar's shoulder. He led me back towards our box. "Would the competitors of the bloodrite event please come forward?"

Pétur passed me on his way down to the ring, only granting me a quick smile. By the time we reached the box, I was shivering from my time in the river. Georg draped a thick fur around my shoulders. I wrapped it around my body tightly as Gil and Óskar pressed me close between them.

By the time I turned towards the ring, Pétur had already won, his opponent caught in a sphere of air. The whole match lasted no longer than five minutes.

The final event of the tournament was two-on-two combat. Hákon entered the ring, a pair of axes in his hands, with Sigrún by his side. In her hands were a pair of weapons I had never seen before. Long, viciously sharp blades stuck out from her closed fist and climbed up her arm. Sigrún held the wooden handles in her hand and swung them around once before she settled into her fighting stance.

The siblings fought with the same ease that Gil and Rúna shared. They effortlessly flowed around each other as they anticipated what the other would do. Hákon's axes were a blur as he swung at his opponent, constantly maintaining the offensive. He managed to disarm him and held an axe to his throat.

With his opponent defeated, Hákon turned to help his sister finish the fight. Sigrún's fighting style was different than her brother's. It was a mixture of attacks and blocks rather than trying to constantly be on the offensive. Her movements were more fluid as she spun and jumped to avoid attacks. Sigrún slowly maneuvered her opponent back towards the edge of the ring as Hákon came up behind him. She trapped his swords between her blades as Hákon placed an axe across his throat.

We were quick to leave once the tournament was declared closed. Gil picked up Rúna as Georg and Pétur moved to make room through the crowd so that she wouldn't be bumped. Óskar wrapped an arm over my fur-covered shoulders before we made our way through the crowd at a much slower pace due to my frozen muscles.

TWENTY-SEVEN

BRYN

The time it took for Hákon to get to Rúna's room felt like forever.

Gil sat beside Rúna's bunk as he talked to her, his words too quiet for me to hear. I sat by the fire with Óskar and Yugar. The furs were still wrapped around my shoulders as I tried to fight off the chill that seemed to have sunk into my bones.

Our heads all snapped to look at Hákon as he rushed through the curtain that separated Rúna's bedroom from the rest of her rooms.

"I need everyone out of the room except for Bryn," Hákon said. He held up a gloved hand as everyone started to argue. "It's going to be hard enough to heal her to begin with. Don't make it harder with unnecessary distractions. Bryn will be here in case I need an extra set of hands."

Gil nodded dejectedly before he made his way out of the room. Óskar and Yugar followed him out.

Hákon headed towards the bunk and placed his healing

bag on the edge of it. I took Gil's seat beside the bunk as Rúna blinked open her eyes.

They were rimmed with tears.

"Hey there," Hákon said softly. "How are you doing?" Rúna let out a pained hiss. "I know, dumb question, right?" Hákon laid his gloved fingers on Rúna's cheekbone. His healing pooled under her skin, and blue lightning covered her cheekbone.

Rúna let out a strangled cry.

I knew there was nothing that he could do for the bruising when his eyes drifted helplessly over Rúna's body. The lightning crawled up her face to curl around her eye. It lessened the swelling there so that she could see better.

"Thank you," Rúna whispered as her voice broke.

"You don't have to thank me. Honestly," Hákon said.

Rúna sent him a small smile.

His eyes studied Rúna as his cheeks flushed. "To heal your other injuries, I have to take off your armour," he said, causing Rúna to raise an eyebrow. "You can leave your clothes on." Hákon continued on hurriedly. "I just need to have better access to your injuries."

"Alright."

He struggled to take off Rúna's leather chest plate. I was worried that trying to help might make it worse for Rúna. So I sat by as Hákon fumbled with the armour, determined not to help unless he asked for it.

Rúna cracked a pained smile. "Not in the habit of taking armour off a girl?" Rúna asked as her eyes finally lit with something other than pain. "It buckles down the side."

Hákon nodded his thanks before he ducked his head, his cheeks red. Hákon tried to ease Rúna out of the armour, but as he pulled it from her body, she passed out from the pain.

The lightning settled on her collarbone first, and even from where I was sitting, I could tell it was broken clean through. Hákon took his time to heal the bone. The lightning spread and pooled over different areas of the bone.

By the time Hákon finished, the fire was casting long shadows across the room. As the lightning spread to Rúna's fingers, I began to light the lanterns and candles in the room so that it was easier for us to see.

Hákon lifted Rúna's shirt to reveal ribs that were already badly bruised. The lightning covered her. Rúna gently wrapped her hand around Hákon's wrist. I hadn't even realized that she was conscious. I doubted that Rúna even realized that I was in the room.

"Thank you." Rúna's voice was still threaded with pain, but not quite as much as before.

"I've already told you that you don't have to—"

"—Thank you for stopping him."

Hákon's throat bobbed before he cleared his throat. "The Verndari helped you too. It wasn't just me."

"He's your brother. He's your blood. But you still chose to save me."

"Of course I did," Hákon said. "What he did was wrong. I can't believe he would do something like that to you."

"I don't know why. It seems like that's the kind of person he is. He's brutal and cruel." Rúna's words were fading as her body dragged her into slumber. "He isn't like you."

Hákon healed her ribs, softening the bruising around the bones. His lightning pooled on Rúna's temples for a moment before it slowly faded from her body. He gently lifted her from the bunk and pushed all the furs to the ground. Hákon laid her back down before covering her with the furs.

I followed him to the curtain after I blew out most of the

lights. The curtain swung shut behind us as I took a seat beside Óskar. I rested my head on his shoulder.

"How is she?" Gil seemed tired. I could understand why. I felt it, too.

"I've got her in a sleep that should last until morning. I healed as much as I could, but she will still be in pain tomorrow." Hákon sighed and rubbed his head. "Normally, when someone has that many injuries, I wouldn't allow them out of bed for a week. At least. But with everything going on, I don't know if she'll be able to stay in bed that long."

"But she's going to be okay?"

Hákon nodded. "It will probably take a few days, but she will be perfectly fine."

"I am going to go sit with her," Gil said before he ducked back behind the curtain.

Hákon turned to the door and clenched his jaw. "Now, if you excuse me, I have some words to share with my brother."

A PILE OF PRESENTS WAS BESIDE ME WHEN I WOKE UP THE NEXT morning. Each one was carefully wrapped with small tags that listed who they were from. I sat up in my bunk, allowing the furs to pool around my waist as I reached for the gifts. I opened them with just my fingers, carefully keeping my cut-up palms away from the paper.

Rúna gave me a brown fur cloak lined with a dark green fabric. A healing book I mentioned at dinner a few nights ago was Pétur's gift to me. Georg gave me a lovely set of daggers with a set of sheaths that would allow me to hide them under my clothes, while Óskar got me a pair of fur-lined boots that had a good grip on the bottom. They would be perfect for my runs when there was snow on the ground. Fannar got me a new set of leather ties for my hair.

The last gift was from Gil. I opened it up slowly, unsure of what to expect. I lifted the lid off the small box to see a note.

The metal was given to me by Fannar. He said that it was from your home.

I set aside the note with hands that shook. Inside the box was a beautiful necklace. A small pendant, about the size of my thumb, hung on a leather cord. The metal pendant was engraved with my family crest. I clutched the pendant in my fist as tears welled in my eyes. I finally slid it over my head.

I got changed for the day before I tended to my hands. Ma would have been furious with me for going to bed without tending to my wounds. I rubbed the cleansing balm into my hands before I wrapped bandages around them.

A knock sounded.

I opened the door to reveal Óskar. He was dressed warmly with a fur cloak folded over his arm. His eyes landed on my hands. "What happened?"

"I just cut them up a bit on the walls yesterday," I shrugged. "They'll be fine."

Óskar studied me for a long moment. "Does Hákon need to look at them?"

"No. They are all shallow. I cleaned them and wrapped them. They'll be fine in a day or two."

"Alright." Óskar grinned at me. "It snowed overnight. Want to join me for a snow fight?"

It felt like it had been forever since I had taken the time to just have fun. Everything seemed to have a purpose lately, and it almost always involved training.

"Just let me grab my cloak," I said. I grabbed my new cloak and rejoined Óskar. "We should see if Fannar wants to join us. He'd love it."

Óskar agreed with a nod, so we made our way to the rooms that Ma and Fannar shared. When I knocked, there was no answer. I waited a few minutes before I tried again. Still no answer.

"He must be out," I said. "I'll try again after dinner."

We made our way out into the grounds that surrounded the fortress. We passed Pétur, who was in a deep conversation with a man who could only be his father. He hurried to finish his conversation once he saw us and joined our journey to the field.

We spent a few hours outside, and by the time we were done, we were soaking wet. My hair had long since escaped from its braids and hung down my back in a tangle of wild curls. My hands were numb, and my damp cloak hung heavy on my shoulders. I was soaked to the bone, but the grin on my face was completely genuine.

As was my laugh that rang through the field.

I CURLED UP IN A CHAIR IN THE COMMON ROOM A FEW HOURS LATER. I had changed from my soaked clothes into something comfortable before joining Georg and Óskar in the common rooms. Gil was still with Rúna in her room, while Pétur had been dragged away by his father as soon as our snow fight had ended.

I had a healing book in my lap and a warm fire by my side. Georg and Óskar sat across the room, a game board on the table between them. Yugar was stretched out on the rug at my feet as he soaked in the warmth from the fire.

Gier sauntered into the common room, his hands tucked into his pockets. Ragna was at his side. Her hair looked as if it had been perfectly done about a day ago. Her clothes were wrinkled, and dark circles had taken up residence under her eyes.

"Bryn," Ragna said softly. "You might want to come with us."

I lifted my head from my book. "What's going on?"

Hákon skidded into the room, his hair mussed as though he had been running his hands through it. "It's Fannar."

"What about Fannar?"

"We can't talk about it here," Gier led the way out of the room with me hot on his heels. They couldn't just say that and then not tell me anything. Óskar and Georg's footsteps followed me out of the room.

Gier led us towards a cluster of buildings tucked away in a corner of the grounds within the fortress' walls. A decently sized cottage-like building stood flanked by two smaller ones. We went into the larger building and immediately entered what must have been a common area. A basic kitchen was on one side of the room, while various tables and couches were placed on the other side. I followed Gier through the only other door in the room.

A large wooden desk was placed just near one of the walls. One of the walls was covered in bookcases, while another was covered with lists, charts, and maps. There was another door in the room, which was shut, and a window that had the shutters wide open to let in some light.

Ragna took a seat at the desk.

This was Ragna's office—the office of the Chieftain of the Striking Shadows. The buildings must belong to them, too.

Gier sat in one of the chairs in front of the desk while Hákon leaned against it. Georg and Óskar entered the room last and stood on either side of me.

"Where's Fannar?" I asked. "You said this is about him; why isn't he here?"

Ragna sighed, her fingers rubbed at her forehead. "We don't know."

"*You don't know?*" I screeched before I remembered to lower my voice. "What do you mean that you don't know?"

"At the war council, we told you that the response teams haven't been able to return to the fortress. So we had to devise a way to get them supplies," Gier explained, his voice level.

"You mentioned that. Did you start using supply trains?" Georg asked.

Hákon nodded, crossing his arms over his chest. "Yes, with whatever people we could spare, which usually ended up being our best recruits."

"You sent out Fannar," I said. I barely noticed as Óskar rested a hand on my shoulder.

"He's taken to his training surprisingly well. He's already climbed to the top of the list of recruits for the next position that opens up in the Royal Regiment. His skills with a war axe are very impressive. Combined with the fact that response team four was near Ebonwell, it made sense to send him with the supply train."

"Normally the response team reports in when they have received the supplies," Ragna braced her arms on the desk. "But we've heard nothing."

I bit my lip. "When should you have heard by?"

"Three days ago."

The words were like a punch in the gut. "Are they dead?"

"That is one possibility," Gier said. "But there are various others we must consider as well."

"We don't know what's happened yet, Bryn. But you deserved to know. You see each other as siblings, and he's technically a member of your household," Hákon said.

"I don't care that he's considered a member of my household," I growled as I glared at them. "What I care about is that you sent him out when he has only had a few months of training. I don't care about how good he is with his axe or how strongly he has taken to his training. You sent my brother out to the site of another attack, and you can't even tell me if he is alive!"

Gier shifted in his chair. "He's been training as long as you have, and you have been sent out into the field as well."

"You made it clear that I had no choice about serving as a Verndari. Fannar is not bound by duty and promises like I am." My words shook in anger.

I thought I had longer before Fannar was sent out into the field.

I was silent for a few moments as I waited for Ragna or Hákon to defend their decision.

They didn't.

I stormed towards the door. I couldn't stay in this room any longer. "I'm going for a run. Don't you dare follow me."

I tore out of the building and through the gates before I settled into a hard sprint around the walls. I wasn't dressed to be out in the snow. The cold wind pierced straight through my shirt. I ignored my discomfort as I continued to run. I only stopped when my body was so numb from the cold that I was afraid I was going to collapse.

I made my way into the fortress without thinking about

where I wanted to go. My feet carried me to the door of Rúna's room. I knocked a few times as I swayed on my feet, overcome by the sudden warmth of the fortress and the emotions that surged through me.

I began to shake.

When Gil opened the door, I collapsed into his chest, and I began to sob. "What happened?" Gil asked. His voice rumbled under my ear. "Why are you freezing?"

"He's gone," I sobbed. "*He's gone.*"

I barely noticed as Gil led us towards the couch closest to the fire. He wrapped a fur around my shoulders as I continued to sob. His hand slowly ran over my back as he tried to comfort me, but my tears refused to stop.

"*He's gone.*"

CHAPTER
TWENTY-EIGHT
GIL

I had always been the person that everyone ran away from. While the Verndari and a handful of others would stand by my side, only Rúna or my sisters would ever seek me out for comfort like this.

The fact that Bryn sought me out like this and what it could mean was new to me.

Bryn was practically lying on my chest with her fingers fisted in my shirt and her tears soaking through the fabric.

My hand shook as I stroked up and down her back.

"Who's gone?" I finally asked.

"Fannar," Bryn whimpered, my chest tightening at her response.

There was nothing that I could say to make this better, and her mind was probably racing with the worst-case scenarios.

Mine was, but then again, mine always did.

I should have told her it would be okay, but I couldn't guarantee that, and I refused to lie to her.

So I decided to be honest.

"I'm here," I said hoarsely.

Bryn sniffled, somehow tucking her face closer to my chest.

I froze for a moment before allowing my body to relax.

Bryn's body shook as she continued to sob. There was nothing I could do to make the situation better except for being there. For whatever reason, my presence brought her comfort.

And I would do whatever she needed.

Eventually, her tears slowed, and she lifted her head to reveal her swollen, red eyes.

"Hi," she whispered.

My lips twitched. "Hello."

"Thank you."

"You don't have to thank me for this, Bryn," I said.

She was silent for a moment before shifting her body away from mine. I immediately dropped my arms, leaving her free to move away, finally coming to her senses.

But she simply tucked her feet up behind her on the bench and laid down, resting her head in my lap. I tensed but slowly relaxed as Bryn patiently waited for me. As she always seemed to do.

I hesitated for a moment before slowly running my fingers through her hair. The vibrant red strands were soft against my skin, the curls springing back as I reached the bottom.

"Is Rúna okay?" Bryn asked.

Fury ignited in my stomach. "Her body's healing. But what he did to her—I don't know how long it will take her to move past that."

"I don't know what she sees in him," Bryn admitted. "He's awful to her, but she still spends all of her time with him."

"He isn't who I thought she was interested in."

Bryn was quiet for a moment. "Does she normally do this when she is courting someone? Disappear like that?"

"No. She doesn't."

TWENTY-NINE

BRYN

After the chaotic events of the tournament, I hoped for a moment to myself. Fannar was gone, Ma still wasn't speaking, and Rúna was withdrawing from us more. I was trying to keep an open mind about who the traitor may be, but it was difficult when everything Rúna did made it harder and harder to trust her.

Hell, Rúna had been spending more time with Baldur than the Verndari that she grew up alongside. As soon as Hákon cleared Rúna to finally leave her bunk, I barely saw her. She only showed up to training half the time, and she was at meals even less.

Regardless of what I had hoped for, the King Commander summoned us to the gathering hall just a short week after the tournament. I dressed in my leathers and tucked the necklace Gil gave me behind my chestpiece.

Gil and Georg were also in their leathers when I met them in the common rooms. Pétur was dressed in common clothes, but his furs had the symbol of the Verndari embroidered on a patch strung across his shoulders. Óskar stumbled into the room shortly after I had gotten there, dressed very similarly to Pétur. Yugar sat by his side, his black fur shiny.

"Are we just waiting for Rúna then?" I asked.

Gil shook his head. "No."

"But Hákon cleared her to leave her rooms. I thought that meant that she was well enough to come?"

"Rúna is still having a hard time moving due to the bruising on her ribs," Georg said as he ran a hand over his head. "But she will be there. We aren't waiting for her because she will be sitting beside Baldur for the meeting."

"She should stand alongside her fellow Verndari rather than sit beside the Commanding Son who constantly tries to undermine us," Óskar crossed his arms.

Georg dropped his hands to his sides uselessly. "There's nothing I can do about it, regardless of how much I may want to."

"If we don't leave, we will be late," Gil reminded us before sending me the smallest smile. It was barely more than a twitch of his lips.

"Bryn, you and Óskar will lead. The three of us will be behind you," ordered Georg.

Óskar smiled at me before he nudged my shoulder with his and nodded towards the door. I made my way towards the gathering hall with Óskar on one side and Yugar on the other. I nodded at the guards who stood beside the open doors to the hall and straightened my shoulders. I lifted my chin as I made my way inside.

The guards closed the doors behind us as I continued to make my way towards the thrones. I bowed towards the King Commander before straightening up and allowing my eyes to drift around the room.

Unlike the last time I was there, the room was eerily empty. The tables and benches were deserted. The Commanding Family were on their thrones with a smaller, less ornate chair where Rúna sat. Ottó stood off to the side with his hands clasped behind his back. Emilía stood beside him with Svanna on her other side.

"Thank you for coming," the King Commander said even though we had no choice in our attendance. His eyes drifted over Emilía and me. "It is important that we all share the same knowledge about the upcoming trials scheduled to begin a week from today."

"A week, sire? That is hardly enough—" Ottó said before cutting himself off as the Queen raised a hand.

"You were the one that claimed Emilía was ready to become a Verndari a few moons ago, Jarl Ottó. If anything, she should be more prepared now. There should be no problem with the trials beginning a week from today." The Queen's words were laced with iron.

Ottó nodded. "Of course, Your Majesty."

"Now that we are all on the same page, it has been decided that the best test of skill would be a series of three trials," Ragna explained. "Each test was specifically chosen to reflect an essential aspect of the position in question. Whoever wins the majority of the trials will be officially appointed as the final Verndari."

"And who has chosen these trials?"

"I did." Georg stepped forward. "As a trainer of the Verndari, I am in the best position to determine what skills are the most important for not only their own survival but also for the survival of the Verndari as a whole."

Ottó's face turned a shocking shade of red. "You will have chosen trials that give that girl—," he flung a finger out towards me, "—an unfair advantage over my daughter. I will not stand for this!"

"I had the final say over the trials, Jarl Ottó. I would suggest that you remember your place." The King Commander's hand was curled into a fist on the arm of his throne.

Ottó clenched his jaw before he once again bowed his head.

"It is hard to limit the skills required of a Verndari to only three core aspects; however, many of the expectations are not easily tested. I was able to divide the testable skills into three key categories: combat, horsemanship, and bloodrite. In this case, considering the position within the Verndari that needs to be filled, I have determined that the three trials will be horsemanship, demonstration of the control of a bloodrite, and combat with daggers," Georg said.

My stomach knotted.

I still couldn't control my bloodrite, which meant that, unless some miracle happened within the upcoming week, I had to win the other two trials.

"We have decided that we will not reveal the order that the trials will take place." The King Commander turned to Emilía and me in turn. "I expect each of you to uphold honour and respect for the other. No intentional maiming, death, or anything of the sort. You are of no use to me if you are unable to fight. Am I clear?"

"Yes, Commander," I nodded my head in respect.

"Yes, sire," A small smirk graced Emilía's face.

The King Commander rose from his chair. "Very well. The next time we shall gather will be for the first trial at the tournament grounds."

～

THE LARGE TABLE was strewn with maps and reports. Many of us had gathered to try and figure out what had happened to Fannar's supply train. Ragna, Svanna, and Gier were there providing any information and reports that the Striking Shadows had gathered. Gier was the most helpful as he shared what he had seen on his numerous dispatches since the attacks had started.

Hákon was there to share any insight that he could into the actions that the supply train may have taken. Training, he had explained, impacted every decision you made in the field. If we understood how the Royal Regiment was trained, then we would have a greater chance of understanding what actions they may have taken.

Georg, Pétur, Óskar, Gil, and I were all there as well. I suspected they were there to support me, but I knew they all had good insights they could provide. I was just thankful that I didn't have to face this alone. From my spot between Óskar and Gil, I almost felt strong enough to face the fact that Fannar may be lost or injured—or worse.

"The protocol in place states that the response team is to send word when the supply train reaches them. Numerous things could have happened that would have prevented that from happening." Gier braced his arms on the table. "The bird could have been intercepted or attacked, the response team may be unable to send one, and the supply train may never have arrived. There are too many unknowns to form one logical explanation of what may have happened."

"There is no reason to jump to the assumption that they are dead. I chose these people specifically because I believed they had the best chance of returning alive," Hákon said.

Pétur shifted in his seat. "The land in that area of Drysden is very hilly, bordering on mountainous the closer you get to the ruins of Graythorn. In this weather, it's a hard journey, especially when you consider that it is a supply train. They could simply be bogged down somewhere along the path," he proposed.

"Are you from around there too?" I asked. His explanation was completely accurate. The roads in that region were notoriously bad during the rain and snow seasons.

"No. I've just done a lot of research into the different terrains of Drysden. My father insisted on it."

I shrugged. "You could be right, but Fannar grew up in Ebonwell with me. He knows what roads and paths to avoid and which ones are the safest at this time of year. It's not very likely that they are bogged down somewhere."

"I haven't received any reports of a Skolli attack in that region, so that is the most unlikely scenario," Ragna explained as she shuffled the parchments in front of her. "There have been rumours of civil unrest in the region, but nothing expansive."

"What do you believe is the most likely scenario?" Georg asked.

Ragna studied the maps and reports in front of her for several moments. "I believe that there are three scenarios that are equally likely to have happened. The first, and what I hope is the case, is that the response team is simply overwhelmed and forgot to send us the bird notifying us of the supply train's arrival. The second is that they have encountered trouble on the road and have not yet been able to reach the response team. But for this to happen during the snows, there are all sorts of complications that could be dangerous for the supply train, such as the weather."

I intertwined my shaking fingers in my lap. Gil's leg

pressed into mine. He was a steady presence at my side like he had been since Hazelpeak.

"And the third?" Georg asked.

Ragna swallowed before her eyes landed on me. "With everything the way it is, I think we have to prepare ourselves for the possibility that those in the supply train may not have survived the journey for a variety of possible reasons."

"You won't give up looking, though, right?" I asked desperately. "You won't assume they are dead until there's proof?"

"We won't stop looking until it seems like the most likely scenario," Gier said.

That wasn't good enough, and I refused to let it stop me. If it came down to it, I would not stop looking until I found Fannar's body.

CHAPTER
THIRTY
BRYN

Gil was waiting for me at the gates when I finished my run the next morning. The guards gave him a wide berth even though he simply stood there with his arms crossed. They expected the worst of him like they always did, making my blood boil.

"Gil!" I grinned at him. "I didn't know that you were waiting for me. I would have taken a shorter route if I knew you were."

He shook his head. "It was a last-minute decision. I also know how much you need your runs. I wouldn't want to disturb that."

"What brought you here?" I asked as I wrapped an arm around his to prove to the guards that he wasn't someone to be afraid of. Gil only tensed for a second before he relaxed in my hold. He still struggled to initiate any form of physical contact outside of combat, but he was becoming more comfortable with me reaching out to him.

"The King Commander has asked me to do something," Gil

said hesitantly before he cleared his throat. "I was hoping that you would be willing to accompany me."

I studied him for a long moment before I pulled him into one of the shadowed corners of the grounds. We were close enough that his breath brushed across my cheeks. It hung between us, nothing more than a white cloud in the cold winter air. "What does he want you to do?"

I was smart enough to know that *asking* was a rather diplomatic way to say that the King Commander had ordered him to do something. Something that made him rather uncomfortable if Gil was hoping that I would go with him.

"He is getting desperate. With a fractured court on one side and the Skolli on the other, he is in a tough position. He wants to gather as much information as he can. That means turning to the previous generation of Verndari."

"He wants to talk to your ma?"

"No," Gil said softly. "He wants me to."

I knew how hard this would be for him. His ma represented everything that he was terrified he would become. Not to mention the fact that she had succumbed to the monster. She has been consumed by the darkness and controlled by it.

"Of course, I'll go with you," I said as I rested a hand on his cheek. "You don't have to face this alone."

He pressed his face into my hand as his eyes fluttered closed. "I don't know what she may say or do. I can't prepare you for what to expect."

"I'll be alright, don't worry about me. Are you okay with this?"

His eyes opened, and he looked down into my face. "I don't have another choice."

"When do you want to go?"

"Can we go now?" Gil asked hesitantly. He was a big man, a

full head taller than I was, with wide shoulders and a well-built physique from all our training. But in that moment, I could see him as the scared little boy who watched his ma be consumed by the same darkness he fought.

"Of course," I said.

Gil led us through the fortress to a door hidden in the entry hall. It opened into a dark stairwell carved into the earth beneath the fortress. It spiraled deep into the ground before finally opening into a large hallway. The hallway resembled more of a cave than anything else, with roughly hewn earth walls lit with torches. Large pieces of stone were spread evenly down both sides of it.

Gil led us to a heavily guarded door at the end of the hallway. Two of the guards stared at him as they tightened their grip on their weapons. I glared at them. I knew they had been exposed to what the darkness could do—they guarded his ma, after all. But Gil was still in control of his darkness, and they didn't care. They only cared about the times when he lost control.

"Are you going in or not?" the guard barked. My eyebrows rose as I took a step closer to Gil. I knew that they didn't like him, but his position as a Verndari demanded and deserved more respect. A moment passed before the guard realized his mistake and corrected himself. "Are you going in or not, Jarl Egill?"

Gil straightened his shoulders. "Yes. Open the doors."

The guard pricked his finger and rubbed it across the stone. He took several steps back as the stone began to move. The other guards quickly moved into spaces in front of the steel door that was revealed behind the stone.

Two guards came forward to unbar the door before they rejoined their comrades in line with their weapons. Gil took a deep breath before he led us into the room. A loud grating sound meant the guards had put the bar back in place. We were locked inside. Gil paused just inside the doorway, his hand quivering at his side.

The room looked very similar to the one that Fannar shared with Ma. Regardless of the lack of sunlight, it was well-lit from the various candles and lanterns around the room. Footsteps from another room came closer and closer to where we still stood in front of the door.

"That better be my food, or I swear by the gods that I will skin you alive. It's been a while since I've gotten to hear the sound of screams. I've missed them," his ma stepped out from behind a curtain that separated the rooms. Her dark hair, the same colour as Gil's, was messy, and her eyes were completely black.

"I don't have any food for you, Mother," Gil said as I watched the woman carefully. I trusted that Gil would look out for me and knew I could protect myself. But I didn't want to be caught off guard. "The King Commander wanted me to ask you a few questions."

She let out an inhumane cackle. "And you just did whatever he wanted, didn't you? Just another one of his pet fighters that only exists to obey his every whim."

"The Verndari are more than that, Ma. I should hope that you would know that since you were one for several years."

"One of the biggest mistakes of my life if you ask me. Look what it cost me."

Gil hesitantly moved closer to his ma as she took a seat on the couch. I stayed close by his side. "It wasn't a mistake, it was your duty."

"It was just as much of a mistake as having you and your sisters."

Gil backed away from the couch, almost bumping into me in his haste.

"I would say that was the best thing that you did," I said as I stepped in front of Gil. He reached for my wrist, no doubt to pull me back to his side, but I didn't let him. "Your son is a good man who cares very deeply. I know you are consumed by the darkness inside of you, but I will not let you talk to him like that. He doesn't deserve it."

"And you think you could stop me, girl?" His mother sneered. Gil reached for my wrist again, and this time, I allowed him to gently pull me back to his side.

"What do you know about the Skolli?" Gil asked.

"Only as much as it was deemed 'appropriate' for me to know," his ma leaned her head against the back of the couch. "Sounds like they got to have the freedom that I always dreamed about. The things that they can do." Her eyes took on a sick gleam.

I reached for Gil's hand. "Please. Tell me everything you know," he begged.

"I know that I was always impressed by the stories we were taught about them. To have that much power and to use it to refine murdering to an art—"

"Mother! I did not come here for you to go on about a monster's murdering habits!" Gil yelled. "I did not want to come here. I never wanted to see the door to your prison. But the King Commander ordered me to ask what you knew. We need to know whatever you know because the Skolli are returning, and people are dying!"

"All I know is that if the Skolli have returned, then people will die. I would be out there supporting them if I could," his ma said. Gil turned his back on her and began to head back to the door with me beside him. "You say you don't want to be here, but we both know you will be. You're just like me."

Gil banged on the door until the guards let us out. He didn't say a word as the door to her prison slammed behind them. When we finally reentered the fortress he left me in the entry hall as he turned on his heel and stormed off down the hall.

I let him go. Right now, he needed to be alone more than he needed my comfort. I would give him the time he needed before I tried to prove that he would never end up like his ma.

I refused to let that happen to him.

I SPENT HOURS EACH DAY TRAINING. SOME DAYS I SPENT WITH PÉTUR or Georg sparring. Over and over. My body felt as though it had been cut apart and pounded into the ground for the past few days. Hákon had taken to visiting my rooms each night before dinner to heal whatever injuries I had acquired from that day's sparring.

The afternoons were spent with Óskar as we worked on my horsemanship. I had trained for the tournament to maintain my illusion, but I was sure I wouldn't compare to Emilía. I could count on one hand the number of times I had ridden a horse before arriving at the fortress. I didn't doubt that Emilía had learned to ride young and hadn't stopped since then.

After dinner, Gil and I would lock ourselves in the small room we had deemed ours. We would spar as we tried to get me to control my bloodrite. Gil was still trying to keep his bloodrite from overwhelming him when he used it. He tried to get Rúna to join us, but she refused every time.

The nights when the moon hung high in the sky were

reserved for Fannar. I poured over the copies of reports that Ragna made for me. Maps were spread out across the floor of my room as I desperately searched for any possibility. He was out there somewhere; he just needed to be found.

The night before the first trial, I was once again in my room. I had changed into some loose clothes and pulled my hair from the tight braid I had it in. I poured myself a tankard of water as a knock on the door drew my attention. Hákon was earlier than he normally was, but with everything going on, I knew it was all he could do to fit me in every night.

I opened the door, my eyes closed as I sipped my water.

"Bryn."

My eyes flew open at the sound of the voice as I dropped the tankard on the ground with a clang.

Fannar.

His face was bruised, his lip cut. His hair was dirty, but his clothes were clean. Someone must have told him to take the time to change even if he didn't take the time to wash up.

I flung my arms over his shoulders and buried my face in his neck. He smelt of smoke and sweat and blood. But Fannar was here.

And he was alive.

Fannar guided us into my room and towards the couch. The fire warmed my back as I clung to him. If I had lost him, it probably would have broken me. But now, with him here in front of me, everything I hadn't let myself feel before consumed me as I began to soak Fannar's shirt with tears.

Grief.

Heartache.

But most of all—relief.

"I thought—they said—" I said, or tried to say, through my sobs.

"Shhh. I'm here now," Fannar's voice was a soothing balm to my nerves. "It's alright."

"It's not alright. You were *gone*! They couldn't find you!"

Fannar wrapped his arm around me, his hand cradling the back of my head as his fingers curled in my hair. "I know, I know. But I'm here now, and I'm alright."

I sniffed but didn't say anything as I waited for my tears to dry. Once I had a chance to collect myself, I raised my head and allowed my eyes to roam his face. "What happened?"

"Hákon asked if I would go with a line heading towards a small village where a response team had run out of supplies. It was in the same area as our village but further out along the edges of the realm," he explained as his hand smoothed over my hair.

"When they told me that you were gone, Hákon said that you were becoming pretty skilled at fighting."

"Yeah, he said that as soon as a spot opened on the Royal Regiment, I would have the opportunity to join," Fannar gave me a small smile. "I'll take my oath after the trial is done tomorrow."

My eyes widened. "As a member of the Royal Regiment? But I thought there were no spots open."

"There weren't before this trip."

My breath caught. "What happened?"

"The people here may realize something is going on, but they have faith, for the most part, in the King Commander and the Verndari. The cities and villages in the centre of the realm, or those that are relatively sheltered by the land around them, don't believe that anything is wrong," Fannar cleared his throat. "But the small villages along the outskirts of the realm? They are scared. They know what's going on and don't put much faith in the King Commander."

I bit my lip. "Like at home. Many of the villagers didn't think that the King Commander could, or would, do anything to help them."

"Exactly. An early rainy season is hard on crops. You know that as well as I do. But these people are having nightmares. Their neighbouring villages and their merchant caravans are being attacked. They're terrified, and they're desperate."

"Desperate people do things that they shouldn't."

Fannar nodded. "Like attacking a Royal Regiment supply train."

"No," I gasped.

"We tried to fight them off without seriously injuring any of them. We knew that they normally wouldn't do that. At least not to a caravan with the Royal Regiment insignia on it. But then two soldiers were killed." Fannar cleared his throat. "Some of their comrades demanded revenge and started killing the civilians. It took us some time to take care of the aftermath, and then we had to report to the village to provide the supplies. By the time we arrived, a group of people were claiming that the Royal Regiment had been ordered to attack the civilians. Someone must have forgotten to send the bird in all the commotion."

My head spun, so I just asked the one question that truly mattered. "Are you alright?"

Fannar gave me a sad smile. "I'm heartbroken that I'm part of the group accused of doing such an awful thing. But other than that, I just have some cuts and bruises. I'll be right as rain in no time."

"I should have figured that I would find you here," I lifted my head at the sound of Hákon's voice. He leaned against the door frame to my room. "Just let me take a quick look at you, Fannar, before I heal Bryn."

Fannar's head snapped to me, his eyes searching my body. "You're hurt? What happened?"

"It's nothing. Training has been pretty intense because the trials start tomorrow." My cheeks warmed.

"By 'pretty intense,' she means that I have been healing her every night; otherwise, she would barely be able to move," Hákon said as he moved to stand in front of Fannar.

"Bryn, you can't do this to yourself," Fannar shook his head. "If you kill yourself in training, then you will be no good if something does happen."

I was silent for a moment as I watched Hákon's blue lightning settle over different places on Fannar's face. "I made Da a promise, and the only way I can keep that is if I win the trials."

"How do you expect to do well in the trials if you kill yourself training?" Fannar asked.

"I don't know," I whispered. "But I don't know what else I'm supposed to do."

Hákon knelt before me and gently laid his gloved hands on my arm. His lightning flowed through my body. "The only thing I know is that a promise to someone else is rarely enough to keep us going when it seems like there is no hope left," Hákon's voice was soft. "It may be enough for now, but you are going to need to find your own reason to fight, or you'll never make it out of a battle alive. You need to give *yourself* a reason to survive."

THIRTY-ONE

BRYN

On the day of the first trial, I dressed in the same leather uniform that I wore for the Crepuscule and my hair was tied back in my typical braids. I strapped on my belt with two daggers sheathed on it. I also slipped two daggers into the tops of my boots and two on the outside of my thigh.

I made my way to the common rooms. The others had agreed to wait for me before we entered the tournament grounds together. Óskar waved me over to join him on one of the couches. "You alright?" he asked.

"I'm terrified." I sent him a weak smile. "So, pretty much what you would expect, right?"

"If you weren't worried, I would be concerned. You'll be fine. You're ready for this, Talon."

Pétur and Georg entered the room and wished me luck before they took a seat to wait for the others. Gil entered the room alone and took up his usual spot along the wall. "Gil," Georg said, grabbing my attention. "Do you know where Rúna is?"

"She is sitting with Baldur," Gil said before he cleared his throat. "And entering with him too." Gil's words caused my hands to shake.

Georg stood from his seat. "I see. We should be on our way then."

Georg led the way out of the room with Pétur by his side. I followed along behind them with Óskar and Gil beside me. We stopped to rearrange ourselves outside of the door to the grounds. I took my place in the front with Gil and Óskar a step behind me. Georg and Pétur took their places at the back of our arrangement as planned. I allowed myself one last calming breath before I pushed the door open with my head held high.

My steps almost faltered as I realized that the stands were filled. I had hoped that this would be private, or at least as private as possible. Óskar wished me luck as the others left to take their places in our box. I took my spot in the centre of the grounds and turned to face the Commanding Family. Hákon and Ragna flashed me smiles as we waited for Emilía to arrive. It didn't take very long. When we were both ready, with the crowd in their seats, the King Commander stood.

"Thank you for coming to watch as Jarl Brynja and Lady Emilía compete to earn the final position in the Verndari," the King Commander said as the crowd cheered. "One of the most critical duties of the Verndari is protection. In order to protect us, they must be able to fight. In this case, we have determined that they shall demonstrate their skill with daggers, the traditional weapon of the lost family. The first to be incapacitated or unable to continue will lose."

I took my spot in the sparring ring that had been used in the tournament. I rolled my shoulders in an attempt to loosen my muscles before I drew two daggers and settled into my fighting stance. I took a deep breath as I tried to settle the nerves that threatened to overwhelm me.

A horn sounded to start the spar.

I charged towards Emilía, my daggers flashing through the air. I slashed at her faster than she could block, cutting into her arms and hands. Emilía began to catch up with her attacks, so I snapped a kick at her ribs to throw her off balance. Emilía slashed wildly. I ducked and stumbled backwards to avoid her daggers.

I dropped back and began to circle around the edge of the ring.

I quickly sheathed one of my daggers before grabbing one of the thinner ones from its place on my forearm. I threw the smaller dagger, forcing Emilía to spin to dodge it. I surged towards her, drawing another dagger from my belt as I did so.

I landed several slashes on her but winced as she landed a few lucky ones on me. I managed to disarm her before I crouched down and swept her legs out from under her. As I moved to pin her, Emilía pulled one of my daggers from my boot.

At Emilía's pained hiss, I looked down to see her slicing her arm with the dagger. I stumbled back from her in shock. Emilía moved the dagger to her other arm, leaving a river of blood behind. I froze in my tracks as my daggers dropped uselessly to the ground.

Emilía climbed to her feet. "What's wrong? Is the wannabe Verndari scared of a little blood?" My heartbeat pounded in my ears. I knew that I should do something, but I couldn't.

I was frozen.

"Are you just going to stand there?" Emilía asked.

Her dagger flashed as it landed cuts on my arms and hands. Emilía grabbed ahold of my hands and forced them up in front of my face. The blood glistened as the sunlight caught it. My body tensed as I stared at the blood, unable to move.

Emilía snapped her foot out suddenly, catching my knee and forcing it sideways. I screamed out as I fell and landed hard on my hip. Emilía released my hands to rest the dagger against my neck.

I had lost.

The world blurred as I lost focus on what was happening around me.

It wasn't until a cloth gently cleaned my hands and arms that I regained focus. "It's alright," Óskar said gently. "The blood is mostly gone." Gil and Óskar knelt beside me. Óskar's arm was wrapped around my shoulders as Gil ran the cloth over me. I bit down on my lip as it began to tremble. "Let's get you inside." They tucked their hands under my arms as they eased me off the ground. I tried to walk, whimpering when I put weight on my leg. "What's wrong?"

"My leg," I whispered as tears began to slide down my face. "She slammed my knee sideways, and now it hurts to put weight on it."

Gil reached out and hesitantly wiped the tears from my face. "Never let her see you cry," he said before he looped his arm around my waist. "Lean on me."

With both of their arms around me, they were able to hold most of my weight as we slowly made our way out of the tournament grounds. Luckily, Georg and Pétur went ahead of us to clear our path, allowing us to make it back to my rooms without anything happening.

Gil eased me onto the couch in front of the fire before he ducked behind the curtain into my bedroom. Óskar sat beside me as Gil returned with my medical kit in his hands. He knelt in front of me, placing the medical supplies off to the side. "I am going to clean the cuts first, then look at your leg."

"Alright," I said softly. I laid my head on Óskar's shoulder and closed my eyes. The stinging feeling in my cuts was familiar to me. I had sat in my kitchen many times as Ma cleaned whatever cut I had gotten.

Gil cleared his throat. "I'm going to have to cut your pants until here." His finger tapped just above my knee.

I nodded before I leaned back. The cool metal of the knife Gil was using slid up my leg. He pulled aside my pants to reveal a nasty bruise over my knee. He prodded my leg, causing me to whimper. Óskar ran his hand up and down my arm as tears began to slide down my face.

"It looks like it's a bad bruise. If it hasn't gotten any better by the morning, Hákon should look at it."

"Okay," I said softly as Gil began to rub bruise paste into my skin. The more he rubbed, the more the pain dulled. By the time he set aside the past, it was only a dull ache rather than a sharp pain. Gil wrapped a roll of bandage tightly around my knee.

When he finished, Óskar hugged me close for a moment before he stood from the bench. "I should let Fannar and the others know how you are doing. I'll check on you tomorrow." I sent him a smile before I nodded. He made his way silently out of my room and closed the door behind him.

"You should wash off the blood that I missed. It's dried now." Gil suggested. I sucked in a breath and made no move to follow his suggestion.

"I don't think I can," I finally said.

My eyes slowly drifted to land on Gil's face to see his eyes already on me. They studied me for a moment. "I can do it," he offered.

I nodded slowly.

Gil made his way into my bedroom again. This time, he returned with a basin and a scrap of cloth.

He dipped the cloth into the basin and ran it over my hands. Gil gently scrubbed at my hands before he eased my sleeves out of the way to reach my arms. My eyes drifted closed, soothed by the warm water.

My eyes eased open as his arms slid behind my back and under my legs. Gil lifted me and held me close to his chest as he made his way into my bedroom. He placed me on the chair that still sat at the side of my bunk before he handed me some loose clothes. I waited until he had closed the curtain behind him before I changed. A few minutes later, his head popped around it.

Gil pulled back the furs on my bunk before gently lifting me into it. He watched as I made myself comfortable. "Is there anything else I can do?" he asked.

I shook my head.

He covered me with the furs. His fingers lingered by my own for a moment before Gil turned towards the curtain. "Wait," I said. He turned back towards me. "Stay. Please." His eyes widened for a moment before he slowly made his way over to the chair. I patted the empty spot on the bunk beside me.

Gil lingered by the chair for several moments. I had started to regret asking when he finally took a step toward the bunk. A smile blossomed on my face. Gil climbed into the bunk, carefully to ensure there was plenty of space between us as he lay on his side facing me.

"Are you okay?" Gil asked softly, his voice barely louder than a whisper.

"I don't think so." My voice broke.

"What can I do?"

I moved closer to him and rested my forehead on his chest. His arms slowly came up to wrap around me. The warmth from his body sank into me and eased some of the aches in my muscles. "Just stay with me. I don't want to be alone."

"I will." Gil's fingers began to trace a gentle path up and down my spine. "I'll stay for as long as you'll have me."

My eyes closed as I allowed his heat and comfort to surround me.

THIRTY-TWO

BRYN

I quietly eased myself out of my bunk the next morning, so I wouldn't wake Gil. I had barely slept that night; flashes of the night Da died had played through my mind on a loop every time I closed my eyes.

My body ached from the day before, but it gave me some form of twisted comfort.

I had failed. I knew that I needed to win that trial so I wouldn't have to count on my unreliable bloodrite. But I didn't. I allowed my fear of blood to cripple me—I froze.

I pulled on my fur cloak over the loose, comfortable clothes Gil had given me the day before. As much as Gil and Óskar had engrained themselves in my life, I needed my family. I needed Fannar, and I needed Ma.

As I made my way out of the Verndari wing, I stumbled over my own feet. Georg said that no one was to know about my reaction to blood because it showed a weakness that we could not afford. Only the Verndari knew about my fear. A Verndari would have needed to tell Emilía about it.

They had wanted me to fail.

I bit my lip and hoped the sting would keep my tears at bay.

I pulled the hood of my cloak over my head to keep anyone from recognizing me as I walked through the fortress. The hallways were mostly empty as I made my way toward the rooms that Fannar and Ma shared. Even though Fannar was to be sworn in as a member of the Royal Regiment later that day, he insisted on staying with Ma until she showed more improvement. Neither Fannar nor I believed that drifting mindlessly around the room was a significant amount of improvement. There had to be more.

I eased open the door. The iron hinges must not have been oiled for a while because it let out an awful screech. I slipped into the room with a wince. I turned to close the door as the cold kiss of an axe was pressed against my throat.

"It's a little early for house calls," Fannar's voice was rough with sleep. "Care to tell me your name and why you're here?"

"Fannar, it's me," I said as I slowly reached up to push back my hood. I had no idea when he had become such a light sleeper. Or that he kept an axe nearby for close access.

"Gods, Bryn." Fannar pulled the axe from my throat and propped it up against a wall. "I couldn't tell it was you with your hood up like that."

I wrapped my arms around Fannar's shoulders and buried my face in his chest. As his arms came up to wrap around me, a small smile flitted across my face. When we were like this, I could pretend we were still just plain old Bryn and Fannar.

"How's Ma?" I asked. My words were muffled by Fannar's chest, but as his arms tightened around me, I knew that he heard me.

"She was doing better," Fannar said. "Ma was starting to respond to us. Not verbally, but if we asked if she wanted a drink, she would reach for the tankard. She still wasn't eating on her own, but she no longer fought us, which we took as a good sign."

I pursed my lips. "Was?"

"Hákon thought that some sunlight would do her good, so I took her to the trial yesterday."

I jerked out of Fannar's arms, my eyes searching his face. "You did *what*?"

"We thought that you were going to win," Fannar said as his hand rubbed the back of his neck. "But then Emilía started to cut you to pieces, and there was blood everywhere." He cleared his throat. "I think it reminded her of that night. It certainly reminded me."

"Has she gotten worse?"

"She no longer seems like she even hears us. If we lift a tankard to her lips, she'll drink, but she won't reach for it herself."

My knees buckled. Fannar reached out to grab me, but I still collapsed to the ground, my knees burning from the impact. I fisted my hands in my curls and clenched my teeth to keep from screaming.

I had done this.

It was my fault.

I curled my arms around my knees and began to rock back and forth. Fannar's arms wrapped around me as he pulled me closer. His hand guided my head to rest on his shoulder.

"I did this," I said, my voice thick with tears.

"No, Bryn. *No*," Fannar whispered.

I sniffled, feeling as though the volume of my tears would choke me. "I made her worse. I failed her like I have failed Da."

"You have failed *nobody*. Do you hear me?"

"I have." My voice broke. "I promised myself that I would look after her, and I made her worse. I promised to become a Verndari, and I've failed. My last words to Da were nothing but a waste."

Fannar's arms loosened around me as his hands lifted my face. His thumbs tried to wipe the tears from my face but more simply replaced them. "Ma would have died without you, Bryn. You saved her life. You found her a new home. You've trained so that you would be ready if something like that were to happen again." Fannar's words were soft but laced with a newfound confidence. "Ma is bound to have setbacks—that's just life. But she is safe, she is healthy, and she is cared for. Don't *ever* think you have failed her."

"Okay."

"Do you believe me?"

I tried to duck my head, but Fannar gently wrapped his fingers around my chin, forcing me to look at him. I closed my eyes with a sigh. "No. Not yet. But I'll try to."

"That's all I can ask."

"I'm still going to fail Da, though."

"How?"

I finally opened my eyes to look at Fannar. "He asked me to do my duty, and I've already lost the trials. There's no way I can fulfill my promise."

"You lost one trial. One out of three. You can still win, Bryn," Fannar said.

"I have a shot with horsemanship, I suppose. Óskar has been relentless with my training for it." I sighed. "But I can't control my bloodrite."

Fannar gave me a small smile as his hands clasped mine. "The Bryn I know is furiously stubborn and was never one to back down from anything. I really hope you don't start now."

"I don't know if I can do it," I said as another tear coursed down my cheek. "Ever since that night in the village, I've been different. Gil says that I'm war-scarred."

"Of course, you're different. That night changed me, and it changed Ma. You don't go through something like that without becoming different in some way." Fannar squeezed my hands. "But I like to think that we are still who we used to be and have just been altered."

I swallowed thickly. "I don't know how to be who I used to be."

"You don't have to know. At heart, you are still the same Bryn from Ebonwell. You're still infuriatingly stubborn. You are still the girl who loves to run and who would have snowball fights with me in the yard. There will be scars from that night, and you have changed since then. You know how to fight and have fought. You've discovered a voice that people from our village could only dream of having. But when I look at you, I can still see the Bryn with wild red curls that streamed behind you as you ran through the village."

I tipped my head forward to rest on Fannar's shoulder, and this time he let me. We sat in silence for a long time, with only the crackle of the fire to keep us company.

"Do you really think I can do this?" I asked hesitantly.

"I do," Fannar said softly.

"And if I do fail?"

He ran a gentle hand over my back. "Then you find another way to fulfill your promise to Da. There's more than one way to protect people, and if I know you, Bryn, you won't stop until you find your own way to do so."

The sun had risen by the time Fannar walked me back to the Verndari wing. The halls were filled with people going about their day. There was also a group of people near the entrance to the wing. They were gathered around Emilía and Ottó. Ottó was regaling the people with his tale of the trial.

"The worthless girl thought she had the upper hand in the fight," he said. The crowd watched him closely, hanging onto every word that he said. "She got lazy, and she got complacent. That girl fits right in with the others if you ask me."

"I saw my chance and attacked. She couldn't keep up with me. It really makes you question their training in the Verndari," Emilía said. There was no mention that the only reason she could land those attacks was because of that underhanded trick. Emilía only won because someone told her how to cheat. She wouldn't have won a fair fight.

Fannar and I pushed by the edges of the group as we made our way to the entrance of the wing. "You know, for someone trying so desperately to become a Verndari, she does say a lot of negative things about us," I spoke loudly enough that the fringes of the group could hear me but not loud enough that Emilía and Ottó could.

The people who heard sent me a small smile as I passed by. Those that didn't sneered at me. I did my best to smile back as I ignored the glares I was getting.

I pushed open the door to our wing. Gil was pacing the length of the entrance hall as Óskar lounged on one of the couches with Yugar. Gil's eyes snapped to me as we entered the room. He quickly made his way towards us as Fannar turned to close the door. Gil's arms reached out for me before they dropped back to his side, his eyes shining with uncertainty.

I smiled softly as I closed the gap between us and gently wrapped my arms around him. Gil tensed for a minute before one of his arms came up to wrap around me.

"I woke up, and you were gone," Gil said, his voice threaded with worry.

"*I woke up, and you were gone?*" Fannar squeaked. "What the hell is going on?"

"Well, well, well, Talon, I didn't know you had it in you." Óskar winked at me. "Well done."

I pulled back from Gil, ducking my head to hide my burning cheeks. "It's not what you are thinking. I was scared after the trial and asked Gil to stay with me so I wouldn't be alone."

"Do not hurt her. You will not like what will happen if you do," Fannar said as he stepped up beside me.

I jabbed Fannar in the ribs with my elbow. "I don't need you to play the overprotective brother. I can look after myself."

"I know you can. I also know you will make the decisions that are best for you." Fannar smiled before he turned back to Gil and crossed his arms over his chest. "Just like I know that he will never hurt you. Am I right?"

"I'll do my best to never hurt her," Gil said.

Fannar studied Gil for a long moment before he turned back to me. "See? There's no problem here." I just rolled my eyes.

"Are you feeling any better?" Gil asked.

"I'm feeling as good as can be expected," I said with a sad smile.

"Then it is time to keep fighting."

CHAPTER
THIRTY-THREE

BRYN

Óskar claimed me for training before Gil had a chance. I barely had enough time to agree to meet Gil for training that afternoon before Óskar dragged me out to the stables. I was finally feeling confident on a horse. I was not as skilled as Óskar, but that was probably an unfair comparison. After all, his entire bloodrite revolved around animals.

I completed the course in the fields several times that morning. There wasn't a single moment where I didn't feel in control. Although it wasn't enough to fully ease my anxiety. Emilía had performed well in the horsemanship competition.

By the time we finally agreed to stop for lunch, my body was one solid ache. A morning working on horsemanship with Óskar always made my muscles sore. But when I was already in rough shape from the trial the day before? I felt like I could barely move.

Óskar and I met Gil in the common rooms for lunch. Gil watched me hobble into the room with a raised eyebrow but thankfully didn't mention it. Hákon joined us for lunch, making the maid scramble to find another plate for him to use.

"Fannar warned me that you decided to continue your training today instead of resting for the trial tomorrow," Hákon said as he took the plate from the maid and filled it with food. "I thought it would probably be best to check on you and heal anything I could."

"Thank you. I'm doing okay, though," I lied. I really did appreciate him coming to heal me, but I didn't want to appear weak after the day before. I didn't want to admit to my pain even though I knew that it was nothing to be ashamed of.

Gil set down his tankard and turned towards Hákon. "Bryn lies. She is walking like an elder who has lost her cane."

Óskar choked on his food as I glared at Gil. Once Óskar cleared his throat, he began to laugh in earnest.

"Fine," I said, narrowing my eyes at Óskar. "I may be a little sore."

"I'll fix that. Are you attending Fannar's appointment tonight?" Hákon asked.

I nodded. "Of course. I wouldn't miss it. I'm hoping to bring Ma as well."

"I want to come too," Óskar said. "I've become close with Fannar and will be able to help Bryn with her ma that way."

"I would like to be there as well," Gil added.

Hákon took a sip from his tankard. "Very well. I'll make sure that a spot is clear for you."

"Hey, Talon," Óskar said through a mouthful of partially chewed food. "Since you consider me a brother, does that mean I get to escort your ma to the appointment?"

I shrugged. "I don't see why not." I grinned at Gil. "I guess that means that you are escorting me then."

"Perhaps," Gil said gravely.

It didn't take long for Hákon to heal me after we finished our meal. He eased the tenderness in my knee, which, thankfully, wasn't anything worse than a bad bruise. Hákon alleviated enough of the stiffness in my body so that I was able to walk comfortably to the little room that Gil and I used.

With the next trial tomorrow, we had no time to focus on my fear of blood. We had to get me to shift.

We *had* to.

We stretched out our muscles before settling into a fighting crouch across each other. I palmed a pair of daggers while Gil swung two swords lazily in his hands, waiting for me to make the first move.

I knew that he was expecting me to charge towards him. That was what I always did. Instead, I threw one of my daggers at him, hoping to catch him off guard. I quickly replaced it before surging towards him.

Gil stepped to the side, knocking it out of the air with his sword. He swung the other around to meet my dagger as I reached him. Our weapons met with a clang.

He brought his knee up towards my stomach, forcing me to jump away from him. Gil slashed out with his sword as I spun away from him. I sank low to the ground and swept a leg towards him, but Gil saw it coming and easily leapt over it.

I rolled away and popped back onto my feet. I threw both my daggers at him before I charged towards him. I wrapped my arms around Gil's stomach and tried to knock him off balance.

His swords sang as Gil re-sheathed them. His arms wrapped around me.

He hooked a leg behind mine, easily knocking me to the ground. He crawled on top of me, his legs pinning mine as one of his arms pressed down on my shoulders and the other pressed into my throat.

My anger coursed through me. I hated getting pinned this early. I hadn't been pinned this early in *weeks*.

"That's it, Bryn!" Gil's voice held more cheer in it than I had heard before.

I looked down to see my skin bubbling. I tried to allow the anger to flow through my body, but now that I was aware of what was happening, I couldn't seem to get it to work.

I watched as the last of the bubbles sank back into my skin before allowing my head to fall to the wooden floor with a sigh.

Gil's forehead pressed to mine, his eyes dipping down towards my mouth before locking with mine. Our gazes held as we breathed the same air. His chin dipped, his face slowly easing closer to mine. I closed my eyes, desperate to feel his lips press on mine.

He pressed his lips to my cheek, then the corner of my mouth, before he rolled off of me and lay beside me as he caught his breath.

Gil propped himself up on one of his arms to look at me. "That was the closest you have come to shifting by will. What were you feeling?"

My head was spinning from how close he had come to kissing me. It took me a minute to focus on what Gil was asking me. "Angry."

"We know that both anger and fear can trigger your blood-rite. That is more than we knew this morning."

"So what now? I just get incredibly angry the day of the trial?"

Gil gave me one of his rare grins. "Well, at least your anger towards Emilía can serve some kind of purpose."

I chuckled despite the frustration that had tightened in my chest. I sat up and crossed my legs under me. "Why were you upset by me saying that you should escort me since Óskar is escorting Ma?"

"It is expected that a member of the Verndari would escort your ma because she has no husband or sons to do so. If I were to escort you, it would be different."

"How?"

Gil rolled onto his back. "If I were to escort you, it would appear to be a declaration of intent to the more traditional households. Many do not bother with the traditional customs, but the traditionalists still put a lot of value into them."

"What kind of declaration would it be?"

"It would declare that we were romantically involved with each other."

I was silent as I considered what he said. "And if I'm alright with that?"

"Then it would be my honour to escort you," Gil finally said.

THE SUN HAD SET AS I MADE MY WAY TO MA'S ROOMS WITH ÓSKAR and Gil by my side. We were all dressed in our leather uniforms with fur cloaks draped over our shoulders. Large patches were slung around our shoulders with the Verndari symbol embroidered on them.

A maid was just finishing Ma's hair as we arrived. She was dressed in a stunning blue gown lined with grey fur. A grey cloak was clasped over her shoulders with dyed-blue fur in its hood.

"Thank you," I said, nodding to the maid.

The maid bowed her head, "It's my pleasure, Jarl Brynja." She took one last look over the gown and the outfit before she curtsied and made her way out of the room.

I made my way towards Ma and knelt down in front of her. "I know that you may not understand what's happening, Ma, but Óskar's going to escort you down to the gathering hall. Fannar's being sworn in as a member of the Royal Regiment, and it would mean a lot for him to have his family there."

Ma blinked but didn't say a word.

Óskar helped me ease Ma to her feet. He tucked Ma's hand into the crook of his elbow before he led her towards the door. Gil held his arm to me and allowed me to rest my hand on it.

The people we passed in the hallways stared at us. When we came to the doors that lead into the gathering hall the people around us were completely silent. Gil led me towards the herald. His eyes were wide as they took us in before they drifted towards Óskar and Ma behind us.

The herald stepped into the gathering hall and tapped his heavy staff three times on the floor. The crowd inside the hall fell silent.

"Jarl Egill and Jarl Brynja of the Verndari," the herald announced as Gil led us into the room. A few seconds later, the herald spoke again, "Jarl Óskar of the Verndari and Lady Hanna of a Verndari family."

Gil led us to the spots closest to the throne. Even if we weren't required to be there, we were still entitled to a position of prominence. Óskar and Gil stood on either side of me and Ma as a shield from the rest of the people in attendance.

Fannar stood in front of the steps leading to the thrones with a girl by his side. He was dressed in his finest clothes. I sent him a large smile as the King Commander and his family filed into the hall. Rúna walked in on Baldur's arm. She barely spared us a glance as she took her place in front of the small chair beside Baldur's.

I sank into a bow.

"Rise," the King Commander said, taking his seat. The rest of the Commanding Family followed suit except for Hákon, who stood two stairs above Fannar and the young woman.

"Do you, Fannar, and you, Elva, intend to become a sworn member of the Royal Regiment?" Hákon's voice rang through the hall.

"Yes, Hersir," they answered in unison.

"Then kneel." Fannar and Elva knelt on one knee before Hákon with their heads bowed. "Do you swear to uphold the laws of Drysden, to serve in times of peace and turmoil, to protect the strong and the weak, and to remain loyal to the crown of the King Commander?"

"We do."

Lúdvík approached the stairs with a weapon in each hand. Hákon took the war axe and gave it to Fannar. He drew his thumb across the blade, and a small amount of blood clung to the metal. I swallowed down the lump in my throat at the sight. Hákon took a bow and a quiver of arrows from Lúdvík, which he passed to Elva. She pulled an arrow from the quiver and pricked her finger on the end.

"Then you are hereby proclaimed members of the second company of the Royal Regiment commanded by me," Hákon said. "You are assigned to line two to serve under the leadership of Sergeant Lúdvík."

Cheers rang through the crowd as Fannar and Elva rose to their feet. I smiled so widely that it hurt as I clapped for Fannar.

He had come with me to the fortress so we wouldn't be parted. So that whatever was left of our family remained together. He found a life for himself here. Fannar had found a purpose, and I was incredibly proud of him. One day, if things worked out, I would be honoured to fight by my brother's side through whatever we may face.

After shaking hands with Hákon, Fannar turned towards us with a grin. He pulled me into a fierce hug.

"I'm so proud of you," I murmured to him.

"Next time, it will be you up there taking an oath," Fannar whispered back.

THIRTY-FOUR

BRYN

I sat on the edge of the wall that surrounded the fortress. Fannar was by my side with his head tilted up towards the sky. The wind blew the hair out of our faces as the summer sun warmed our skin.

I smiled at him. "Everything turned out alright, didn't it?"

"It did," Fannar said, his eyes shut tight to fully enjoy the warm sun. "It turned out better than I thought it would."

"Who would have thought that we would be here?" I asked. "Who would have thought that we could be happy here?"

"Not me," Fannar said gravely. He turned towards me slowly as blood dripped from his eyes.

I screamed.

Fannar spit blood as more poured out of a large cut on his stomach.

"No, no, no," I cried. I pressed my hands over the cut to try and stem the flow of the blood. It didn't work.

Fannar's face was pale as he began to sway in his spot. I tried to grab ahold of him, but I was too slow.

I watched helplessly as he tipped off the edge of the wall. He didn't scream as he fell.

But I did when he hit the ground.

I shot up in my bunk with a cry. The furs pooled around my waist as I panted, my eyes searching the room desperately. I worked up enough courage to leave my bunk to relight the fire and all of the candles in the room.

I collapsed back in bed and pulled the furs up to my chin. My eyes drifted around the room, catching on every dancing shadow on the walls. I knew that I needed to go back to sleep so that I was rested for the second trial. But each time I tried to close my eyes, I was scared. Da wasn't here to check the shadows for the Ógn like he did before. Ma wasn't here to reassure me that everything would be okay.

I was on my own.

I tossed and turned for the rest of the night. If I had gotten even an hour more of sleep, then I considered myself lucky. I finally dragged myself out of bed as the bright winter sun streamed through my window. I pulled on my leather armour and had just finished braiding my hair when someone knocked on my door. I pulled open the door to reveal Gil standing on the other side.

"May I come in?" he asked.

I simply nodded and stepped to the side. Once he was in the room, he shut the door behind him.

"How are you feeling?" Gil asked as he leaned against the wall beside the bookshelves.

"Today, I could break the last promise I ever made to my Da," I said softly.

"That will not happen."

I shook my head, my eyes fixed on my feet. "You don't know that."

"You do not know that it will happen," he said firmly. "There are still two trials left. You have not lost yet."

"What if I can't do it? What if I fail?"

"Then you fail." I whirled around to stare at Gil. "You would lose these rooms and your position as a Verndari. But you would not lose the legacy of your family." Gil walked closer to me as I spoke. "You could still fight to protect those that you care about. Hákon would appoint you to the Royal Regiment if you asked."

I closed my eyes. "What about the friends—the family—that I have made here? Would I lose them, too?"

"Georg will always see you as one of us. I have never seen someone more loyal to the people they care about than Pétur. Óskar treats you the same as he does his sister. I cannot speak for Rúna right now, but I do not think you would lose any of them."

"What about you?" I asked softly.

Gil was close enough that his breath brushed across my face. "Nothing would change. It might even be easier if you lost. There has never been a relationship between two Verndari like the one we share. People are going to fight it," Gil said softly as he rested his forehead against mine.

I swallowed thickly. "Promise?"

"I promise." Gil pressed a hand on my cheek. His fingers trembled against me as he rested his forehead against mine. "I should have kissed you yesterday."

"Why didn't you?"

His eyes flickered down to my mouth. "What I feel for you scares me. I am constantly drawn into your orbit, which can put you at risk."

"Can I tell you a secret?" I ask.

Gil nodded. I rose up on my tiptoes, his hands automatically finding my waist. I leaned in close to his ear. "I wanted you to kiss me. I *still want* you to kiss me. And I would rather be by your side helping you fight the darkness than kept safe away from you," I whispered. His hands tightened on my waist. "And even if there was a risk, I would still want the exact same thing because you are worth it, Gil."

His body was tight, his jaw clenched as though he were fighting to cross the last wall he had built between us.

His muscles loosened as his eyes flared with heat. He walked me backwards until my back hit the wall behind me. He pressed his body close to mine, his heartbeat pulsing through my body.

"Please tell me that I can kiss you," Gil groaned, his mouth hovering close to mine.

I didn't bother to answer as I tangled my fingers in his hair and rose to my toes to press my lips against his. His hand tightened on my hip as the other knotted itself in my curls.

He kissed me hard, his body pushing me back into the wall.

Our lips moved over each other, neither of us holding back.

I wrapped my arms around his shoulders, trying to press myself even closer to him.

Gil's mouth drifted to my cheek and down my neck. He wrapped his arms around me as he rested his head on top of mine. I tucked my face into the crook where his neck met his shoulder.

"What now?" I whispered, too content to break the silence that surrounded us.

"Now you fight like hell to win."

∼

I TRIED TO WALK WITH MORE CONFIDENCE AS I ENTERED THE tournament grounds for the second trial.

I had agreed to fight, so that was what I would do.

The King Commander stood from his seat once Emilía and I were in position.

"Welcome," the King Commander said as the crowd roared. Fannar sent me a grin from the front row. "Since a Verndari spends a lot of their time in the saddle, it has been determined that today's trial will be horsemanship. The competitors will race to complete our track as fast as they can. The first to do so will be the winner for this trial."

The mirrors from the tournament were wheeled in as two stable hands led in our horses. I mounted mine smoothly and followed the stable hand to the start of the course. Emilía took her place beside me with a sneer. When the horn rang through the air, I kicked my horse into a gallop.

We raced through a weaving path neck and neck with each other. A series of jumps that alternated with low-hanging planks loomed up ahead. I settled into the proper position for jumping and trusted my horse to know what to do. The horse jumped with ease, allowing me the time to duck to avoid the low plank that followed. I was quick to push myself back into the proper position. It seemed as though the second jump was shorter, but the third jump was closer than the last.

My horse was clean through the jumps, but Emilía's horse stumbled on the last jump. Determined to gain as much of an advantage as I could, I bent low over my horse's neck. We charged into a clearing where two riders were dressed in house colours. I set my eyes on the one in blue and silver and followed him into the forest.

He led me through many twists and turns, trying to lose me. Eventually, we reached the end of the forest, and I could see a bridge tied up ahead. The rider stayed off to the side as I flew towards the bridge. I dropped my horse's reins and pulled two daggers from my belt. I threw them both at the ropes holding up the bridge. It slammed down onto the ground, allowing me to gallop across it.

When we reached the end of the bridge, flags outlined a trail for me to follow. I risked a glance behind me to see Emilía turning onto the track. The flags got closer and closer together until they were just wider than the horses.

A large block of wood came up on the left side of my horse. I unhooked my foot from the stirrup and swung my body over the horse's other side. Once we were past, I pulled myself back onto my horse's back. I quickly swung to the other side to avoid a second piece of wood. This one was much longer, and by the time I was able to pull myself back up, my muscles were trembling. Up ahead, rather than the wood simply blocking one side, it formed a tunnel.

"*Shit.*" I scrambled to pull my feet from the stirrups. The closer I got to the tunnel, the longer it looked. I slowed my horse down to a fast trot before I hesitantly stood on its back. Once we were close, I jumped onto the wooden roof as my horse disappeared into the tunnel. A crash sounded behind me, followed by a cry. Emilía must have hit the tunnel. I sprinted across the wood as I tried to listen for the sound of hoofbeats underneath me. Once I reached the end, I took a step back and waited for my horse to get closer.

When it sounded like it was right under me, I jumped off the bridge. I landed hard on my horse, which stumbled as it tried to keep me on its back. I pulled myself into the saddle as I urged the horse into another gallop.

The trail led me back toward the fortress, and the cheers from the audience were thunderous. I galloped around the walls before the trail led me back inside the gates. My horse charged through the courtyard. We followed the path as it twisted and turned around the buildings before it led me back to the tournament grounds. The cheers were deafening as my horse skidded to a stop in front of the Commanding Family's box.

The King Commander stood to speak, but I didn't hear a single word he said. I had won the event. Baldur scowled, his hand clutching Rúna's wrist. Rúna's lips were pressed tightly together, but her eyes shone. Fannar stood to cheer for me with a giant grin on his face. Gil was on his feet as he clapped with a grin. I slid from my horse as Óskar ran towards me, whooping and hollering. I crashed into him, his arms wrapped tightly around me before he swung me around.

I had done it.

THIRTY-FIVE

BRYN

B ells rang loudly through the fortress. I jerked out of a deep sleep, searching for what caused the noise. I scrambled out of my bunk and pulled a cloak around my body. I ran into the hallway to find Óskar charging down it.

"What's going on?" I called out.

Óskar turned around, his face white as a sheet. "Those are the alarm bells." He turned back down the hall. "Gear up!"

I sprinted down the hallway after Óskar. Once I reached the armoury, I quickly changed into leather padded pants and a tight shirt with extra padding over all the important organs in my body. I allowed myself the briefest of moments to study my choices for armour before I took a leap of faith and chose one.

The one I chose was a risk.

It was armour designed for shifting.

It was made from leather that was covered with metal disks. Even though I would be at the front alongside everyone else, shifter gear was often more lightweight than other forms of armour. I strapped on both my chestpiece and the additional protection for my neck. I buckled on my arm guards but didn't put on the leg guards. They would just get in the way if I shifted. My weapons belt was next, as well as my daggers. Six went into my belt, four more went into my arm guards, and eight lined my chestpiece. I pulled my hair into tight braids to be out of my face before I charged towards the meeting room.

The men were already there when I arrived. The sight of Gil in his metal armour made my heart jump into my throat. He would only wear that if he thought he would be in heavy combat.

Close combat.

Pétur and Óskar were both in armour, similar to what Gil was wearing. Georg wore armour that was closer to mine than Gil's. The doors had just shut behind me when they slammed open to reveal Hákon and Ragna, covered in weapons and armour. Hákon wore metal armour, while Ragna wore leather armour with added metal protections over her neck and organs.

Gil quickly made his way over to join me. "That's shifter gear. You need to shift, or you'll be vulnerable."

"I know. I can do this—I *have* to do this," I said. My eyes met his, and I could see an understanding shining in them.

"As long as you are sure."

"I am." I grabbed his hand and gave it a squeeze. "I can do this."

The doors slammed open again to reveal Rúna with Baldur and Emilía hot on her heels. Rúna's metal armour shone in the firelight. Georg didn't waste any time once Rúna arrived.

"We have a large horde of Skolli approaching the fortress. Fast. Luckily, they seem to be concentrating their forces for a ground assault rather than a two-pronged attack from ground and sky," Georg said gravely. He paused as his eyes roamed over each of us before they settled on me and realized what I was wearing. "Do you think you'll be able to shift, Bryn?"

"I do." I nodded. Óskar's eyes widened as he realized that I was in my shifting gear.

"We are gathering the Commanding Family and anyone not fighting in the Gathering Hall. We need to stop the assault before the Skolli have the opportunity to get past the walls. Bryn, Óskar, Gil, Rúna, Pétur, and Hákon—" Georg pointed to each of us in turn. "You six will lead the defence on the front line. Station them amongst the Royal Regiment and other warriors as you see fit, Hákon."

I nodded my agreement. I didn't trust my voice right now.

Baldur growled as he crossed his arms over his chest. "No. Rúna will be in the Gathering Hall with the rest of my family who are not fighting."

Rúna looked annoyed.

No.

She looked *pissed.*

"I am not some kind of doll you can take out and dress up when you feel like it. I'm not some sort of accessory that you can use to elevate yourself. I am a Verndari." Rúna was practically in Baldur's face as she hissed at him. "My duty is to fight. My duty is to protect the fortress and everyone in it. Not to sit by your fucking side like a helpless damsel. Go. Sit in safety. I have a job to do here."

Baldur looked absolutely furious as he stormed out of the room.

"He's not going to be very happy with you," Hákon said.

"Oh, trust me, I know exactly how mad he's going to be. But I'm a Verndari, and it's time I reminded him of the fact."

"Ragna and I will be in the fortress guarding the gathering

hall should any of the Skolli breakthrough," Georg said as he refocused their attention.

Emilía pushed her way past Rúna. "Where will I be?"

"You will be with the rest of the people not fighting."

"You forget who you are talking to. I'm just as qualified as anyone in this room—"

"—no, *you* forget who you are talking to." Georg's voice thundered as he quickly strode towards Emilía. He stared down at her as he continued. "You are nowhere near qualified to fight alongside us, let alone in a position of command. You don't have the training or the bloodrite to give you a chance against the Skolli. If you fought with us, you would be nothing more than a liability."

Emilía glared. "How dare you say that to me when you have Bryn fighting, who can't even control her bloodrite *and* is scared of blood."

"I dare to say that because she has fought more Skolli than any of us and is still standing here ready to fight. She may not have complete control over her bloodrite, but every time she has needed to use it, she has." Georg's words were practically a growl. "Now get out of my sight before I have to take warriors from the fight to escort you to the dungeons." Emilía stormed out of the room, slamming the doors behind her. Georg sighed before he turned towards the rest of us. "Remember, you are not just responsible for your own lives. Protect each other and protect your comrades."

Hákon stepped forward. "Strike hard, strike fast."

"Strike hard, strike fast," we all responded.

Georg nodded at Ragna, and they made their way to the door. He paused before he opened it. "I expect to see all of you when tonight is over. Don't let me down." Georg and Ragna left the room at a run, with the rest of us hot on their heels.

When we reached the end of the Verndari wing, Georg and Ragna turned left towards the gathering hall while the rest of us turned right and charged out of the fortress. The Royal Regiment was gathered in the courtyard. Their armour gleamed in the light from the torches. Fannar was among them with an axe in his hand and another strapped to his back. He sent me a smile that I tried to return.

Hákon wasted no time as he positioned the Royal Regiment in front of the walls. It was one of the hardest things I had to do as I watched Hákon lead Fannar's line outside the walls. Every part of me screamed out to be by his side for the fight. I could only hope that I was positioned near him.

The fear of the Royal Regiment was so tangible that I could almost smell it. Hákon led us towards the front lines in our pairs. He evenly spaced us out in front of the regiment. I couldn't see Fannar or Gil around me. I just had to hope to see them after it was over.

Pétur used his bloodrite to carry his voice over to us. He was able to link all our voices together on the wind so that we could hear each other. "Someone has to speak to the warriors. The fear is practically rolling off of them."

"It should be Bryn," Gil said.

"Why me? I'm not even technically a Verndari!" I argued as I shifted my weight anxiously. I felt incredibly vulnerable in my limited armour when surrounded by so many heavily armoured people.

"You've faced Skolli twice and lived to tell the tale," Rúna said. "Not to mention you are like them. You weren't raised a Verndari like the rest of us."

I bit my lip. I wasn't ready to tell the men and women about to fight that they would live to see the sunrise when I didn't know that for sure.

But what if I didn't, and the last thing they ever felt was fear?

Not hope or courage or camaraderie.

I sighed after a moment. I rubbed a hand against my forehead. "Alright."

"I'm going to use my bloodrite to magnify your voice so everyone around the fortress can hear," Pétur explained. "Just speak like you normally would."

I took a moment to gather my thoughts. "Comrades!" My voice echoed through the air. "We can all see the threat approaching, so I'm not going to waste time telling you what you already know." Óskar's hand found mine and gave it a squeeze. We would face this together. "Just a couple of months ago, I was like you, facing a monster I had never seen before. I fought with nothing but the sheer determination to protect everyone I loved. I held my father as he died—I failed him that night. But that won't happen tonight. Each of you has more training than I did. You have more comrades, more friends, by your side than I did." I swallowed as the thunder of the charging Skolli could finally be heard. "Everyone here has something, someone, to fight for. A mother or brother. A friend or a lover. Your comrades. But most of all, fight for yourselves so you can live to see the sunrise in the morning!"

The Skolli got closer, and I knew I had run out of time.

I allowed my anger to flow through me. Anger at the Skolli for attacking my new home. My anger at being unable to fight by Fannar or Gil's side that night. And my absolute rage over the good men and women who were going to die that night.

Burning spread through my body.

My legs, my hands, my teeth.

I grew taller as my legs shifted to become Skolli legs. The warriors behind me cheered. I walked forward with Óskar by my side as my talons and fangs formed. The other Verndari walked forward from their positions until we were all a short distance ahead of the warriors. The cheers grew louder as more and more people were able to see my bloodrite in action at last.

Óskar began to call out orders to the warriors behind us. Rúna and Hákon were doing the same from their positions further away. I sunk into a fighting crouch as I watched the Skolli get closer and closer.

I wasn't fighting to uphold my promise. I was fighting for my family, for the Verndari. I was fighting for myself—to defend the new life that I was making.

And this time, I would not fail.

CHAPTER
THIRTY-SIX
BRYN

I watched as the Skolli got closer and closer. I had to wait until they were close enough that the warriors behind me could join in the defence. If I charged ahead, I would be overwhelmed in seconds.

"Ready your weapons!" I yelled as I pulled two of the thin daggers from my chestpiece.

I rushed forward to meet the Skolli as Óskar yelled out, "Charge!"

Horns rang out down the line as an almighty war cry filled the air.

I threw my dagger at the first Skolli. It fell as it impaled its throat. A second Skolli fell with a dagger in its eye. The one beside it fell with an arrow through its throat.

I launched myself at the closest Skolli with a cry of my own. I hit the first Skolli hard. I ducked out of the way of a wicked slash of its claws. I flipped over the top of it and slashed its throat open with my claws. I used my momentum to carry me over to the next Skolli.

It landed a slash across my cheekbone. The sharp sting was

easy to ignore as I leaned close and ripped out its throat with my fangs.

"Duck!" Óskar yelled. I dropped down to the ground as three arrows flew over where I had been.

I rolled out of the way as one of the Skolli fell towards me with an arrow through its eye.

Two Skolli approached me from either side. I popped to my feet as I drew two more daggers from my chestpiece. I threw a dagger at each of the Skolli. I didn't wait for them to hit the ground before I rejoined Óskar.

I would protect his back like he did mine.

HÁKON

It was mayhem. I had been separated from Pétur as soon as the Skolli reached us. My axes dripped with black blood. The Skolli pushed forward with a harsh assault faster than the warriors could handle.

A Skolli charged towards me and knocked me to the ground with a vicious blow. I rolled to my feet with a wince. I caught the Skolli's claws with my axes and forced it back with a kick to his chest. It stumbled back off balance. I didn't let it recover as I beheaded it with a swing of my axe.

I needed to find Pétur; we needed to stick together.

I began to fight through the Skolli as I tried to find Pétur. I could only see the warriors closest to me as the Skolli towered over us. I turned towards my right, where Pétur was earlier, but I couldn't see him.

The wind rushed around me as a bunch of Skolli were blown into the air. That was where Pétur was. I fought my way through the Skolli that divided us. I tried to ignore the screams of the wounded. I could heal them later, but only if we survived the night.

I finally made it to Pétur. We fought side by side against the never-ending stream of Skolli. My axes were a blur, a never-ending defence against the horde. I slashed a Skolli's neck but didn't wait for it to hit the ground before I pushed off its back. I cleanly beheaded the Skolli that was behind it.

Pétur screamed in pain. I cursed as I spun towards him. Pétur's shield was on the ground, his shield arm cut badly at the shoulder. He still fought, his sword slashing at all the monsters trying to take advantage of his state.

I knew that I couldn't waste my bloodrite healing all the wounded. But if one of the Verndari went down, our chances of survival would plummet. I had no choice.

"I need you to hold them off while I heal you," I said over the noise of battle around us. Once Pétur nodded, I dropped my axes on the ground and pressed my gloved hands over the wound.

"It's about to get real hot around here." Pétur pulled out a piece of flint from his pocket. "Just thought I would warn you." He struck the flint against a rock, and the small spark suddenly turned into a massive flame.

"Great. Try not to burn me, yeah?" I tried to ignore the sweat that dripped down my back from the fire. I needed all my focus on the healing.

Pétur winced. I didn't have time to waste making the healing comfortable. "I'd stick close to me then," he said through gritted teeth.

The fire only cut close to me once as I healed his shoulder. Once I finished, I took a moment to catch my breath. The combination of the fight and having to use my bloodrite would eat through my energy if I wasn't careful.

Pétur wielded the flame like a massive whip as he snapped it at the Skolli. To our right, the Skolli began to break through the line.

"Hold the line!" I hollered. My voice was nearly swallowed by the chaos around us. I stooped down to pick up my axes before I charged for the weak spot. "Fill the gap! Don't let them break through!"

A Skolli knocked me sideways. I hit the ground hard. I wheezed as I tried to get air back into my lungs. The Skolli let out an awful screech as it was encased in a sphere of fire. The fire formed a wall around me until I could get back on my feet.

I grabbed my axes as the fiery wall opened on one end. I didn't hesitate as I ran through the small opening towards the rapidly weakening spot on the line.

"Sergeants on me!" I roared. Only Lúdvík was close enough to hear me. "Ingvar's line is failing. We need to reinforce it. Spread your warriors out behind the weakening spot. I'll call the line back to fill in the holes once we are in position. Send Fannar to me. I'll be in the centre of the new line."

I quickly headed for my position. Fannar appeared by my side, a long slice down his eyebrow painted half his face red.

"You're fighting with me. Normally, one of the sergeants would be with me, but I can't risk weakening a spot in the line by moving a sergeant," I explained as I studied the warriors taking their place around us. "I'm commanding here, but I also need to fight. I'll be keeping an eye out for wounded or tired warriors and calling in replacements. I need you to watch for any that I miss while we are fighting. Can you handle it?"

"I have to. I have no choice otherwise."

I flashed him a grim smile. "That's the spirit." I checked the line before turning back to the front. "Ingvar! Fall back!"

We only had to last until sunrise.

I just had to hope that we lasted that long.

BRYN

"Stay in formation!" Óskar yelled as an arrow sank into another Skolli. "You leave your comrades open if you don't!"

I swiped at a Skolli with my claws. The burning wetness of its blood splashed across my face. I pressed my lips into a thin line before turning towards the next Skolli. I knew that I couldn't stop moving. The moment I stopped moving would be the moment I was overrun.

"On your right!" Óskar cried. I spun, but I was too slow.

A Skolli slashed me brutally across my ribs, sending me crashing to the ground. I rolled onto my back as I fought to get air back into my lungs. I rolled to avoid its next attack. I didn't have time to get back on my feet before I had to roll again.

"Óskar!" I screamed as I avoided another attack, scrambling backwards on the ground.

I rolled again.

Two axes flashed through the air. I looked away, knowing instinctively what was going to happen. The only way I would make it through this fight without freezing was if I tried to avoid the sight of blood.

A large hand appeared in front of my face. I didn't hesitate to reach out and grab it. I was pulled to my feet, face to face with the massive raider from the shipyards.

"Thank you," I said.

"Don't mention it." His voice was gruff.

"Bryn!" Óskar yelled over the noise around us as he reached my side. "The wall!"

I whirled around, trusting the raider to have my back. Some Skolli had broken through the line and were climbing up the wall.

I looked down at my own Skolli legs for a moment.

Then I began to run.

GIL

Rúna and I fought back to back as we always had. It didn't matter that Rúna was tangled up in things that I didn't agree with. I would protect her as I always had and fully trusted her to do the same.

My swords were black with blood, droplets spraying in the air each time I swung them. I was desperately trying to avoid having to use my bloodrite, but it looked like I wasn't going to have a choice. Rúna's staff crackled with her light; the smell of burnt flesh filled the air around us.

But we were still being overrun.

A Skolli charged towards me, its wings tucked close to its body. I slashed at it with both of my swords. It dodged the first strike before it blocked the second with its claws. I spun as I swung at its knees. The Skolli bent down to block the strike. I continued to spin as I slashed the back of its neck with my second strike.

The Skolli's head bounced off the ground before it rolled to a stop.

I turned to face Rúna as a Skolli attacked her from her blind spot.

"Spin right!" I roared as I tapped into my bloodrite. I didn't bother to check if Rúna had listened to me or not. I knew that she would.

I sharpened my darkness until it was razor sharp and sent it hurtling toward the Skolli. The darkness skewered the monster clear through the neck. I bent the darkness, forcing it to impale four more. I dissolved the darkness and tried to maintain control of the monster inside of me.

"I need you to take over command," I panted as I turned towards Rúna. "I am going to need all my focus to remain in control. We need my bloodrite."

"Of course." Rúna nodded. Her eyes widened as they landed on something over my shoulder. "Archers!" she bellowed. "The wall!"

I whirled around. A handful of Skolli had broken through our defences and were scaling the wall. I spun back around towards the attack. I dropped to a knee as Rúna took her position at my back. Her whip crackled against the ground as she extended its length with her light.

Rúna's whip cracked above us, now over twenty feet long. I sank down into the darkness inside of me. I allowed it to rush out of me as I sharpened it to points. As soon as I impaled a Skolli, I dissolved the darkness and reformed it into a new weapon.

I couldn't help the archers take care of the Skolli on the wall.

I needed all my attention on the ongoing assault we faced.

～

BRYN

I used the stronger Skolli legs to charge towards the wall. I was the only one that could make it there in time. Archers began to pepper the Skolli with arrows, but only four fell from the wall.

One still climbed, with no arrows to slow it down.

A lone, large eagle raced back towards where Óskar was. I ignored it.

I pulled two large daggers from my belt as I got close to the wall.

I pushed off hard with my Skolli legs. I soared through the air as I spun the daggers in my hands so they stuck out in front of me. The Skolli was almost at the top of the wall, but I wouldn't let it reach the grounds behind it.

I landed hard on the Skolli. My daggers sank deep into its back to keep me from falling. It roared. I pulled one dagger out and hung from one hand. I grunted as I tried to pull myself high enough that I could slit its throat.

The Skolli reached back with a giant clawed hand and ripped me from its back. It slammed me hard into the wall. I screamed as I fumbled for another dagger. The Skolli swung me into the wall again. The dagger in my hand tumbled down to the ground.

I pushed my Skolli legs into the wall behind me and forced both of us off the wall. We tumbled through the air. I ripped out its throat with my talons, but I had no way to stop my fall. The warriors below me fled, clearing the ground under me.

"*BRYN!*" Óskar bellowed as he spiralled down towards me on the back of the eagle. He pulled me roughly into his lap as the eagle fought to keep us steady. The Skolli crashed down onto the ground with a loud thud. "Gods, Bryn. Try not to die on me, yeah?"

"I didn't really have another choice there," I said breathlessly.

Óskar flew us back to our positions. It was already easier to see as the sky began to brighten. Once we were safely on the ground, Óskar's eagle flew back towards the walls.

The raider threw an axe at a Skolli before he turned towards me. "That was one way of handling that."

"It worked, didn't it?" I thrust my claws through Skolli's eye. "Stay strong!" I roared to the warriors behind me. "Dawn is almost here!"

I lost myself in the chaos, my only focus on defeating every Skolli that crossed my path. The thrum of Óskar's bow was as steady as my heartbeat, a constant companion in the midst of the fight.

I didn't even realize that the sun had risen until the Skolli began to flee. Some of the warriors chased after them. "No!" I yelled. "Let them go! We need every single one of you to help us recover the wounded!"

"Anyone who is hurt but can walk on their own is to make their way into the fortress immediately!" Óskar called out as we walked through the warriors we had commanded. "Anyone who is not hurt, or is only mildly hurt, is to assist the wounded that cannot walk with support! Any severely injured are to remain where they are, and the healers will tend to them first!"

About half the warriors made their way into the fortress alongside their comrades or with an arm slung over someone's shoulder. Others stayed in the field alongside those too wounded to be moved. They would keep them company until the healers reached them.

My legs burned as they returned to my normal ones. My pants hung in tatters around my legs, and my boots were completely destroyed. Óskar passed me his bow and quiver before he knelt so I could climb on his back.

Gil and Rúna were already at our meeting place, a small area just inside the gates when we arrived. Gil gently pulled me from Óskar's back as his hands travelled lightly over my body, searching for injuries. I winced as they reached my head.

"What happened?" Gil asked softly after he pressed a kiss to my forehead. He spun me away from him so that he could see my head.

"The Skolli were climbing the wall." I winced as his fingers pressed my scalp.

"Yes. We told the archers to get them."

Pétur and Hákon joined us as I answered. "Well, they missed one. So I got it."

"And almost killed herself in the process," Óskar added as Hákon laid his gloved hands on his arm. "She threw both herself and the Skolli off the wall."

I glared at him. "I was fine."

"Someone should go check on everyone inside," Hákon said as he moved on to Pétur. "I have to help the wounded out here after I finish with you all. Someone should ensure that everyone is fine in the fortress."

"I'll go," Pétur said as Hákon finished healing him and moved on to Rúna. I turned to him in shock. "What?"

I shrugged. "I just thought that Rúna would want to go, seeing as Baldur is in there."

Rúna snorted. "I'd rather be out here checking on the warriors and defences if you don't mind," she said before stalking off.

THIRTY-SEVEN

BRYN

After Hákon healed me and I helped gather all of the dead, I collapsed into my bunk. I didn't wake until the sun was low in the sky. I made my way down to the common rooms to see if anyone else was awake.

Hákon and Georg sat in armchairs near the fire as Gil lounged on the couch. Óskar lay on the furs in front of the fire with Yugar curled up by him.

Óskar noticed me first. "Talon! Come join us!"

"Alright, alright." I joined Gil on the couch after I poured myself a tankard of water.

Georg leaned forward in his seat. "Óskar was saying that you have gained control of your bloodrite."

"Yeah." I leaned my head against Gil's shoulder. "It's a relief. I feel a little more in control of everything."

"I heard that the King Commander believes the final trial would be a waste of time with the most recent attack, now that you have control over your bloodrite and Emilía doesn't have one."

I placed my empty tankard on the table before I lay down

with my head pillowed in Gil's lap and my legs curled up behind me. He tensed under my ear for a second, but he slowly relaxed as his fingers began to toy with my curls. I allowed myself to finally let my guard down as I lay in the comfort of the common room.

A knock on the door drew my attention.

"Sorry to interrupt." The maid curtseyed. "Ísak is here." I sat up, sharing a look with the others.

"Please show him in," Georg said. It didn't take long for the old scholar to join us. He took a seat on the couch across from where Gil and I sat.

"You all look exhausted."

Óskar snorted at the scholar's words. "Gee, thanks. You don't look very bright-eyed and bushy-tailed either."

"The events of last night troubled me."

"They troubled all of us." Gil sent me a half-hearted glare as he spoke. He was rightfully concerned that I had thrown myself off the wall with no plan to save myself. But he also knew it needed to be done, so he supported my decision. Even though I was sure that he would much rather I play it safe. After all, I felt the same way about him.

But we didn't have that choice.

"I was *fine*—" I tried to reassure him, but Ísak cut me off with a rough shake of his head.

Ísak ran his hand down his beard. "I was more concerned about *how* the attack happened. Not what happened during it."

"What do you mean?" Hákon asked. I simply gasped as I realized what Ísak was talking about. Hákon's head snapped to mine.

I explained the story of the exiled Commanding Family. I told them everything I knew. The result of the Great War. The barrier. The traitors. What the Skolli returning must mean.

"So you're telling me that there are two traitors in the fortress." Hákon's eyes darted from me to Ísak. "No, not just in the fortress. But within my *family?*"

"Do you have any idea who they are?" Georg steepled his fingers under his chin. "I've tried to keep an eye out since you came to me, but my relationships with the Verndari and the Commanding Family made it hard for me to see past what I already knew."

I licked my lips, hesitant to reveal what I thought. "Baldur," I said. "And Rúna."

"Rúna?" Hákon was incredulous as Gil remained silent beside me.

"She withdrew from all of us, speaking to us only when she couldn't avoid it. She also pushed us away." I chanced another glance at Gil to see his eyes fixed on me, hearing out what I had to say. "Not to mention that she aligned herself with Baldur seemingly out of nowhere."

Georg looked deep in thought. "Why Baldur?"

"He opposed my position of Verndari the most. There would be no benefit of Emilía taking my position unless he sought to weaken it. The only reason I can think of that he would want to weaken it would be—"

"—if he was the traitor," Georg finished as he began to pace. "The Verndari are going to be essential when dealing with the Skolli. By weakening us it makes it easier for the exiled Commanding Family. If this does end up in war, it would weaken us for that, too."

"Rúna does not do things to hurt anyone. She also would not put up with how Baldur treats her without a reason." Gil looked pained as he spoke. "If they were both traitors, it would explain why they are together."

Ísak's face was grave. "That all makes sense, but that isn't what worries me right now."

"What could be worse than traitors?" Hákon asked with furrowed brows.

"From what I was told, there were many more Skolli than there was in any other of the attacks that have been reported."

"That is true," Gil said. "What is your point?"

"Up until last night, the most Skolli to attack was twenty because of the barrier."

I felt sick as I put the pieces together.

"They weakened the barrier as much as they could," Georg said. "Probably as much as they could without the blood of a member of the Commanding Family."

"That's what I believe, yes." Ísak's eyes met each of us. "If I had made that move, I would know that it wouldn't be long until someone caught on to what I was doing—if they didn't already know."

"I would have left." My voice was soft. "I would have headed for the barrier to join my allies." I shared a wide-eyed look with Óskar before I took off for the door.

I raced down the hallways towards our private rooms. If Rúna was the traitor—if she was gone—it would destroy Gil. Once I reached the door to Rúna's room, I didn't bother to knock before I threw the door open, fully expecting her to be gone.

Óskar slammed into my back as I froze just inside the door. I let out a pained hiss. I may have been healed, but I still felt as though I had been trampled. Gil, Hákon, and Georg filed into the room, but I didn't pay them any attention.

Because there, in the middle of the room, was Rúna.

"What are you doing here?" I asked as I stared at Rúna, my mind blank from shock.

Rúna rubbed at her brow. "This is my room. Shouldn't I be asking why you are here?"

"We thought you would be gone." Gil stepped forward. "Did you have anything to do with the attack?"

"No. Not only is there no way for me to have any control over that, I would never do something like that," Rúna recoiled a bit from Gil. I couldn't tell if Rúna looked more horrified or more hurt. "I thought you thought better of me than that."

I shared a look with Georg. There was no way that she could fake that. Suddenly, it dawned on me. "Holy shit," I muttered. Everyone turned to stare at me. "We were wrong." I left the room at a run. They followed me, calling out as they tried to figure out what was going on. When I finally reached the door she was looking for, I burst through without waiting for everyone to catch up. The rooms were empty.

It was as if Pétur erased his existence from this room before he took off.

"It wasn't Rúna," Georg said. "It was Pétur."

"The letters he got, the knowledge of the terrain on the outer reaches of Drysden," I listed before I spun around to stare at Gil wide-eyed. "The Skolli in the forest. Georg said to keep the fire down to embers so that the Skolli wouldn't see us, but when I left the tent—"

"The fire was huge," Gil growled in frustration.

"Emilía always knew more than she should because Pétur fed her information the *entire time*."

Rúna raised a hand. "Would someone care to explain what in the gods' names is going on?"

"He would have ridden hard all day to put as much distance between him and us as possible," Georg said as Gil filled Rúna in on what was happening. "If Óskar uses his bloodrite to increase the speed of the horses, we may reach him before he reaches the barrier, but it will be close."

"We have to try," Óskar's voice was soft. "He's one of us."

"We leave in five minutes."

I tore out of Pétur's room. I pulled on a set of travelling clothes and grabbed my saddlebags. I had kept them packed with necessities since I recovered from the trip to Hazelpeak. I barely had enough time to grab my daggers before I had to meet everyone at the stables. Everyone was dressed the same as I was. There wasn't enough time to don armour.

"I can't leave with you, not after that attack," Hákon said. "I need to be here in case I am needed. For combat or for healing."

Georg clapped a hand on his shoulder. "You do what you need to do." He swung himself up into his saddle before he turned to Óskar. "Are you going to be able to get us all the way there?"

Óskar set his jaw as he fiddled with the reins in his hands. "I can do it." He led us out of the stable and through the gates. "Brace yourselves."

That was the only warning he gave us before the horses surged forward.

We rode hard throughout the night. We took short breaks every hour to ensure the horses were cared for throughout the harsh journey. I had small scratches across my cheeks from the branches that I had been too slow to avoid.

Finally, as the sky lightened above us, we reached the corner of Drysden where the Commanding Family had been exiled. My fingers shook as I took in the sight of a fortress carved into the mountain. The barrier must have been weakened enough to reveal what was hidden behind it.

Pétur and his horse stood between two massive rocks. The evenly spaced rocks had to be the boundary line.

Pétur guided his horse between the rocks towards the fortress that lay beyond them. There was nothing we could do as he left his horse by the steps of the fortress. We were too far away to stop him as he disappeared behind the giant stone doors.

We were too late.

WE RODE BACK TOWARDS GOLDHELM IN SILENCE UNTIL THE SUN WAS high in the sky. We finally stopped when I almost fell out of the saddle.

My eyelids were heavy as we cared for the horses. Georg wanted to get back to Goldhelm as soon as we could, but he was also realistic. We needed to sleep, or we would never make it back. A nap would do us all good.

Rúna sat on the snow-covered ground, her arms wrapped tightly around her legs. Her hair was a tangled mess from the long ride, and her eyes were tired. "What did I do?"

"What do you mean?" Óskar asked tiredly. He lay on the ground with his head propped up on his saddlebags and his arm tossed over his eyes. A blanket lay under him to protect him from the cold.

"What did I do that made you think I was the traitor? What made you think I would *ever* betray you guys?" Rúna's voice broke.

I shared a long look with Gil before I finally squared my shoulders and turned towards Rúna. "That was my fault. I thought that your relationship with Baldur never made sense. Ever since you started to spend time with him, you pulled further and further away from us. You didn't stand up for Gil or Óskar or me when people came for us."

Rúna fisted her hands in her hair anxiously. "That was never my choice!" she cried.

"What do you mean?" Gil's voice was soft as he knelt down in front of Rúna. "What was not your choice?"

"Any of it!"

Georg crossed over his chest. "What does he have on you?"

"I can't tell you," Rúna sobbed.

"You can trust us."

Rúna shook her head. "I can't risk it. *I'm sorry.*"

"As soon as we get back to the fortress, you can leave him. We will protect you from whatever happens," Gil said softly. "You do not have to be with him out of fear, Rúna."

She was quiet for several moments before she turned towards me. "You think that Baldur is the other traitor."

"I do," I nodded. "It makes the most sense."

"He thinks that with what he has on me, I will be loyal only to him," Rúna straightened her shoulders. "Gil said that for the barrier to fall, both traitors are needed. I'm your best bet to keep that from happening."

Gil shook his head. "No. That is too much to ask of you."

"It's our best option."

"I saw how he treated you at the tournament. I have seen you withdrawing further and further into yourself. I will not support an option where that is the result."

Rúna gently laid her hand on Gil's with a small smile. "I'm strong enough to deal with it."

"You should not have to be strong enough to deal with it. It is still abuse, Rúna."

"I know it is, but I need you to let me do this. I need to regain control of the situation I am in. What I need, more than anything, is your support," Rúna smiled softly at Gil before she turned to the rest of us. "I need all of your support. I have people I need to protect, too."

Gil turned towards me. I smiled sadly and nodded. I didn't like this any more than he did, but we had no other choice. We couldn't force Rúna to make another decision. We had made our argument for why we thought this was the wrong choice. All we could do now was offer her our unwavering support. After all, Rúna deserved nothing less.

"Fine," Gil finally said. "But the second he lays another hand on you, or I see you withdrawing into yourself, you end it. We will shelter you from whatever fallout comes from it."

Rúna threw her arms around Gil. He didn't tense from it. It was almost like he was expecting it. She smiled at the rest of us over his shoulder. "Deal."

THIRTY-EIGHT

G il pulled me close just outside of the doors to the Gathering Hall. I rose up on my toes as though to kiss him but pressed a kiss to his cheek and the corner of his mouth instead. I spun away from him with a wink.

"Now you know how it feels," I teased before I led the way into the Gathering Hall.

The Gathering Hall was filled with people, yet they parted like a wave as I entered with Georg, Óskar, and Gil at my back.

The maid had pulled my hair out of my face with braids, but I insisted that she leave my curls to tumble unrestrained down my back. I wore the same glittering black uniform from the last time I was meant to be appointed. The black furs trailed behind me as I made my way to the centre of the hall.

For once, the Commanding Family was already seated.

I sank into a curtsy in front of the thrones, my eyes meeting Rúna's. She sat by Baldur's side but wore the same formal uniform as me. A barely noticeable smirk was all that she could give me.

"Rise," the King Commander said as he stood from his throne. "Today, we stand in the same position we stood months ago. Jarl Brynja has more than proven herself as a worthy member of the Verndari." Hákon sent me a small smile while Ragna merely nodded her head. "As such, today, Jarl Brynja will be appointed Verndari as she should have been the last time we gathered here." Sigrún pursed her lips as Baldur's hands clenched into fists on the arm of his throne.

"Commander, I believe that the trials stand tied at one apiece," Ottó argued from his place near the throne. "With all due respect, the trials have not been completed, and as such, the girl should not be appointed."

The King Commander descended the stairs to stand in front of Ottó. "I was unaware that you had the power to contradict my decisions. Because of you, we wasted several moons to allow your daughter to make a play for the Verndari. She *failed*. If you challenge me again, you will find yourself in the dungeons." The King Commander turned towards the gathered crowd in the hall. "What Jarl Ottó says is true. The third trial, which was to be a demonstration over the control of a bloodrite, never occurred. However, many of you witnessed Jarl Brynja's control over her bloodrite when she fought to defend the fortress and all those inside it. If that is still insufficient proof for you, I invite Jarl Brynja to provide said demonstration."

I made my way towards the open area in front of the stairs that led to the thrones. My eyes drifted over the crowd. My shoulders loosened as I realized that most of the people that stood closest to me were familiar to me.

Gier and Svanna.

Georg and Óskar.

Ma and Fannar.

Gil.

I took a deep breath, the now familiar burning spread to my fingertips and teeth. I opened my eyes.

I raised my hands to reveal claws as I opened my mouth to reveal my fangs.

The crowd roared.

"As Jarl Brynja has demonstrated control over her blood-rite, I *officially* declare her the winner of both the third trial and of the trials as a whole," the King Commander's voice was laced with iron as he re-took his place in front of his throne. Almost as if he was daring anyone to try and contradict him again. "Jarl Brynja, if you would please approach the thrones."

I climbed halfway up the stairs. I sank into a curtsy before I knelt on the stairs, leaving my furs to drape behind me.

"Do you, Jarl Brynja, swear to uphold the laws of the realm and to represent the authority of your King Commander and his family with honour, grace, and dignity?"

"Yes, Commander."

"Will you protect the old and the young, the rich and the poor, men and women?"

"Yes, Commander." My throat was dry.

"In times of war, will you lead your warriors with determination and passion? Will you fight with skill and strength?"

I swallowed. "Yes, Commander."

"Then stand, Jarl Brynja." I rose as the King Commander descended the stairs to meet me. He carried a fine gold chain that held both the crest of the Verndari and the crest of my family. The King Commander placed the chain around my neck. "May this serve as a reminder of the oath you have taken and as a symbol for your position within the realm." He turned back to the crowd. "May I present Jarl Brynja, a Verndari of Drysden."

The crowd's cheers were deafening.

I did it.

I was a Verndari.

My fellow Verndari clapped wildly. Óskar was even whooping and hollering. Gil's eyes were bright with pride. I turned towards Fannar as he cheered for me, and for the first time in months, Ma smiled.

Snow lay in a white blanket over the ground. My thick cotton pants were tucked into calf-high boots lined with fur. My thick cotton shirt was covered by a fur-lined vest while my cloak was attached to my shoulders. My curls were tied back in two braids that streamed behind me as I ran.

I glanced to the side as Fannar huffed. He was dressed similarly to me, with a reddened nose and flushed cheeks from the cold. The wind streamed through his hair, allowing his close-cut locks to bounce as he ran.

Our feet crunched in the snow as we ran across the previously undisturbed ground.

If I ignored the Royal Regiment insignia embroidered on the shoulder of Fannar's shirt, I could pretend that he was the same man that he was in Ebonwell.

And if I ignored the chain with the Verndari crest bouncing on my chest, I could pretend I was the same person I was just a few moons ago.

Even though I knew we were the same deep down, it was hard to remember when we now had to spend our days training. Training for something that had only ever been a fairy story for us.

I showed up at Fannar's door that morning, desperate for

something to ground me. For my brother in everything but blood to be by my side as we hurtled towards what was sure to be bloodshed.

He had taken one look at my clothes, so similar to what I would wear for my runs in Ebonwell, and had changed to match me.

Regardless of how overwhelming everything felt, we still had each other.

I smiled at Fannar as he kept pace beside me. "If you don't turn back to look at the fortress, we could be back in Ebonwell right now."

"I don't know," Fannar's voice was winded. "I would only run when you forced me to back in the village."

"Well, if Da was here, he would say that it's about time that you started to run. Especially if he realized that you joined the Royal Regiment."

"I can imagine the conversation now."

I sent Fannar a positively wicked grin. "His intensity for your run would have gone up tenfold as soon as you joined."

"You know, you worry me whenever you have that look on your face. Half the time, it usually means that something is going to happen that I don't like."

"I'll give you a thirty-second head start to try to beat me back to the fortress," I said.

"Gods, Bryn, there's no way—"

"Twenty-nine, twenty-eight, twenty-seven..." Fannar took off towards the fortress, kicking up the snow behind him.

I paced where I was as I counted down the thirty seconds I had given him. As I reached one, I slung my braids over my shoulders with a grin and launched into a sprint towards the fortress.

It didn't take me long to close the gap between me and

Fannar. He had only begun to train when we reached the fortress, and very little of that was in the snow. I wiped away a tear as I remembered the last time I had done something similar with Da.

"Faster, Fannar! You've got to be faster!" I called out. "You will never be able to outrun anyone if you don't get any faster!"

THIRTY-NINE

LEIFUR

The sound of my boots on the stone floor echoed throughout the stone hallway. The torches cast the long corridor in an eerie light, the flames causing my shadow to climb up the walls. I stopped outside the large double doors at the end of the hall to check that none of my clothing was out of place. Pushing open the doors, I approached the two thrones on the platforms, my parents already in their seats.

My sister stood at the bottom of the dais, steps away from a kneeling man. I took my place by her side before I bowed to my parents. No matter how long I had been trapped with them, it still unnerved me to see them after they drank the life-extending elixir made from the harvested souls. They seemed to have lost thirty years of age and looked like they could be my older siblings rather than my parents.

"You summoned me, Father?"

"Yes. How is your work coming along, Leifur?" my father asked. His voice made the hairs on the back of my neck rise.

"Very well," I tucked my hands behind my back as I spoke.

"Many of the families I have reached out to have already pledged their support and their soldiers. Others have provided me with information with the hopes that it would be enough to appease me to overlook their choice not to support you."

"Will it?"

I swallowed. "Of course not."

"Very well. There is someone I would like for you and Katrín to meet." My father rose from his seat and descended the stairs. He turned towards the man who still knelt before the thrones. "Rise." The man stood. "Pétur, may I present my children, Leifur and Commanding Daughter Katrín." My father turned back towards us. "Children, may I present Pétur. Once a member of the illustrious Verndari and now one of the newest warriors in our army."

My mother descended the stairs to stand beside my father before she tucked her hand into his elbow. "It won't be long until we are once again free to reclaim what is ours." My father started to lead them from the room as my mother continued to speak over her shoulder. "For now, it is time to get to work, my darlings."

ACKNOWLEDGMENTS

Writing a book is a deeply personal, deeply isolating, thing. You design whole lives for your characters, create an entire world (of which, only the smallest part makes it to the book), and weave together multiple plot lines simply from your imagination. Hours upon hours are spent just you and your laptop as you write tens of thousands, if not hundreds of thousands, of words to complete your book.

But luckily, you get to choose the team that you bring in to really make your book shine.

Samantha from Ravens Wing Editing Services made my story sing. Her support, encouragement, and feedback helped me take Nightmares of Nightfall to the next level.

My incredible map maker, Rachael from Cartographybird, brought my world to life with the most breathtaking map.

The entire team at MiblArt were amazing. Not only did they design my logo, they also designed my cover and some marketing materials. It was joy working with them and their work is phenomenal.

I knew that with my full time job I wasn't going to be able to give my launch the attention that I wanted so I hired David from Lawson Digital Strategies Limited. Not only did he build my website for me, he also ran my digital marketing campaign. He helped me get this book into hands of readers and I cannot be more thankful.

To my family, friends, and my dog (who was the inspiration for Yugar), thank you for your endless support and encouragement.

And thank you, dear reader, for picking up my book. I can't wait to share the next one.

ABOUT THE AUTHOR

Aspen Sherwood is a self-published author from Southwestern Ontario who loves all things fantasy and romance. As a 20-something herself, she loves writing about 20 year olds who are exploring their worlds and discovering themselves just like she is. When Aspen is not writing she can be found cheering on the Toronto Maple Leafs or the Toronto Blue Jays.

Follow Aspen Sherwood on TikTok (@aspen.sherwood), Instagram (@aspensherwood) on Facebook (Aspen Sherwood), or by joining her email list on her website (www.aspensherwood.com).